I0685034

Project J

Sean Brandywine

To my wife,
for years of putting up with me,
and immeasurable support and love

CONTENTS

1. AUDITOR IN A BLUE CORVETTE

Tamara Graves looked at the buildings and smiled. Leave it to security people to make a site always look like high-security. There was the chain link fence with barbed wire atop it, the guard gate, the armed sentries, a large sign proclaiming "No Trespassing" and "Use of Deadly Force Authorized"; all the things you need to shout to the world: look here, a High Security, Top Secret Place.

If she had her way, it would look nothing like a security installation, more like a small office building, an appearance enhanced by a concrete sign out front proclaiming an insurance company, a couple of legal firms, and, larger than the others, "Coast Medical Data Repository". Make it look bland and ordinary, and of no interest to anyone. Easier to keep your secrets that way.

Oh, and don't put it out in the middle of nowhere where it was the only sign of human activity for miles around.

But there it was, in the middle of the New Mexico mountains not more than twelve miles from Los Alamos, where a hell of a lot of other secrets are kept. The sign in front proclaimed "Chronodyne Corp." and below that "Project Dry Wells", whatever that meant.

At least the scenery was pretty: pine trees, a clear blue sky, and fresh air.

She pulled up to the guard gate and began getting her credentials from her purse. The guard was not military but from a private security agency. Still, he had the look of former military about him. Probably a veteran. He gave her ID a good going over, looking up at her face several times as if he doubted it was the same face as on the ID. Finally, finding no reason to turn her away, or arrest her, he gave back the cards and waved her through. She could almost see him fight the urge to salute. Military training is so hard to overcome.

The place looked much like a military base, with a couple dozen large buildings that could almost have been hangars but were not, and a few that could pass for office buildings. It was to the closest one of those, the one marked "Main Offices," that she drove up and parked in the lot. In a stall marked "Visitor" of course. Her car lacked the required parking permit.

Standing beside her metallic blue Corvette, Tamara enjoyed a deep breath of the mountain air, and sighed. She missed her Colorado hometown, and she was seriously worried about her health spending most of her time in large cities, breathing in car fumes and heaven only knew what. The site had all the lovely pine trees cut down to the fence line, which was a shame for a girl who was born in a pine forest and lived there for her first eighteen years.

But this was not a vacation and she had work to do. Clasping her purse solidly to her side, she marched up the concrete walkway to the front door. Within there was a receptionist, but not a pleasant looking female. Instead, it was another of the private security forces type. Again, Tamara's ID was carefully checked several times, the receptionist consulted a computer twice, and finally reached into a drawer to hand her a Visitor's Pass.

"I will need to see Dr. Stryker as soon as possible," she told him.

"I will get you an escort." It was, of course, another

armed guard who was none too subtle giving this young lady a good going over that neatly undressed her with his eyes. But she was used to that.

"This way, ma'am."

The office she was led to was on the top floor, which was not saying much considering the building was only two stories. A simple sign on the door read: "Dr. Brian Stryker, Project Director."

Inside, she was handed off to another receptionist, or secretary, it was hard to tell, but at least a female one this time. Not a bad looking younger woman with a body that filled out the business suite nicely, and long blonde hair. Dr. Stryker knew how to pick them for looks at least.

"I need to see Dr. Stryker."

"Have you an appointment?" Her voice was much like Marilyn Monroe singing "Happy Birthday, Mr. President."

"If I had an appointment, then this wouldn't be a surprise audit, would it?" Tamara informed tartly.

The blonde pursed her lips and seemed on the verge of flatly refusing to let this intruder anywhere near her boss. But the ID card did say "Department of Defense", and that pulled a lot of weight in a place that might be private enterprise but got a great deal of money from government contracts.

"I'll see if he's free," she said, sounding as if it would be a serious imposition.

She got up and entered the inner door without knocking.

Tamara was quite certain that the woman could have called him far more easily, but wanted to let him know in person that the DOD was paying a surprise visit – never a pleasant experience. She waited, as she had in many other outer offices.

"Dr. Stryker will see you now," the secretary informed. It

would have been nice had she held the inner door open or been polite in some manner, but she went right back to her chair and seemed to forget about the visitor.

'The Project Director should teach his staff that DOD auditors are important people,' she thought as she opened the door herself.

The office was much as she expected. Oak walls, several cabinets, scientific awards in frames, photos of him with a few top scientists and politicians, a window looking out over rooftops and on to the distant mountains still retaining their caps of snow. There was a computer, but she noted it was not on his desk but a side table. The doctor was standing, and he came around the desk to greet her. He was middle aged, receding hairline, about half gray, and a bit of a double chin. All in all, he looked like a businessman going to pot slowly as the years drifted by. Perhaps a banker, but not the classic image of an award-winning physicist that he was. His handshake was firm but not overpowering. For a brief couple seconds they eyed each other carefully, and then he asked her to have a seat.

"Coffee? Tea?" he asked.

"Tea would be nice. Herbal, if you have it," she told him. She really did not feel like a drink, but asking for it would mean that the secretary would have to get it, and that petty imposition pleased Tamara. 'Really shouldn't be that way,' she told herself, but it was just part of the game.

As predicted, he pressed a button on his phone and asked "Miss Swanson" to fetch coffee and tea, herbal.

"Have you been to this part of the country before?" he asked politely while they waited.

"My job takes me all around the country," she told him. Actually, lately she had mostly been visiting companies in

California and Texas. But she was familiar with the East Coast defense industries also. She did like what she saw of the mountains in northern New Mexico, and she told him so. They reminded her very much of her hometown.

The tea and coffee came in quickly, and the next minute was taken up in preparing the drinks. The Doctor liked his coffee with lots of sugar; Tamara preferred her herbal tea straight, but after sniffing it and discovering it was orange flavored, she put sugar in it to dull the taste. She much preferred mint teas.

"Dr. Stryker, let's get right down to business," she said after taking a sip. "I'm here to do an audit of your Project Dry Wells."

"We had an audit from DOD just last February," he mildly protested.

"Yes, but that was a science review audit. I'm here to do a financial and records audit."

The doctor's face turned a little paler. "Oh," he said, then busied himself with his coffee while he thought about that.

"Yes," she went on. "I'll need access, of course, to your financial records, and, of course, someone to help as liaison. Will also require security clearance on your computer system."

"Miss Graves, we are classified at the highest level of clearance here. I don't believe I can just give you unlimited access to our computers."

"My clearance is also of the highest level. You should receive a communication from my boss, telling you to grant every consideration. Probably in an encrypted email. May already be in your email."

The project director looked unhappy. Which she was used to. Nobody likes to have an auditor prowling around inside their books and files. Might find too many secrets they would rather keep hidden.

Before he could react, she continued, "I am well aware of the level of your security clearances here. In fact, I was not able to find out just what it is you do here, even though I tried, it is that high. And few things escape my attention. Dr. Marcus, my boss, said that you would give me a briefing about the nature of your project, so I can have a better idea of you expenditures and such."

"I will need to confirm your security clearance before any briefing. Perhaps tomorrow morning?" he suggested.

"Check it now," she said firmly but without raising her voice. "I would like to get started this afternoon." She had learned over the years that if you wanted people to jump, you had to sound as if you expected no other reaction. And don't give them time to plan a defense.

"Hmm..." It was clear he wanted to have time to get together with his department heads and give them time to get things in order – and hide that which should be hidden. She had seen this kind of delaying before.

"You have come on rather short notice..." he began.

"It is a surprise audit," she cut him off. "Wouldn't be, if I call ahead, now would it?" She smiled and tried to keep any gloating expression off her face.

He would comply because he had no other option. Much, if not all, of this project's funding came from the Defense Department, and they dared not antagonize the hand that feeds them, to misquote a phrase.

"I would suggest that you begin by checking your inbox."

He made an unpleasant noise but turned to his computer. The man was just not used to some young woman waltzing into his office and giving him orders. After a minute, he found and read the encrypted email she had mentioned, frowning as he did. She could see his face reflected on the monitor's screen. But when he turned to her, there was a smile on his face; not a warm smile but a polite one. He knew when he was beat.

"Of course, Miss Graves. I'll have my secretary clear my appointments and give you a briefing myself."

"That will be fine, Doctor."

Informing Miss Swanson to hold his calls and cancel all appointments, he also told her to have a Dr. Crane meet them in Conference Room A. Tamara did not think that the doctor had any real appointments, but she kept that to herself. Conference Room A was on the ground floor but only a short walk downstairs and along a corridor. It had the usual screen for projections, a couple white boards, U-shaped table, chairs and a couple side tables, all looking well used.

After a minute, another man came in. He was mid-thirties, slender, a hand's width over six feet in height, and looked like a nerd – but one tall enough to make the basketball team. A scraggly van Dyke beard adorned a slender face with a hawk-billed nose, on which perched a pair of thick-lensed glasses.

Introductions were made, with this man being Dr. Marshal Crane, the Chief Scientist and Assistant Director for the project.

"Miss Graves needs to have a briefing on our project," Dr. Stryker told him. "She's an auditor from DOD."

Tamara did not like the look she got from Dr. Crane, but that was not unusual. No one likes auditors.

"How much science have you had, Miss Graves?" Crane asked.

"A few science classes in college," she told him. Actually, she had had more than a few, but she liked to not let people know just how much she knew. They tend to make mistakes that way.

"Well... I'll keep it basic." Turning to Dr. Stryker, he received a nod and began his lecture.

"Quite simply put, what we have developed is a time machine." He paused to see her reaction.

"I've heard that time travel is impossible," she said, not showing any surprise. "Unless by time machine, you mean a better clock."

"Time travel is impossible," he agreed. "For a number of reasons. There are the classic paradoxes that time travel could create – like someone going back in time and killing his own father so that he would never be born. But then how could he go back in time in the first place?"

He paused again, but continued when Tamara only nodded.

"Another reason is conversion of matter/energy. If I were to travel back in time and my body appear in, say, 1880, that would mean that this time would be short the mass of my body. And that can't happen because you cannot create or destroy matter and energy. You can convert them from one form to another, but not create them from nothing nor make them disappear into nothing. E equals M C squared and all that.

"Time travel, as most people know it, is therefore impossible. But..." He smiled. "But we found a way to create something from the past in the present. It does not break the conservation of matter/energy because no matter or energy is exchanged between the point in the past and the present.

"Are you familiar with entanglement, Miss Graves? Quantum entanglement?"

"Explain it to me."

"Under certain conditions, two particles of matter can become connected in a way that is buried deep within quantum theory. When the state of one particle, such as the position, momentum, spin, or polarization, changes, the same measurement of that state of the other particle will also change. It will be the opposite, actually. And this happens no matter how far apart the particles are. And it happens instantaneously. No time lag at all. It is the only phenomenon we know that can apparently exceed the speed of light. Two entangled particles can be light years apart and still change simultaneously."

"But Einstein's theory of Special Relativity states that nothing can travel faster than the speed of light," she protested. "How does the second particle know...?"

"Correct. But entanglement does not involve anything traveling. In fact, entanglement was first suggested by Einstein himself, along with Boris Podolsky and Nathan Rosen in a 1935 paper. Erwin Schrodinger, of the live/dead cat fame, did several papers on it shortly thereafter.

"When you make an experiment that causes one member of an entangled pair to take on a definite value, the other member will be found to have the opposite value from that point in time on. This can happen with any particle: photons, electrons, even molecules. In quantum entanglement, the transfer of state happens instantaneously, no matter the distance between the objects. Well, maybe not instantaneously, but recent experiments have shown that this transfer occurs at least 10,000 times faster than the speed of light. Those experiments only give a lower limit to the speed. There probably isn't any upper limit, since it may well be truly instantaneous.

"In our original research, we found that it was possible to

entangle two particles even when they were separated by both distance and time. We found a way to make particles today assume the state of particles days ago. Well, after allowing for reversing the measured property of the particle. Do this for all the particles in an object and you've created an exact copy."

"That doesn't seem right," Tamara said. "You can entangle two particles across a period of time?"

"That's right. We can entangle a particle here and now with any particle from anywhere and from any time. The original experiments were carried out ten years ago. We've come a long ways since them. This is mostly because larger, faster computers are available now. You know what a FLOP is?"

"Floating Point Instruction. A measure of computer speed," she said.

Giving her a weary glance, he continued, "Right, a FLOP is a floating point operation per second. Right now the officially fastest computer in the world is in China. It's called the Tianhe-2 and runs at 33.86 petaFLOPS. That's thirty-three quadrillion instructions per second. Ten to the fifteenth power.

He smiled. "But Lightning, that's the name for our main computer, runs at one hundred petaFLOPS!" Turning to Dr. Stryker, he added, "It's too bad we can't tell the world about Lightning."

"You know it's classified," Stryker responded.

"Yes. Well, as I said, we have been developing this entanglement of particles between the past and present until now we can actually reproduce an object from the past in the here and now. Since each particle of the object will be identical to the original, it will be the same object. There is absolutely no way you could tell the two apart. Assuming, that is, you had some way of bringing them together. Which would normally be impossible.

"We've run a number of tests of this principle and believe me, it works! Gobbles up computer power like you wouldn't believe! But then you have to understand that we have to be able to entangle each and every particle in the object, reproducing it here and now precisely as it was at an instant in prior time.

He paused, and looked at Tamara for reaction. But all he got was a frown. She had seen plenty of top secret projects in her work, but never anything as weird sounding as this.

"And what is the good of this?" she finally asked. "Besides an interesting and expensive science experiment."

"Don't you see? The military potential alone is tremendous! Let's say you want to know some technical secret hidden deep within a foreign country. You just scan back in time to when that secret was written down, locate it – which is another development we discovered almost by accident – and you copy that piece of paper right here into the lab. Would work well for industrial secrets. Of course," he admitted almost shyly, "a hell of a lot of historians, anthropologists, paleontologists and such would beg to get their hands on this if they knew about it."

"Which explains why this project is classified at the highest level," interjected Dr. Stryker.

"Yes, well, someday..." Crane muttered.

"Just how far along are you?" she asked.

The two men glanced at each other.

"Pretty far. Marshal, why don't you show her the museum?"

"Yes. Good. Come along, Miss Graves, I've got some interesting things to show you."

2. TRINKETS

The "museum" was just an office on the main floor, not far from the conference room. But, unlike most offices, it lacked a desk or even chairs. In fact, the only furniture was two tables and a couple filing cabinets. The only adornment was a single framed picture on one wall. Tamara walked over to it. On a plain white background was a single piece of paper, only a few square inches, brown with some black markings on it.

"That was our first object retrieved from the past," Dr. Stryker told her. "Well, except for test items from the near past. This was the first real piece of history we retrieved. It is a piece of papyrus dating from one thousand BC. Not much to look at, but it was a scientific breakthrough standing right up there with the printing press and the splitting of the atom."

She looked a little closer. Yes, those could be hieroglyphics. But they lacked the faded look she had seen on other papyrus documents. It looked as if the printing had been done only yesterday.

"In case you're wondering, it's part of a legal document. A deed to some land being granted to a noble by the pharaoh," added Dr. Crane.

Directing her attention to one of the objects on the nearest table, he held up a frame containing a large piece of dull gray paper on which were lines of tightly packed writing.

"In 1215 a bunch of barons ganged up on King John of England and forced him to sign the Magna Carta. This is the original document with the king's signature and all. There are four surviving copies from that time. We compared it with the copy in the British Library. It is identical. You will note the ink seems fresh. It is.

"This," he said, putting down the framed document and picking up a small, dull gold colored rock, "is the first piece of gold discovered at Sutter's Mill in 1848. John Marshal was supervising the construction of a sawmill and found this in a creek. It started the gold rush in California.

"That dirty black top hat was worn by President Lincoln while he gave his Gettysburg Address. Those sparkly red shoes were worn by Judy Garland in 1938's 'Wizard of Oz'. That somewhat battered sword there belonged to Hernán Cortés, the guy that overthrew the Aztecs and conquered Mexico. It has bloodstains on it.

"That beat up wooden box there was the portable writing desk designed and used by Thomas Jefferson. In 1776 he wrote the first draft of the Declaration of Independence on this desk. And that frame next to it has the actual first draft."

He was warming up to his task, and apparently enjoyed showing off the items they plucked from history.

"This is a freshly minted 1804 silver dollar."

"Is it worth much?" she asked.

"Well, actually, quite a bit. Has an interesting history. I'm sort of a coin collector and have studied this one. In 1804 the US Mint records indicated that 19,750 silver dollars were minted. However, it was the practice at the time to use old dies until they were worn out. All of those coins minted in 1804 were dated 1803. Silver dollars with the 1804 date did not appear until 1834 when a set of coins was minted as gifts to certain rulers in Asia. The mint employees knew that 1804 was the last date for those types, so they produced a set with that date. They only produced seven copies since they were supposed to be gifts, not for release to the public. Then, between 1858 and 1860, a number of these coins were illegally struck by a Mint employee. He sold them to collectors in a store in Philadelphia. However, Mint officials hunted them down and seized all but one.

"Anyway, to answer your question, the last one sold at auction fetched just over four million dollars."

Tamara pursed her lips. "I can see the potential for acquiring a great deal of wealth with your time machine."

"Oh, we take precautions to assure that none of these items ever gets out of here," Stryker immediately said.

"Okay, if you're not making money with it, what do you use the machine for?"

"Mostly for research," Crane said. "We have a small staff of university professors here who are collecting artifacts for study. We're making wonderful strides in many areas of historical study. And we are constantly working on ways to make the process faster and less resource draining. You'd be surprised at how much electrical power the Machine requires. And lots of computer time. Oh, and we don't have any fancy name for it; we just call it 'the Machine'."

"And that's all?" she asked them, her investigator's nose sensing there was something more.

"Ah, well, there are certain government agencies who use some of our resources," Stryker said. "Of course, I cannot..."

"Tell me who they are or what they are doing," she interrupted. "I'm familiar with the routine. I don't have a need to know."

"I'm sure you understand."

"Of course. Well, this has been interesting, especially that little side tour into the world of numismatics. I think I have an idea what your project is all about. If you'll just provide me with a desk and computer terminal, I'll get about my job. And I'd like to have one of your staff available to answer questions and assist."

"I'll attend to that immediately," Dr. Crane offered. "You do realize, of course, that everything you've seen and heard is classified at the highest level?"

"Of course. I won't say a word to anyone," she said as she made a zipper motion across her lips. She smiled at them.

As they walked down the corridor, she suddenly asked, "Is the project name what I think it is?"

"You mean Project Dry Wells?" Crane smiled widely.

"Yes. Would that happen to be a reference to H.G. Wells?"

His smile widened. "Of course. He was the author of 'The Time Machine', wasn't he?"

3. THE GOOD BOOK

The Machine took a lot of power to run, and the lights dimmed every time it was turned on. Williams glanced up at the dimmed lights and grimaced, hoping that no one else would notice. There was little chance that anyone else would be working this late at night, but with scientists, one never knew.

The lights resumed their normal glow, and he turned his attention to the massive control panel before him. Half a dozen display screens overflowing with numbers and codes spoke of what was happening inside the chamber and in the support equipment around it. Two keyboards plus assorted other input devices allowed him to give orders to the most highly advanced electronic device ever built by man. His eyes tracked the main power gauge as its red line slowly crept towards the right end of the scale. When it stabilized at 100%, he touched a few keys to initiate the probe imaging. The largest screen flickered, the numbers disappeared and a picture took their place.

The picture was blurry, out of focus, but seemed to show the inside of a room with a small slit window allowing a shaft of sunlight in to fall upon a table. As the computer subtly nudged the fine settings, the image became more focused until one could see the texture of the stone walls behind the desk, the tiny motes of dust in the sunbeam, and the leather-bound book sitting on the rough wooden table. The brown cover was detailed with gold leaf inlay along the edges and across the spine where the words *"Biblia Sacra"* could be read, also in gold.

Glancing up at a second screen, he nodded to himself. The time and location were right on: March 1454, Mazarin, Germany. Using twin knobs with extreme delicacy and care, he placed a red square around the book. A few typed-in commands and the view of the book rotated until the sides of the pages were visible. Again he positioned a red square of lines on the screen. With the book properly defined, he typed some more and the red lines began blinking. He was smiling as he punched the final ENTER key.

The low background hum increased as the Machine began operation. Most cruelly it twisted the fabric of time-space, digging a tunnel through it, linking that book with the empty platform in the chamber. Subatomic particles called quarks were forced into entanglement at either end of that tunnel; billions then trillions, and then far greater numbers of quarks, the building blocks of matter, were linked in a strange manner that defied the laws and logic of physics. Incredibly thin beams of photons focused on the center of the platform. Slowly, molecule by molecule, a copy of the book was being built from the bottom cover upward. Each page appeared magically from nothing, the black text and red highlighting becoming visible for just a moment before the next page overlaid it. The intertwining vines and red flowers used to enliven the text seemed to be growing around the pages.

Eleven minutes later, the Machine ceased weaving the book from nothing and reduced to its background hum. Immediately, the man shut it down. The room became suddenly silent, making his footsteps loud on the metal floor. Swinging open the chamber door, he stepped in and bent to pick up the book. Fighting the urge to stroke its soft leather cover and admire its gold decorations, he closed the chamber door. The book he placed on a cart, along with a squat clay bowl decorated with black and red primitive images of dancing deer and leaping wolves. Next to those were two other artifacts, a flint spear point and an oval piece of wood with crude symbols carved on the surface, looking almost more like scratching than a language.

The other items were enclosed within glass boxes with sealed lids. But the book he simply covered with a towel.

Leaving the large room where the Machine was housed, he took an elevator up to the office level where he deposited the glass boxes on a table. In the morning, the scientists who had requested those items would pick them up and take them to whatever lab they had, to do whatever it is they did to them. Williams really did not know or care. His job was simply to take the list he was given, search for, find and duplicate those items.

His last stop was the small office he shared with the other operator who ran the Machine during the daylight hours. Looking around to make sure that no one was present, even though that was highly unlikely, he took the towel off the book and lightly ran his fingers along the spine. Almost reverently he opened the cover and touched the black letters on the page. He could not read the Latin, but he knew what it said – more or less. This was a copy of the Bible. But not just any copy. This was a very special copy. This was a Gutenberg Bible, the first major book ever printed. In 1454, Johann Gutenberg used moveable type on his invention, the printing press, and changed the world. No longer did books have to be painstakingly printed by hand. The information explosion he had created ushered in a whole new world of technology and innovation the world was still recoiling from.

Williams had done his homework. A little research on the Internet had told him all he needed to know about this item. It was historical, very rare and very valuable. Gutenberg had printed only about one hundred and eighty of the two volume, thirteen hundred page book, of which only forty-two copies were known today, and only twenty-two of those were complete copies. The last complete Gutenberg Bible to be sold had fetched 2.2 million dollars. Those were 1978 dollars. One website estimated that a copy today would be worth between twenty-five and thirty-five million dollars – if one were available. Virtually all copies were in museums. Even leaves from that book were expensive, running between twenty thousand and one hundred thousand dollars each, depending on the size and condition.

Almost unable to take his eyes off this prize, he had to force himself to put it in his briefcase. In a few hours, he would go off shift and take it home. He would then show it to Daisy – not that she would understand how special it was – and explain to her how he would break it into small sections and sell them individually through an antiquities dealer who asked no questions. Individually, the leaves would not bring as much in total as a complete copy, but would be much easier to pass.

And it would make him rich.

Flopping down in his chair, Williams let out a big sigh and put his feet up on the desk. This was one sweet job he had fallen into! And so easy. For the first few months he had simply done his job, using the Machine to fetch objects for the research staff. Then one day, a random comment about how valuable an ugly looking piece of parchment was set him to thinking. All he had to do to fetch an additional object for himself was to use the Machine a little longer after his regular night's run to make an extra copy of something valuable. His first foray into stealing from the past was to make for himself a copy of the Hope Diamond, all 45.52 carats of it. It was only later that he realized he could not sell a stone that big without attracting too much attention. But after a while he got to thinking about what other things he could grab that would be worth the risk. That exact replica of the Hope Diamond was currently sitting atop the dresser in his bedroom next to a watch that needed a fresh battery.

He spent the rest of his shift filling out paperwork and daydreaming about what he would do with all that money. He and Daisy would travel around the world. She always said that she wanted to see the Pyramids in Egypt. Not that he figured they were much to look at; just a pile of stones. His tastes ran more to expensive cars, good booze and maybe – just maybe – a sharper looking girlfriend. Yeah, that was it! He'd have so much money that the gorgeous babes would be crawling all over him. Daisy was fun in bed but not the best looking dame in the world. Or the smartest. He deserved better.

A few hours later, he signed out, walked to the parking lot whistling a happy tune and swinging his briefcase, and then drove away with a very rare book on the seat next to him.

4. SMILEY

"Most people who work here stay in the nearest town, White Rock, but a few live in a small apartment building we have on the facility," Dr. Crane told Tamara. "Since you're only going to be here just a few days – I assume that's right? – staying in the Mountain View would seem the best. Also, it saves you a drive each day."

"I'm not sure how long my work will take," she told him. "Depends on what I find." It was a thinly veiled threat but she had found that being tough with clients worked best. Let them think you're weak, and they'll try to take advantage of you.

"If you want, I'll take you over there as soon as we're finished here."

"That will be fine."

Looking around the small office she had been led to revealed about what she expected: a desk, side table, and a cabinet and only one guest chair. At least a small window looked out towards the Jemez Mountains. And at least the walls and furniture were not the dull gray that seems to be prevalent in most government offices. These were of wood, and the walls were painted a pleasing shade of light blue. Immediately she went to the computer terminal sitting on the desk. With quick, sure motions, she flipped the on switch, and then began typing as soon as the screen showed a response.

"Windows 11.5," she said, somewhat sarcastically. "You're two versions behind."

"You can log into our Unix system, if you prefer. Or

Linux Mint 14. Or Omni 2.4. Whatever you're most comfortable with."

"Good. I'll assume that I will have an account and password before the day is out."

"Of course." He said that with a straight face, so she could not tell if he was also being sarcastic or not.

The afternoon passed in getting her a permanent visitor's badge that would give her access to the entire facility, and showing her around. The latter task was delegated to a secretary, or something much lower than Dr. Crane, who then made his excuses and left Tamara, his promise to personally show her to her apartment apparently forgotten. The young woman who was now in charge of the auditor was of Latin descent, witnessed by her brown skin, dark eyes and shiny black hair.

"My name is Carla. I'll be happy to show you around."

"That will be acceptable. Tell me, Carla, are you normally a tour guide?"

"Oh, no. I'm a programmer. Spend most of my time cutting C Sharp code. We don't really have any tour guides. Top secret place and all that."

The woman seemed to be honestly friendly and not at all put off by Tamara's strict and aloof attitude. That made Tamara soften a bit. "My dad used to be programmer," she told the young woman. It was always good to make friends. Might learn something from them. "He even goes back to the days of COBOL."

"Gosh, he must be old!"

"As the mountains," Tamara said with a smile. "He used to tell me stories about the early days of computing. He even knew how to use a keypunch. Nowadays no one even knows what a punched card looks like. Used to be called IBM cards."

"I think I heard of them. From one of the older scientists."

"Well, you picked up that phrase from someone. Only the old programmers like my dad used the term 'cutting code'. Everyone else would say 'writing' code, or programming."

"Yes, we had an old guy in our department. Died two years ago. Very nice guy. Used to complain about programmers being called software engineers instead of programmers. Maybe your dad knew him, both being programmers."

"I doubt it. Well, let's begin that tour. Got a map?"

By the time she had been given a tour of the place it was lunchtime, so they adjourned to the cafeteria. The tour had been superficial; they entered few of the buildings, but it did give her a sense of the layout. The cafeteria itself was small but the food was very good, and they had outside tables so Tamara could enjoy the fresh mountain air and view.

"Have you worked here for a long time?" she asked of Carla.

"Since the project moved here from California. 'Bout five years now."

"You like the work?"

"Yes. I like working for Chronodyne and I like this area. Big change from smoggy LA. Only thing bad is that it's such a long ways from Disneyland. I used to drive down there a couple times a month. I like the place."

"Happiest place on Earth, Walt used to say."

"Yeah. I think so. I love watching the children looking around with wide eyes and not believing what they're seeing. You ever see a little girl run up to Mickey Mouse and give him a big hug? Priceless!"

"Is the staff here good?" Tamara was just making talk,

but she was also paying attention. You never knew when casual chats would reveal hidden secrets.

"Yeah. I like most of the people. 'Course, some of the scientists look down on those of us with only a B.S. You know, PhD snobbery. But others are fine."

Finishing the chicken cordon bleu, Tamara began attacking the apple pie. "I find Project Dry Wells pretty amazing. What do you think of it?" She was probing to see if this low level programmer knew about the time machine.

"Amazing isn't the word for it. Incredible! Impossible! To actually recreate a..." Suddenly she cut off. "Well, you know," she finished lamely.

Tamara laughed. "Don't worry! I have the highest security clearance, and a definite need to know." She pointed to her badge, which gave her clearance for the whole project. "I've already been given a briefing by doctors Stryker and Crane. I know what kind of time machine you have here."

Carla looked a little embarrassed but relieved. "I think it's fantastic for research. We only have a small team of scientists other than the physicists, but they're finding out the most interesting things about the past. Dr. Brown has found four new species of dinosaurs! And Dr. Borodin thinks he has located a partial play by Shakespeare that was never published. Isn't that wild?"

"That would be interesting," Tamara agreed, even though it was a lie. She had read one of his plays and thought it the most boring thing ever. "Anything really spooky going on here?" she asked.

"Spooky? Well, there are the spooks! You know, the CIA guys. At least, I think they are from the CIA. They won't talk about what they're doing, but every once in a while they come in and take over the Machine. Lot of guessing going on about that they're using the Machine for but I doubt anyone knows for sure. Maybe not even Dr. Stryker.

"And then there's the secret projects."

"Secret Projects? You mean there are parts of this project you don't know about?"

"Sure. There's five of them. They don't have any names, but are called Project A, B, C, D, and J. Real mysterious like. But everyone pretty much knows that Projects A and B are bringing back extinct animals."

"What?" Tamara's ears picked up. "You mean they can create living animals from the past?"

"Sure. About a year ago they began experimenting. Apparently they had troubles at first and had to redesign parts of the Machine and reprogram a lot also. A lot of animals didn't make it or died almost immediately. But they got it down. The first really successful test was a cat. Fluffy it was named. It was picked up from 1966. It's not official, but most people think that it was Dr. Grossman's pet a number of years ago and he wanted it again. Well, anyway, he kept the cat and it's still living with him. Pretty wild, huh?"

"Yes, pretty wild." Her mind was racing with the possibilities that would open, the least of which was resurrecting extinct species. But why hadn't they told her about that capability of the Machine? Were they keeping it secret? Or did it just not come up?

"Come on, I'll show you something," Carla said.

The something was a small pen behind a building not far from the cafeteria. In it Tamara saw what she first took to be a turkey, but as she got closer it took on a strange look. It was fatter than most turkeys she had seen in the wild, had large yellow feet, but most strange was the large, hooked beak in green, black and yellow. The plumage was a brownish-gray. It stood just over three feet tall and was busy munching on an apple.

"Hi there!" said a voice from the side. Tamara turned to see a man walking up. He was late forties, somewhat on the heavy side and sported a bushy gray beard along with overly thick eyebrows. "I'm Dr. Brown," he continued as he came up and offered his hand. "I'd guess that you're the auditor from DOD."

"Word certainly gets around fast," Tamara commented dryly.

"Small place here. How do you like Arnold?"

"Is that what I think it is?" she asked him.

"Well, if you're thinking *Raphus Cucullatus*, then you're right. Also known as the Dodo."

"They're all extinct," she said. "He doesn't seem very dead."

"In the wild, sure. The last one died in 1662, only a hundred years after their discovery on the island of Mauritius. This was our first success at reviving an extinct species."

"And what is that... that thing over there?"

The thing she was pointing to looked like a small horse or mule, but the front half of the body had white strips like a zebra's over its brown coat while the back half had none. It was munching on some hay.

"That is Herman. He's a Quagga. An extinct form of zebra. Last one died in an Amsterdam zoo in 1883."

"Quagga and dodos! Please don't tell me that you've got a yard filled with T-Rexes on the other side of the building," she said.

"No, all the T-Rexes we had escaped last week. They're up in the forest now, hunting anything they can find and terrorizing the natives."

She looked to him sharply, only to see a wide grin and knew he was kidding her.

"Well, it would be possible, wouldn't it?" she asked.

"Well, sure, but we're more interested in perfecting the Machine than creating a Jurassic Park. Besides, the Machine is limited in the size of the object it can bring back. Dr. Carlyn has some very small dinosaurs, but a T-Rex would never fit in the chamber."

"You have any more animals around?" she asked carefully.

"Well, just one right now, he said with a smile. "Come on, I'll show you."

Inside the building there was a laboratory, including a lot of testing equipment and cages.

"This here is Smiley. Of course, he's just a juvenile now."

Inside a wire cage was a large cat with light brown coat. When it looked up at her, she saw a blunt forehead and small, rounded ears. But what immediately caught her eye were the teeth protruding from the upper jaw. It looked like a cross between a cougar and a vampire.

Before she could ask, he told her, "This is a Smilodon, also known as the Saber-Toothed Cat." He opened the cage and reached in. When he turned around, the cat was in his arms and licking his face. It was big enough that he could barely hold it.

"Smiley here is quite affectionate, but that maybe partly because he was raised here, not in the wild. Human company is all he knows. We picked him up right after he was born. He was bottle fed by humans and has become rather domesticated. Of course, now we feed him nice, juicy chunks of raw meat. Even so, he still plays rather roughly at times. Tries to bite the hand that feeds him and such."

"A Saber-Toothed Tiger," Tamara said in wonderment.

"Cat actually. Calling it a tiger is wrong. Would you like to pet Smiley?"

"I'll pass. My aunt had a cat once, and every time I tried to pet it, it bit me."

He scratched Smiley's head, which the cat seemed to like very much, then put it back in the cage.

"Smiley's in here for some tests. Later I'll take him for a walk and put him in the larger cage. It's big enough for him to roam around in."

"How big will Smiley get?" Tamara wondered aloud.

"Oh, that depends. My field is not paleontology, so I'm not totally sure which species of *Smilodon* this is. If he's a *Smilodon Gracilis*, then he'll max out at about 220 pounds. If he's a *Smilodon fatalis*, then about 600 pounds. But if he's a *Smilodon Populator*, then he'll get up to 800 pounds. That's about the size of the largest Siberian Tigers." He sighed. "I'm afraid we'll have to get rid of him before then."

"What will you do with him?"

"That hasn't been decided yet. I'm hoping that we can announce our project before then so we can openly give him to a zoo. But our little time machine is top secret right now and is likely to stay that way for a long time to come. I'm pushing to announce him as a cloning project using DNA from a Smilodon crossed with a modern day tiger. Smilodons, you may know, became extinct only a few thousand years ago. They were contemporaries with man. Cloning them without the Machine would be completely possible with modern techniques. There's been talk about cloning a mammoth. Why not a Smilodon?"

Tamara thanked him, and left shaking her head.

"See, I told you we had some fantastic results from the

Machine," Carla said. "Come on, now, I'll take you over to Personnel and they'll get you assigned an apartment in Mountain View. That's what the apartment building is called."

It was done as Carla said. After going through the usual red tape and delays, Tamara found herself later that afternoon standing in a second story apartment, looking out over the Dry Wells Project. The apartment reminded her of a small studio apartment she had in West LA once. Small kitchen, small bathroom but a fair sized single room with TV, desk, computer terminal, a picture on the wall of a fiery red sunset at the beach scene, and a sofa that opened out into a bed. Nothing fancy, but good enough for her. It made her nervous when some company tried to put her up in an expensive place, and wine and dine her.

The sun was low in the sky, but it was on the other side of the building so she saw its rays illuminating the low mountains to the east. If the mountains were a higher and had more snow, they would have reminded her more of her home.

A great deal was going through her mind. Usually she absorbed the technical details of a project while maintaining an intellectual attitude and remained impartial towards the possible results of them. But this project was different. It made her feel uneasy. She tried to tell herself it was just because this one was such a giant leap in technology, but a nagging portion of her mind told her it was more than that; more than just high level technology. Illogical as it might seem to an educated person such as herself, but she could not help but wonder if this was a tool that could be terribly misused in the wrong hands.

She had trouble getting to sleep that night, and it was because of more than a strange bed.

5. QUESTIONS

The man sitting back in the chair, legs outstretched and hands crossed on his lap, looked older than his thirty-six years. His hair was long, a dark brown, as was his full beard, although traces of gray appeared at the temples and some in the beard. His eyes were closed as he sat in the warm sunshine, absorbing its heat as it chased away the last of the night's coolness. His face was worn, creases radiated out from his eyes, and the skin was tanned as with someone who had spent most of his life out of doors. He wore tan slacks and a blue UCLA sweatshirt. His feet were in sandals. Had he stood up, he would be barely over five feet in height.

The scene was a courtyard, twice the size of a tennis court and adorned with shrubs and several small, incongruous palm trees. It was surrounded by a high wall, broken only by a few windows and two doors.

"Good morning," said another man, walking slowly up to the seated man. This man was easily at least twice as many years, yet they both looked much alike. The newcomer had a beard, neatly trimmed, almost totally gray matching his thinning hair, and more than a few lines creasing a face with pale blue eyes. He walked with a cane and a pronounced limp. He spoke not in English but in the native language of the seated man.

The seated man slowly opened his eyes to look at the newcomer, and then closed them again. "You are come to ask more questions," he said wearily. It was not a question.

33

"If you feel like it. There is much I would still like to learn."

"Why is it you wish to know so much about me?" he asked. "I failed. What was to be, did not happen. I was wrong."

"You did not fail." When that did not evoke a response, he continued with, "You did what you could and what you believed in." Still there was no response. The man eased himself down into the adjoining lawn chair and changed the subject.

"I would like to know about your home. The town in which you were born and lived as a child."

"I have told you. It was nothing. Just a small village."

Taking a folded piece of paper out of his pocket, the older man slowly opened it and spread it out on his knees.

"I have a map of your small village here. Would you please show me where your house was?"

For a while it seemed as if the man had no intention of answering. Then, with a sigh, he straightened up and looked down at the paper.

"This is not right," he said.

"I know it is not accurate, but please try to see it the way you remember it. Can you show me where your house was?"

Looking down at the hand drawn map, he frowned. "This word here... It means water?"

"A well, yes."

"Then our house was here."

6. DIVING INTO RECORDS

The next morning, Tamara was up early and heading towards the administration building as a few early arriving cars trickled into the parking lot. She found the cafeteria had just opened, and she dined on *huevos rancheros,* which she found to be quite good. Twenty minutes later she was at her desk, ready to begin her audit.

'God, I hope they aren't hiding anything,' she muttered to herself. 'I hate when things get nasty and I have to nail people to the wall.'

She chuckled because that was not exactly true. She loved nailing people to the wall – if they tried deliberately to slip something past her. Honest mistakes were another thing and usually dealt with in a kinder manner. Truth was, she enjoyed the hunt when she sensed something was amiss. A challenge, a battle of wits, the bad guys vs. the good auditor – that sort of thing.

And so she plunged into the books, records, computer files, and anything else she could get her hands on that might tell her the story of how this project was spending the money granted to them. And a large amount of money it was, larger than most research projects funded by the OSI, DOD or any other government agency. She was humming to herself as she began tracing fund allocations within the project.

It was not until the afternoon of the second day of the audit that she began to sense something was not quite kosher.

7. LATE NIGHT MEETING

Three men met in a quiet office long after business hours. It might have been an executive's office; good quality furniture, soft carpet and a window looking out over to the scattered lights of the city. In the distance, an airliner was tracing its path over houses and businesses, lowering all the time as it approached the long line of lights marking the airport. Only one lamp was turned on in the office, as if these three wished to meet in darkness in hopes no one would see them.

The oldest man was heavy set, doubled chinned and a bulging waist that even the expensive black suit could not hide. On the pudgy fingers was a large gold ring bearing a dark red ruby and the chi-rho symbol on both sides. He sat in the chair behind the desk, filling it so much that it creaked every time he moved.

The second man stood behind the fat one in an attitude of subservience. His clothing was also black. He was late thirties, slender of build and marked with a forlorn face and thinning hair.

The third man was standing before the desk, nervously shifting his weight from foot to foot and glancing at the window every few seconds as if worried that someone was watching. He seemed not to know what to do with his hands.

"Please tell the... us what you told me before," said the man behind the chair.

The chair creaked as the fat man leaned forward, his dark eyes intent upon the nervous one.

"I... Well, you see, I work at..."

Once started, he blurted out the essential fact he had come to say, then spent the next few minutes trying to make these two believe him. When the questions began, it was the fat man who asked them, and who did not seem to believe the man's story. Or did not want to believe it. But, try as he might, the fat man could not find fault with the story. At least this man was consistent with his facts. Which was not difficult, as he was telling the exact truth to begin with.

"I think you can see why I came to you."

"You did the right thing, my child. I promise you, I will look into this."

The fat man rose with difficulty from the chair and offered his hand to the storyteller. He remained calm, and even smiled as if this man had told him something that pleased him. But as soon as the man left the room, his countenance turned dark and his voice took on a hard edge.

"Have you checked out this man?" he snapped.

"He seems to be who and what he claimed," answered the other. "I will, of course, check further into his story."

"You must! If there is the slightest shred of truth in what he says, we *must* know!"

"And act upon it," added the slender man.

"What?!" The fat man froze for long moments as that idea churned around in his mind. Then he slumped back into the chair. "You are right, of course. We have never faced a danger like this before. We may have to act, and swiftly!"

8. CONFRONTATION

Charges for computer time did not match the logs for Machine use.

That might not sound like much – perhaps just a clerical error, but to a snoop like Tamara it was like waving a red flag in her face. Since the computer time usage was greater, that suggested the Machine's use was not all being logged properly. Mistake? Probably not. Especially since it occurred on more than one occasion. So what was going on? She continued comparing the data. The largest of the discrepancies occurred just over a month prior, with smaller ones trickling down to the present, but the story it told her was that someone used the Machine and did not want others to know about it.

After a break for lunch, she began charting the Machine use by project. An interesting pattern emerged; one that set her thinking. The power usage logs also corroborated that the Machine was being used for some unknown purpose. Again, small drains here and there, but one large one a month prior. All projects had an occasional discrepancy, but the biggest – again a month ago – was for that Project J.

Tamara printed out some of the key data, and then got on the phone to Brian Stryker's secretary, informing her that she wished to see the boss immediately. After the usual protests that he was a busy man and maybe she could make an appointment, the DOD auditor got tough.

"Look, either I see him within an hour, or you won't believe the report I'll be submitting to my bosses in DOD."

The threat was delivered in her professional, calm tone, totally devoid of emotion – and carried all the more impact because of that. She was a pro at manipulating secretaries.

Ten minutes later she was ushered into Dr. Stryker's office. He was behind his desk, and did not rise politely as he should have when a lady entered the room. What was happening to common courtesies?

"I've found some discrepancies in some of your records. The pattern demonstrates that someone, or ones, are using your time machine and not logging the proper entries."

She enjoyed the way his face turned pale. Now came the interesting part. She would watch his reactions carefully to judge whether he knew about this or not.

"I... Perhaps it is just a clerical error," he almost stammered, grasping for an explanation.

"I think not. I have here some of the logs and related data. Would you like to go over them now?"

She was surprised when he rose from the desk and, looking her straight in the eye, said, "Yes. Of course." His firm reply told her that he was not aware of any chicanery and really wanted to see her data.

"Perhaps we can find the problem," he said, more in control now.

She had seen this pattern before. Surprise, shock then wanting to dig into it. The classic pattern of a man not trying to hide something. As much as she enjoyed nailing someone's hide to the wall, she was fair about it. It was her immediate reading that he had not been aware of these discrepancies.

Coming around to her side of the desk, he took a seat on the sofa to one side and reached out his hand for the papers she held. Ten minutes later, the Chief Executive Officer was again turning pale.

"My God! Someone has been falsifying the logs!" he said.

"More than one person, I'd say," she told him. "These smaller omissions are spread out across all projects. Could these be something done by the spooks who use your Machine?" she asked, referring to the secret use of the Machine by the CIA, NAS and perhaps some other super-secret agencies.

"No. All usage of the Machine for those purposes is included under Project D. Besides, why would they try to hide usage? Everything they do is totally classified, but totally within their rights. None of my staff knows what they are doing. I don't know what they're using it for. So why try to hide it? But I do know that our government, of which you are a representative, threatened to take over the project totally if I didn't allow them unrestricted and unmonitored use of the Machine. Think of the loss that would mean to academic research! Oh, how I long for the day when our work here can be made public and available to all researchers!"

"So, if it's not the spooks, then who? The biggest hidden use of the Machine was by Project J. Unless whoever is doing this is cleverer about hiding his tracks and just making it look like Project J. What is that project, Dr. Stryker?"

"General research. Trying to make the Machine more efficient, improving the search capabilities and exploring new directions." He paused to look out the window. "The biggest single effort has been to see if we can use the Machine to explore other worlds."

"Other worlds?"

"Oh, yes. We can use the Machine to find and duplicate most anything on Earth. All the way back to prehistoric times. Why not use it to duplicate objects from another planet? Why send an expensive probe to Mars to pick up and return a sample when we could just recreate it in the chamber? It would not be a Martian rock but it would be identical in every respect.

"And then there is the possibility of reaching out much farther than the planets in this solar system. How would you like to have a piece of rock from one of those planets they've found orbiting Alpha Centauri?"

Tamara shook her head slowly. The idea was staggering.

"Of course," he continued, "there are many problems to overcome before this can be practical. New routines have to be written for Lightning. New hardware has to be developed. I believe the best Dr. Fielding has been able to do is copy a food packet from the International Space Station. A few attempts to retrieve a moon rock have failed. But we expect one day to do much more than explore the Earth's past."

"That's incredible. Could it be that this Dr. Fielding has accomplished something along those lines but hidden it?" she asked.

"I don't know." Then he turned to her and smiled. "Why don't we ask him?"

9. CONFRONTATION II

Dr. Conrad Fielding's office was a mess. Papers and books and printouts were stacked everywhere, some atop filing cabinets reaching almost to the ceiling. Charts covered what little wall space was available, and a white board was covered with equations, erased and rewritten over and over. The desk was likewise covered with papers where there was room between two computer monitors and keyboards. The doctor himself was sort of a mess too. Late thirties or early forties, slender, with wispy blonde hair and a couple days' growth of barely visible beard. His pale blue eyes looked out from behind glasses on a face that would not have been out of place on an accountant. Tamara expected to see a plastic pocket protector with an assortment of pens and pencils.

His voice, however, was deep, not at all like his appearance.

"Hello! I guess you're that DOD auditor I've heard about," he said by way of greeting.

Tamara was introduced by Stryker, who then got right down to business. "What are you hiding?" he asked firmly.

A pen almost fell from Fielding's hand. "Hiding...?" he stammered, looking bewildered. Or maybe shocked.

"Your project has been using the Machine and not logging it. What have you been doing? Some kind of secret research?"

Fielding sat back down, looking as though he was going to be sick. "Research... You could say that," he said weakly.

Taking a deep breath, he seemed to regain his composure when he added, "I guess it had to come out eventually."

"What kind of research, Dr. Fielding?" Tamara prompted.

"Let me get Juliette in here," he said. "She's been wanting to tell you from the start." He looked to Stryker and frowned. "We didn't think that we would get approval for it. So we sort of snuck it in."

"What in?" demanded Stryker.

Fielding lifted one finger in the air, and then touched a button on the intercom. "Juliette, would you please come into my office."

Juliette O'Neill was the exact opposite of Fielding; a tall woman of solid build, late thirties, tanned, looking as though she just came in off the tennis courts, and with bright green eyes that went very well with her wavy red hair. A lot of Ireland was in her genes. She smiled a little uncertainly when she saw the Project Director and a stranger standing there, looking more than a little nervous.

"What is it, Conrad?" she asked of her boss.

"The excrement is about to hit the air circulation device," he told her with a weak smile at the old slang term. "It's time to tell them about our little secret."

"Oh, shit!" she said, looking much like a person who has just been told her whole career was about to be flushed down the toilet. Perhaps it was.

"Let's go to the conference room. We can talk better there," Fielding suggested.

The conference room also served as a storage area with more filing cabinets along one wall and two computer terminals sitting along another. At least there was a nice view out over the green mountains.

"Okay, let's have it," Stryker said as he sat down next to

Tamara. "What is it that I would not approve of?"

Taking in a deep breath, Fielding began.

"You are aware of the successes Brown has been having in fetching live animals, the dodo and Smilodon and such. Well, we, Dr. O'Neill and myself, got to thinking that, since the Machine works for animals, it might be possible to fetch a human."

There was a stunned silence in the room for several long seconds before Fielding went on, "A lot of reprogramming had to be done, and some other changes. A human is much more complex than any lower form of life, but the principles are the same."

"A human?" Stryker said with disbelief rapidly shading towards anger. "A human!"

"We suspected that you would not approve," O'Neill cut in. "But think of the possibilities! There is so much we have been learning about the past from artifacts. How much more could we learn from a real person that we could question!"

"But you can't just grab a person from the past..." Tamara began.

"It's not like we grabbed a person," Fielding immediately said. "Any person we fetch would still be in the past. All we would get here is an exact replica."

"How close of an exact replica?" Stryker said slowly, emphasizing his words.

"Well, the animals Brown got are... Well, truth is, it would be an exact replica. The person would be real and alive. Absolutely the same as the original." He paused a moment before adding, "Even down to the thoughts and memories."

"Oh my God! You're talking about creating a real person! You can't just create life!" Stryker's face was turning an unpleasant shade of red.

"We didn't create it; we only copied it," Fielding protested.

Stryker took in several deep breaths. Tamara was on the edge of her seat, staring in disbelief. The only ones who were not in shock were Fielding and O'Neill, but they were edging towards it.

Before Fielding could go on, Stryker pointed a finger at him and asked, "You have actually done this, haven't you? You've brought into our time a person from the past. Who... Who did you fetch?"

"Well, we figured we might as well bring someone here who could answer historical questions. Someone of historical significance. For research, you understand."

"Who. Did. You. Fetch?" Stryker pounded his fist on the desk with the last word.

"Ah... Jesus."

You could have heard a pin drop in the room.

10. CONFESSION

"Jesus! You mean Jesus Christ!"

"Yes, that one."

"Oh my God!"

"I told you he wouldn't approve," whispered Juliette to Fielding. It might have been meant as joke, but no one laughed.

Stryker was shaking his head, and gasping, unable to speak.

Tamara leaned forward. "Did the procedure work?"

"Of course. Like I said, it was the same as we did with animals, only bigger. Took a lot of computer power, I can tell you. Lightning was running full speed for over three hours."

"And he was... is alive?"

"Yes, of course." At least Fielding had the decency to look sheepish.

"Where is he?" Tamara continued.

"I had a couple offices turned into an apartment of sorts, here in this building. He's living there."

Even Tamara ran out of words at that point. This was just too big for their minds to accept.

"I suppose you will want to meet him," Fielding offered.

"Jesus Christ..." muttered Stryker.

It was Tamara who began to grasp the implications before Stryker. "Jesus was a first century Jew. Wouldn't there be a tremendous cultural shock bringing him into our time?"

"Of course," Juliette answered. "That's why we've

isolated him and hidden the whole project from others in the company. To protect him. We wanted to be able to talk with him, ask questions, find out facts." She leaned forward, her green eyes glowing. "Think of it! Here is the chance to learn so much about the most important point in history! And the most important man in history! Think about how much has been said and theorized about him and his time. How many different interpretations of his life and actions there are. How many unanswered questions. Ask a thousand people who, in all of history, they would like to talk to and most will say Jesus of Nazareth." She was warming to her subject.

"We kept him isolated from virtually all knowledge of our society and the world today. He does not know about TV, space travel, heart transplants, the world wars..."

"Or about the church he started?" Tamara interrupted.

"Most assuredly!" Juliette was emphatic. "Of course, he didn't really start the church. Others after him did. But it would be a shock for him to know just how much his teachings have affected the world."

"Then what does he know?"

"He knows that he has been brought forward to a different time and place from the world he knew. It took a lot to convince him that we have the science to do that. He still calls us 'magicians'. That's the only way he could understand what happened to him. At first, he thought... Well, it's complicated. Once we healed him..."

"Wait a minute!" Tamara jumped in. "Just exactly when in his life did you 'fetch' him?"

Juliette looked to Fielding before answering. "We picked him up off the Cross. Just before he died."

"Oh my God!" Stryker seemed to be having trouble breathing again.

"So you had a man who had been crucified and was near death?" Tamara asked.

"Yes. We had a doctor and nurse ready. We treated him for shock, wounds to his hands, lacerations on his back, a wound in his side, and other problems. He was unconscious for a day and a half. But now he's fine."

"Physically maybe," Tamara said. "But what about his mental state?"

"Well, it has been a shock," Fielding told her, glancing to Juliette as he did. The look expressed surprise that this stranger was understanding so quickly. "But we expected that. We brought in an expert on Biblical times and a speaker of Aramaic. That's Jesus' native language, you know. We had someone on hand when he awoke to ease him into a new life."

Tamara was still concerned. "I'm surprised the shock didn't drive him crazy. It's hard to get your mind around how much change he had to cope with. One moment he was hanging on the cross, in agony, dying; the next he's in a world absolutely alien to his."

"We feel he's adapted reasonably well," Juliette said. "We're slowly bringing him along, a bit at a time."

"And have you been learning from him?" Tamara asked. "Academically? Getting the story straight for history's sake?" She was sounding sarcastic and tried to keep it out of her voice but failed.

"Oh, yes. We've learned a lot," Fielding told her. "Myers has been with him every day. Dr. Seymour Myers. He has degrees in Biblical Studies, history, and archeology, speaks Hebrew, Aramaic and Greek."

"And he's Jewish, which helps," Juliette added.

"I'm sure it would. Keep everything kosher." Again, Tamara had trouble to keep from sounding sarcastic.

Before an argument could start, Fielding cut in. "Look, there's a lot to learn here. We recorded every interview with Jesus, and most of the rest of the time he's been here. You can look over those recordings. It would be the best way to understand what we've done." He turned to Stryker. "Brian, I'm truly sorry to have hidden this from you. But this is exactly what we made the Machine for. To learn! To find out the truth, no matter what it is. I hope you understand."

Stryker could only shake his head. "You've got a lot to account for," he muttered in admonishment.

Fielding would not let go of trying to make them understand. "But don't you agree: this is the greatest science experiment of all time!? Our chance to answer so many questions. We couldn't ignore this opportunity!"

"We felt," Juliette added, putting her hand on Fielding's shoulder as she stood behind him, "that we would not be able to do this if we went through normal channels. Too many people would object. Objections would pile on and others would want in and nothing would ever get done."

"You got that right," Stryker told them. Then he sighed deeply. "I suppose we can't just shove him back in time. We're stuck with him. My God, do you have any idea of the legal hassles this brings up? To say nothing of what the churches would say?"

"It is the Second Coming," Fielding said with a smile.

"You promised you wouldn't say that," Juliette chided him. But she could not stop herself grinning also.

Tamara leaned back in her chair, her mind a whirl of thoughts, and not a few emotions.

"Could we meet him?" she asked meekly.

11. ALARM

"If this is true, then we must act!"

The speaker was Cardinal Gaetano Milanesi; the place was an office in the Palace of the Governorate, Vatican City. The Cardinal was one of three men gathered in an emergency meeting after the receipt of alarming news from an American bishop, and was the President of the Governorate, a man who reported only to his Holiness himself.

"Again, I must ask: are you certain of these facts?"

"They have been given to us by a man within that research project, one of the men who helped to build this time machine."

The Cardinal shook his head. "It is impossible to believe. It cannot be true."

"I assure you that we have checked out this man and the evidence he has given us. Bishop White and one trusted man of this staff did the investigation. He is convinced. In addition to his statements, this man has provided photocopies of documents. And there is the photo."

Cardinal Milanesi picked up the iPad and gazed at the photo it displayed. The quality was not excellent, because it was taken originally from a cell phone camera, but it was clear enough to see two men seated on patio chairs apparently in a courtyard somewhere. One man was an older man of prominent Jewish features, graying hair and with a cane resting against his chair. He was in side view. The other man was smaller, of full beard and long hair trailing down to his shoulders. He was facing the camera and looked as if he was speaking, his lips poised in mid-sentence. One hand rested on his knee, a white gauze bandage showing at his wrist.

The Cardinal stared with intensity at that face. It was sun darkened – a man who spent a lot of his time out of doors. There were stress lines on that face, telling of hard times endured.

"Can this be real?" the Cardinal muttered, mostly to himself. "This is... What did you say? An exact copy of Jesus? A living, talking, breathing man who is exactly the same as the Christ?"

"Identical in every respect," Bishop Carabelli said. "Our informant says that this man even has the memories of Jesus. He speaks Aramaic. He knows things that only Jesus would know."

"Have you identified the other man in the photo?"

"He is Doctor Seymour Myers, a highly respected Biblical historian and expert on Aramaic. Also Hebrew and Greek."

The Cardinal finally put down the tablet and turned to the window to his left. The view was of part of the *Giardini Vaticani* with the Leonine Wall and Vatican Radio building, along with a corner of the Chapel of Santa Maria. The sun was shining and it was a fine day in Rome.

"This may be a copy of Christ's body," he said slowly. "I know enough of science to believe the Americans might have built a machine capable of what you described. But," he said, turning back to the other two for emphasis, "it has not the spirit of Jesus Christ. That cannot be."

"Of course, your Eminence," the Bishop immediately confirmed. "The real Son of God cannot be made by a machine."

The third man, who had remained silent thus far, stirred

in his chair and finally spoke. "Of that there can be no doubt. But... Many people will look upon this and believe that it is He."

"The faithful will not..."

"Your Eminence, it is not so much the faithful I am worried about. It is the rest of the world." He paused to let his meaning sink in before continuing. "If the Americans tell the world of this man and present him for the world to see, the impact on the Church would be immense. What this false Christ may say frightens me, because people will take it as the real words of Christ.

"Even if they are wrong and this is not a true copy of Christ; even if this is a fake and a fraud, announcing it to the world would still be disaster for us."

He looked up into the Cardinal's eyes and said firmly, "We cannot allow this to happen."

For the first time, Cardinal Milanesi did not look perplexed or disbelieving. He looked scared.

12. MEETING THE SON OF MAN

"Now you have to understand a few things," Dr. Fielding told the group. "Most importantly, do not tell him anything about the Christian church as it exists today. We have kept much of history from him. We wished to learn about him and his time. It is the opinion of Dr. Myers, as well as ourselves, that the impact of his learning how much has been done in his name would be a dangerous mental strain on him. He is still undergoing culture shock of being in our time. In fact, he doesn't even know how much time has passed since his death.
"

Juliette cut in with, "Some things we have had to explain. How we managed to get him here, for example. Which he accepts as magic. I'm sure he has no real concept of how much the world has changed. One time he saw an airliner pass high overhead, so we had to explain to him about airplanes. He was shocked that men could fly in the sky."

"I am going to introduce you to him as friends of Dr. Myers, who he knows as Seymour and accepts that he is a learned rabbi. Dr. Myers is Jewish, but not actually a rabbi. There is no real concept for a college professor in Jesus' experience, and rabbi fitted best.

"Oh, and, by the way, you should address him as 'rabbi' also. In his time, he acted much like a rabbi. He taught the rules of Judaism: the Torah. And, according to Dr. Myers, he was what we would call a radical preacher: his views differed from those of the established priesthood. But I'll let you talk with Dr. Myers later. Right now, don't ask questions. It's not an interrogation session. You may shake hands with him, that is a universal gesture showing that you hold no weapon in your hand."

Again Juliette added to the rules. "I don't know your religious backgrounds, but please do not look like you're worshiping him. Be respectful, he expects that, but don't treat him like the Pope or some deity."

"Remember," Fielding added firmly, "this is not THE Jesus. Only an exact copy of him."

At that point, another man entered the room. He was walking carefully, leaning on a cane made of hand-carved wood with a leaf pattern. He was nearly bald but had a full beard, although heavily gray. His face was lined with a slight squinting look like someone who had spent most of his life looking at books. Before Dr. Fielding could do so, he introduced himself.

"I am Dr. Myers but you may call me Seymour." He held out his free hand to Tamara first. "Dr. Stryker, I don't believe we've actually met. And this young lady must be Tamara Graves from the DOD or some government agency."

"Correct... Seymour," Tamara said, returning his smile.

"I understand you wish to meet our distinguished guest," he said with a smile.

"I told them you would introduce them as friends of yours," Fielding told him. "It will be a short introduction, nothing more." The latter was directed at the others, even though he was looking at Dr. Myers.

Myers nodded. "That will be good. He has been wishing to meet more people as he heals."

"Heals?" asked Stryker. "From what?"

Myers turned to Fielding. "You did not tell them?"

"We told them."

"You mean the wounds from the cross?" asked Tamara.

"Of course. And more. He hung there for about four hours," Juliette explained. "He was also stabbed in the side with a spear, one of those crude Roman ones. The loss of blood was the first problem we had to work on. And the shock of nearly dying up there."

Again going into lecture mode, she continued, "There were also the lacerations on his back. He was flogged, you know. He was a weakened man when he was put up there. The doctor who treated him told us that he was very close to dying when we 'grabbed' him. Not in good shape at all."

"I'm sure you're anxious to meet our guest," Fielding cut in. "Later, we can talk about the procedures and what we've learned so far. If you'll come right this way."

He turned to open a door but halted and turned back. "One other thing. Do not say anything about God or the issue of Jesus' divinity."

Dr. Myers immediately added, "You have to understand that his concept of God and yours are probably very, very different. He was a devout apocalyptic Jew living in an age totally different from ours."

Stryker looked as if he was about to object somehow, but he kept his mouth shut. Tamara had a fair idea what Myers was saying. She had been very interested in religions as a teen, and studied them more than the average person. Early Christianity in particular had fascinated her.

"Shall we go?" said Fielding with his hand on the door.

Without waiting for replies, he opened the door and walked through, leaving them to follow.

They were outdoors. It was late afternoon and the sun was just above the top of the western wall, casting a shadow that covered the whole courtyard. There was some patio furniture, a table and chairs, and a barbeque. There was also, near the chairs, a brick lined circle only a foot or so high. Inside were black lava rocks. A fire pit. Around the courtyard were a dozen palm trees.

Fielding gestured for them to pause while Dr. Myers went ahead of them. This gave them a little time to take in the man sitting in the chair only twenty feet distant.

He was not at all the image of what Jesus should look like. Every depiction of him had him as a tall man with a gentle, kindly face, a well-trimmed beard and long, graceful hair. This man was hardly kind looking, and his beard could definitely use a trim, giving the impression that he would not allow scissors to touch it. He was dressed in blue slacks, sandals on bare feet, and a dark blue sweatshirt with UCLA in bold letters across the front. Upon hearing voices, his eyes opened and he turned to take in the visitors. When he saw that two of them were new to him, he sat up a little straighter. His eyes were turned towards Tamara as they walked up.

"*Shelama*, rabbi," Myers said. Then, in Aramaic, "I have brought a couple of friends who wish to meet you." He gestured them forward. Stryker looked confused, as if he had trouble grasping the situation. Tamara smiled, and tried to tell herself that this was nothing special, just meeting a man. No need to act or say anything different than she would meeting any other man. Certainly no reason for her legs to feel weak and her stomach tense.

"This is my friend Brian," Myers said, waving his hand at the Project Director. He spoke in Aramaic with only the name coming through clearly. He did not try to explain the man's position. Jesus would have trouble understand what a Project Director was.

"And this is Tamara, a friend."

Jesus slowly got to his feet. Up close, the bandages around his wrists were obvious, sticking out of the sweatshirt's sleeve. There were also almost healed scars on his forehead. It appeared that just standing was somewhat painful for him.

The nails through the feet, she thought. It's a wonder he can stand at all. Then, looking down, she realized that she could see no wounds nor any bandages on his feet. She was certain, however, that under the overly large sweatshirt, his back would be horribly scarred. The old Romans were noted for whipping prisoners with leather whips that had pieces of rock or metal woven into them to cut the flesh. From her studies, she knew that he had been flogged by the Romans before he was crucified.

Stryker stepped forward and offered his hand. There was the "welcome" smile of a politician on his face, one that held no real warmth. It was obvious from his reaction that the handshake was painful for Jesus. It had to be, with nail holes healing in the wrists, Tamara thought with a wince. Stryker could have been a little more considerate.

Tamara came up and offered her hand but only gently touched his, not a real shake. His eyes were a pale brown up close, with lines radiating outward. This is someone, she thought, who spent a lot of time squinting at the sun without the aid of sunglasses. He smiled at her, and she felt some of his animal magnetism come across. This was definitely not a meek and mild little man, even though the top of his head came only to her nose. This was a man who could attract loyal followers and influence crowds of people. She felt it.

"I am very happy to meet you, Rabbi Jesus," she said.

He spoke a few words that she did not understand at all. His voice was soft, but she had the feeling it could rise to a thunderous roar when needed.

"He says that you are the most beautiful woman he has ever seen," Myers told her with a smile. "He has met very few women since awakening, but you are, indeed, the prettiest."

Tamara felt like this was something in a surreal movie. Here was Jesus telling her she was beautiful. And she had actually touched his hand.

Then a thousand questions filled her head, demanding to be let out, and had to be forced down. Maybe later. She bowed her head slightly in thanks. It was hard not to just stand there and stare.

Myers spoke a few words in Aramaic. "I've told him that you two have to be going. Have to be someplace else, but had wanted to meet him."

Stryker turned and left, but cast several glances back over his shoulder. Tamara, on the other hand, asked, "Please tell him that it is a pleasure to meet him. And I hope to do so again soon."

Myers spoke the words. Jesus smiled slightly and a transformation came over his face. The worn, tired, pained man was gone, and a caring, even loving man took its place. He said something to her.

"He says it is a shame you have to go. And he does very much want to meet you again. He finds your earrings fascinating."

Only then was Tamara aware that she was wearing cubic zirconium earrings that looked like three or four karats worth of diamond sparkling in the sunlight. She felt herself blushing for no reason. Again she nodded to him by way of a bow, and turned to leave.

He must think I'm terribly wealthy, she thought as she retraced her steps towards the door. Maybe that's not good, she added. Didn't he say something about it being easier to get a camel through the eye of a needle than for a rich man to enter heaven?

13. ISA COMES

"This I cannot believe," said Abdul Rahman Munif, waving a sheet of paper around.

"The Catholic Church believes it," replied Khurram Murad dryly.

The scene was an office located on the outskirts of Cairo. It looked like a student's dorm room with books scattered around, newspapers piled in the corner and a laptop computer to go along with pizza boxes and empty cola cans. Both men were in their later twenties, bearded but neatly trimmed, dressed like casual college students. Through an open window came hot, humid air and the sounds of a mass of upraised voices from not far off.

"Can these American's actually do this? Bring back *Isa Ibn Maryam*, a Messenger of Allah? Today? With a time machine?"

"There is a man working in that project who fed the information to a bishop of the Catholic Church. He felt they should know. Our spy in the Vatican intercepted the communiqué and sent it to me. He says that the Church is taking this report seriously."

Munif sat down in an old desk chair, keeping the paper in front of him and his eyes upon it. "And what does this Jesus say? What is he telling the Americans?"

"I do not know."

"And what should we do about it? What will happen when this is announced to the world?" Munif shook his head and put the paper down. "No, this must be a fake. A trick of some kind. Jesus? Alive today?"

Murad reached across the desk to take the sheet of paper. It held only a few lines of computer printout but had shaken these two Muslims badly.

Murad, always the more religious of the two, said quietly, "Maybe this is the work of Allah. Is it not written: *It is definitely close in that time that Isa, Son of Maryam descends amongst you as a just ruler. He will break the cross, kill the swine and abolish jaziya. And money will abound in such access that no one will accept it*?

"His second coming will be one of the signs of the End of Days. Perhaps that sign is now."

Munif stared at Murad, open-mouthed. The room was quiet for a long time, save for the distant murmur of voices raised in protest from the daily demonstration.

"Allah is merciful," Munif finally said. "But what if this is not the sign? Not the End of Days? What if this is a trick by these Americans? Then we will have to do something."

"What if it is not a trick?" Murad said softly.

14. BACKGROUND

"Now that you've met our guest and had an evening to think, and, I hope, good night's sleep, are you ready for some background?" Fielding asked the company head and the DOD auditor who had fallen into something far more than she ever imagined possible. "You are welcome to talk to Dr. Myers and see the video recordings we've made of the interviews."

"You've made videos...?" Tamara asked.

"Of course. This is history in the flesh. We have almost every word he has spoken on record, along with Dr. Myer's translations, of course. Well, some of them. He's busy working with Jesus and hasn't caught up on all the recordings yet."

"I really don't care about what he says," Stryker cut in. "But I do care about misuse of company equipment."

Juliette smiled, and asked, "What misuse? We simply put the Machine to the use it was intended from the beginning: gathering knowledge."

Stryker harrumphed and glared at her.

"She's right, you know," Fielding added in support. "Sooner or later we would have gotten around to retrieving a human from history."

"Couldn't you have grabbed George Washington? Made him tell you if he really did chop down that cherry tree. Or someone else? Someone a little less controversial? Jesus, man, why did you have to grab this man!?" His face turned a strange shade of red as he realized his curse was all too true. "I'm going to have to talk with legal about this. God only knows what I'll tell the shareholders!"

"They won't know for a long time," Fielding said. "Unless you want to unveil the whole project sometime soon."

"You know I can't do that. The spooks will be all over me. Probably grab the whole project and take it for themselves. We're lucky they didn't do that from the start."

"Then what have you to worry about?"

Stryker leaned over the conference table and said strongly, "For one, those same spooks who grab chunks of time on the Machine and never say a word about what they're doing. We've been lucky that they're so involved in being secret themselves that they haven't wondered if we might have secrets from them. Can you imagine the cry that will go up when they hear of this?"

"Then don't tell them."

For a long time, Stryker stood there, leaning on the table and glaring at the scientist. Finally, he stormed out of the room, casting back a, "I'll let you know my decision."

After the door slammed, Juliette asked Fielding, "He wouldn't shut down Project J, would he?"

"No. I think that he'll come around to seeing that this is exactly what the Machine was built for. As you put it, 'To learn the truth'."

"While, I for one, would like very much to learn more about... About Jesus," Tamara said. "It's still hard to imagine that really is him I touched yesterday."

"I've met him many times, and I still can't get over it," Juliette commented. "You're not alone."

"Won't the DOD expect you to be finished soon? And expect a final report on your audit?" Fielding asked.

"I'll tell them I'm still looking into matters. They'll

believe me. I pretty much have free rein since I usually get the job done. Besides, I'm telling the truth. I'm just looking deeper into the project." She smiled as she said it.

"Well, you're free to talk to Dr. Myers most any time you want. He is with Jesus every day but not always for long periods. He says that Jesus, although a good orator when he gets going, is prone to being reclusive with periods of intense meditation. We let him have as much privacy as he wishes."

Tamara, an investigator used to seeing the big picture, had to ask, "And what are you going to do with him? Eventually, you'll run out of questions. What then? Send him off to a retired messiahs' home? Or let him go on the TV talk show circuit, giving personal interviews?"

"Oh, not that!" Fielding laughed. "I wouldn't subject anyone to that!" He turned to Juliette and they exchanged looks. "Actually, we're not sure. I guess you could say that, in the heat of desire to learn if we could do this, we didn't think that far ahead."

"But don't worry," Juliette quickly added, "We wouldn't ever do anything to hurt him. And we always show him the respect he deserves."

"How much respect does the Son of God deserve?" Tamara could not help herself from asking.

"Ah... About that," Fielding began, "so far, we've found him simply to be a man. There has been no turning water into wine, no raising the dead, nothing more than a normal man could do."

Juliette added, "We have a religious member of the team, Dr. Hans Buerer. He's Catholic and was concerned about this project from the beginning."

"Actually, he wanted us to not go through with it," Fielding said, "kind of like Dr. Stryker, he said we should try it on some other human in history. In fact, he suggested a totally unimportant person, a nobody."

"But that would gain us little in the way of historical knowledge," Juliette said. "Oh, we might get some knowledge about the period we grabbed the person from, but nothing like we're getting now! It's hard to get anything out of him, but Seymour has gotten him to open up on occasion and we've learned so much! Did you know that Jesus was married? And he had two children!"

"Wasn't there a movie about that a while back?" Tamara asked.

"And we found out where he was during those missing years," she continued without answering the movie question. "You know, the time between his early teenage years and when he began his real ministry at about thirty years of age."

"Juliette, let her learn from Dr. Myers." Turning to Tamara, Fielding said, "You'll find the recordings fascinating. But, by all means, talk with Dr. Myers."

"I'm sure I will. That has always been a fascinating period in history for me."

"Then enjoy!" he said. On a less enthusiastic note, he added, "We'll talk again about this."

As the meeting broke up, Juliette showed Tamara where Dr. Myers' office was. The man was in, and seemed genuinely happy to see the auditor.

"Please come in, come in. Have a seat."

His office, like so many of the scientists, was filled with books, but his desk was very neat, holding only a computer terminal on one corner and a pad of paper before him. Tamara noted that he wrote with a gold fountain pen, a very archaic touch but one that she liked. She had a great-grandfather who used fountain pens and had one almost exactly like that.

After the usual pleasantries, she got right to the point. "Dr. Stryker has given me permission to learn all I can about your Project J – which, I assume, stands for Jesus?"

"It does," he agreed. "But I'll wager that you applied some pressure on him to gain this privilege."

She laughed. "True. I had to threaten him with the report I'm supposed to write. He certainly does not seem happy with Project J."

"No, he's not. But he'll get over that. Dr. Fielding says that he's a grump but will come to realize the tremendous value of this project. And the tremendous publicity it will mean for Chronodyne. He's mostly unhappy that the target was chosen without his consultation."

"Target? Is that how you refer to Jesus Christ? A target?"

"A technical term only." Myers set the gold pen on the pad and pushed both a little way from him. "I am extremely happy that I was chosen to participate in this project. Can you imagine what it means to a scholar who has studied Biblical times and people all his life, especially this man, to be able to talk to him, to ask questions?"

"Yes, I think I can. When I was in college, I was interested in that period. And, to be honest, in the Jesus story. I read many books about it. Even took a class in Biblical History. There are so many interpretations of his life, so many ways of looking at him. Some truly believe he was the only Son of God. Others that he was only a man. Some say he was a political rebel who wanted to overthrow the Roman occupation, others that he was simply a rabbi teaching his beliefs. It is a fascinating story. I wanted to find out the truth for myself."

"And did you?"

"Of course not! There are so many unanswered questions, so hard to know what to believe! I sometimes felt that I could almost grasp a feeling for what had happened two thousand years ago. Then I would read another book and what I thought I understood came into question. But the truth? No. I could find nothing I could point to and label it the truth."

Myers smile faintly. "As so many others have found, there are no easy answers. Until now..."

"I noticed you that called him Rabbi," Tamara asked with a slight frown. "From what I've read, that term wasn't used until well after the revolt in 66 CE."

"Ah, yes, my dear, you are learned on that subject. Well, let me explain. When we began talking, as he was recovering from his wounds, he asked me if I were a Pharisee because I knew so much about the church and laws. I explained to him that I was simply a teacher. It just seemed easier for me to use the term rabbi in the sense it is used today to mean a teacher. He accepted that, then told me that perhaps I should also call him rabbi since he was trying to teach the Jews himself. Of course, he meant about the coming Kingdom of God.

"So he is now an unofficial rabbi. So am I, which would surprise Rabbi Lebowitz, who taught me so much a long time ago," he said with a smile.

"Do you believe that this is really Jesus Christ, Doctor?"

"Please, call me Seymour. Or even Sy, if you wish, although the only person who called me that was my wife.

"And the answer is yes. I believe this man has the exact memories of the man who walked this earth two thousand years ago."

Tamara leaned forward to ask earnestly, "Then what was

he?"

"That, my dear, is a little hard to answer. I can tell you this: he believed that he was chosen by God to prepare his people for the immediate coming of the Kingdom of God on this earth. In that sense, he was definitely what we would call an Apocalyptic Jew. He was a Jew first and foremost, and never intended to be otherwise. In addition, as did many of the Jews of his time, he firmly believed with all his heart and mind that very soon there would be the coming of the Kingdom of God to this earth, and that the power of God would bring justice and peace to a world ravaged by injustice and oppression. And that this Kingdom would be signaled by the arrival of the 'Son of Man', a Messiah. The literal translation of the Hebrew word *moshiach* is 'anointed', which refers to the ritual of consecrating someone by anointing his head with oil. This Messiah would be the man designated by God as an agent for his imminent apocalyptic judgment on an evil world."

He paused and pursed his lips. "Perhaps a little more background, my dear.

"At that time, the Jewish people were under the rule of the Roman Empire. It was not an overly harsh rule, for the Romans were willing to let the Jews believe as they wished and run their own affairs, so long as they paid taxes to Rome and allowed the Romans pretty much free rein. The Roman soldiers could, and did, conscript Jews to work on roads and other projects without pay. But to the Jewish people, with their long history of oppression, this was not acceptable. This was their land, given to them by a covenant with God. They wanted very much to kick the Romans out but lacked the military strength to do it. This was proven in 70 BCE when an open revolt was smashed, the Temple destroyed and thousands of Jews killed. And in other revolts before that big one.

"It was a common belief, and had been for a long time, that God would come to Earth, overthrow the oppressors and restore the Jews to their rightful place. There were even some who believed that in this apocalyptic vision the Jewish people would rule the entire world.

"You should understand that this was the world Jesus was born into. His people were under what they considered a harsh foreign rule; the times were rough and violent, with people often barely eking out an existence. Add to that mix the fact that these were a highly religious people whose worldview did not separate reality from religion. Theirs was a hard world dominated by a dissatisfaction that often spilled over into rebellion.

"Jesus, from the beginning of his life, was taught obedience to God in all things and that God would come to save his chosen people. The Hebrew bible contained many passages that proclaim such, even describing the one who would come to initiate God's Kingdom.

"Am I telling you that which you already know?" he paused to ask.

"Pretty much. That is the picture I had gotten from my readings."

"Well, then, back to your original question.

"From an early age, Jesus was different. He was and is an intelligent person. Very probably irritated his elders with questions that were hard to answer – you know the type. He was also on the quiet, shy side. To understand why, you have to understand the circumstances of his birth.

"First off, to correct a common misconception. Jesus was not born of a virgin. In the first place, the use of the term virgin in the Bible is incorrect. The Greek word *'parthenos'* means 'maiden' not virgin. It was translated into 'virgin' by those who rewrote the gospels, to imply that Jesus had a miraculous birth rather than the old, common method. Second, Jesus himself told me that his mother, Miriam in Aramaic, had told him that she was not a virgin and that Yosef (aka Joseph) was, indeed, his father.

"As a side note, he also told me that he had an older brother by his father with a prior wife, Leah, and three younger brothers and two sisters by Mary. The oldest was James. After Jesus came Jose. The next younger brothers were Judas and Simon. The sisters were Rachel and Tamar. The last one, Simon, was born of Mary by another husband after the original Joseph died. Jesus never got along with this stepfather. In fact, he won't even tell me his name.

"Oh, I see by your expression that I'm boring you with that which you already know."

Tamara protested, "I had heard some of that, but it is interesting that you heard it from his own lips. And this bit about a stepfather is new." She paused for a second. "Say, the Bible doesn't name his sisters, does it?"

"No. But Jesus liked them and told me their names. Tamar, by the way, is the root of your name. It was also one of the daughters of King David.

"Well, Joseph and Mary were betrothed to marry after his first wife died. He had a young son and wanted to remarry for that reason, if no other. And, yes, he was considerably older than Mary. However, as is often the case, they got a little carried away, and when the time for the marriage approached it was obvious that she was with child. She was, as near as I can calculate, only fourteen or so at the time. Not really that unusual in those days. I never asked Jesus how old his father was. Joseph died when Jesus was eleven.

"Well, then as now, having sex and getting pregnant out of wedlock was a no-no, but not all that bad or uncommon. They didn't have the pill, after all. The problem was that Joseph lived in Bethlehem while Mary lived in Nazareth. In the strict Jewish rules, unless she could bring witness to show that she was with the licit father, Joseph, it was assumed that she might have been impregnated by a man outside her community, possibly a prohibited person. Rumor and gossip were no less in those days than they are today. She was condemned for it.

"This made him, in Aramaic, a '*mamzer*'. This is important to know, because it affected his standing in the village where he was born and raised. It was sort of like having to wear a scarlet 'A' on your clothes. The charge that he was illicitly conceived plagued him all his life, even outside his hometown and later in life. See John 8:13." He quoted from memory: "*The Pharisees therefore said unto him, Thou bearest record of thyself; thy record is not true.*

"*Jesus answered and said unto them, Though I bear record of myself, yet my record is true: for I know whence I came, and whither I go; but ye cannot tell whence I come, and whither I go.*

"Well, being a *mamzer* had a strong influence on him. For one thing, it made him more tolerant of those who were considered sinners. It is still a touchy subject with him, so don't call him a bastard."

The twinkle in his eye told her he was making a joke. The very idea of calling Jesus a bastard to his face was ludicrous enough to be comical.

He took in a breath and said, "Sorry, I'm digressing. You asked about who he was. Jesus was born in a poor village, Bethlehem. Oh, by the way, that was Bethlehem in Galilee, not the Bethlehem near Jerusalem. Apparently Joseph took

Mary there rather than have her give birth in her home town of Nazareth. Maybe he thought it would help with the whole illegitimate thing. After he was born, they took up residence in Nazareth. Anyway, Jesus was raised as a good Jewish boy, taught the oral traditions of his people and apparently had quite an interest in religious matters from the start. When he was thirteen, his family made a pilgrimage to Jerusalem for Tabernacles or *Sukkoth* festival. This trip had a profound influence on the impressionable Jesus. The Temple in Jerusalem was the largest religious building in the world. It was not only huge, but also impressive almost beyond imagining. The walls were...

"Oh, sorry, I was supposed to be giving the short version. Well, Jesus was mightily impressed with the Temple, but more so with the feeling of being near God. He was supposed to have gone into the holy of holies, the innermost part of the Temple, you know. This became an important turning point in Jesus' life. In fact, he left his family and stayed in Jerusalem, wanting to be close to the feeling of God he had felt there. Eventually, his family returned to Nazareth without him."

"That was the beginning of the missing years," Tamara said. "That period of his life no one knows about."

"Ah...! But that's not true. I know what he was doing!"

"Well, don't keep me in suspense. Tell me!"

15. JOHN THE BAPTIST

"For a while, Jesus wandered the streets of Jerusalem, begging for food, sleeping in hidden places. He would undoubtedly have gone into the Temple daily but for the fact he had no money and the Temple requires you take a ritual cleansing bath before going in, a service for which they charged."

Dr. Myers was warming to his task, a common trait when a college professor finds an eager audience.

"At that time in history, there was an itinerant preacher wandering around in the wilderness, talking up the coming Kingdom of God and that all should prepare themselves for it by becoming pure. His name was *Yochanan* the Immerser, but you know him as John the Baptist, and it was his contention that being baptized in 'living' water was the best way to renounce your sins and become pure so you will have a place in the coming Kingdom. 'Living water,' by the way, was that which came from springs or rivers, natural sources. Of course, it may be argued that all water comes from natural sources, but many came to listen to him preach of the coming salvation of the Jewish people and to partake of a dip into the Jordan River.

"Jesus had heard of John. What little he had heard of the Baptist's views was much along the lines of what he thought himself. He went out to seek this man and found him by the river, loudly preaching to all who would hear and dunking them in living water. Well, to make a long story short, he approached John, they talked, and he became one of John's followers. Eventually he was baptized by John and it was like a revelation, an epiphany for the young boy. He was filled with confidence that he had discovered what he was looking for: the Truth.

"John was your classic hermit preacher, wild looking, with a straggly beard and long hair matted into dreads. He wore a camel-hair tunic and was surrounded by a small handful of disciples who had chosen to stay with him, learn from him, and help spread the word.

"Jesus stayed and became one of those disciples. It was that or return to Nazareth and a stepfather he hated, a boring life tilling the fields and doing repair work, just as his father, Joseph, had. He would eventually marry and become just another peasant.

"Now, you have to remember, this teenage boy had not been accepted by his own village because he was a *mamzer* and, as such, was ostracized by the elders in Nazareth. Although Joseph openly claimed him as his son, Jesus did not accompany him to the gathering of elders called the synagogue. His fellow villagers kept him from the gatherings, while his older brother, James, emerged as an authority in the congregation. James could claim that he was descended from King David through his father, while Jesus' claim to his birthright was always challenged. This birthright, which Jesus felt was rightfully his also, gave James a special place in Israel. James would go on to become an important leader in the church, especially after Jesus' death.

"I'm sure," Myers said, "that there was a good case of sibling rivalry there. James got to do the things Jesus could not, yet wanted to. But Jesus has never spoken of that to me. Any reference he makes to his older half-brother is polite and respectful, but little more. I think there has always been some resentment there.

"Well, anyway, Jesus found something that had been lacking in Nazareth: a place that accepted him as he was. He stayed with John for years, about five, near as I can tell. He learned the older man's *Mishnah*. A rabbi's *Mishnah* was his repetition, the words and actions that conveyed his teachings. Jesus learned this well from John. John, in turn, gave Jesus something he needed, a sense of belonging to a family.

"Jesus came to accept John's insistence on the relationship between repentance and release from sin, and it became a major part of his own ministry. Release from sin might be best translated as 'forgiveness'. Jesus had a firm conviction that release from sin made every Israelite pure – and thus acceptable in God's eyes."

He paused for a moment and sighed.

"Sorry, I'm getting off on too many sidetracks. Comes from being an old man, you know. You cannot focus your thoughts as well any more.

"One day, eight armed guards of Herod Antipas came into the camp. With drawn swords, they arrested John and took him away. It seems that John had condemned Herod's marriage to Herodias, his half-brother's wife. This was in violation of the basic understanding of purity, and was prohibited by the Torah. Jesus thinks it was much more because John's teachings ran counter to those of the Pharisees and the official priests in Jerusalem. There was also the fact that Antipas might have feared that John would ferment rebellion, something that would be terrible for the people and their king, Herod Antipas himself. The Romans were known for being strict with kings who could not keep their people in line.

"Whatever the real reason for John's arrest, Jesus and the

other disciples scattered in fear of their own lives. A short time later, he heard of John's beheading and experienced a period of fear, disorientation and pain. The man who had become the focal point of his life was dead. It left him aching and lonely. But it also gave him a new sense of confidence and independence. He was a disciple of a great man, a man who had tried to show the people the way to salvation in the coming apocalypse.

"He returned to Galilee and his family. Surprisingly, he was welcomed by his family. Part of that was because his stepfather, whom he still refuses to even name, had died. And another hand could always be used in the fields or as a repairman, which was the trade his father had taught him. There was also the fact that Galilee had heard of John and some of the respect for what some considered a prophet rubbed off on Jesus. Anyway, he settled down in Nazareth, but not to the life he had known. Here was someone who had done things not done by normal villagers. Here was a man who had rubbed shoulders with a local folk hero, John, and now spoke much as that prophet had. He began to tell others of his views. In short, he became a teacher, a rabbi.

"He was twenty years old when this happened. It was the actual beginning of his ministry. Slowly, his notoriety grew and more people came to listen to him. Not all agreed with him, especially the priests, but eventually the small towns around Nazareth were not enough and he switched his base of operations to Capernaum.

"Other changes came about. He ceased the immersion in living water as a means of release from sin. Instead, he emphasized the use of a meal as a festive celebration. He spoke of *lakhma d'ateh*, the "bread that is to come." Bread and other foods came from the land and were pure in God's eyes.

As was wine. He used the meal as a means of spreading the word and as a means of purification.

"Again, I'm getting off the subject. I apologize.

"Jesus taught, moved around, constantly spreading the word of the coming of the 'Son of Man' and the apocalypse, when God would cleanse the land of the impure and install Israel to its proper place. He had troubles with the established priesthood in Jerusalem who felt him a menace. You must always remember that their land was under the rule of Rome, and the Pharisees feared Roman intervention. And the Pharisees just plain did not like anyone teaching against their rules.

"Do not get Jesus off on the subject of the Pharisees. He hates the way they defiled the Temple – at least in his view. One of the main bones of contention was the manner in which sacrifices were made in the Temple. But I won't get into that. Suffice it to say that there was no love lost between him and the ruling priesthood.

"Now here is where I have to back up and explain something." He took a deep breath. "Up to a certain point, Jesus had preached that the 'Son of Man' would come to inaugurate the Kingdom of God during the apocalypse. He firmly believed that this apocalypse would happen very soon. This was a common belief of many Jews at that time. God would step in and set everything right. And any day now.

"But... He taught that this Son of Man was a divine one sent directly from God. He always referred to him in the third person. This man would be as an angel, holy and blessed with powers by God.

"At some point, his view changed. I think he grew tired of waiting. Or something like that. Or maybe he had always been heading in that direction anyway, but at some point be began to think of himself as that appointed agent of God. It was he who would do as God wished, bring in the Kingdom of God, to be the Messiah, the savior of the people.

"He began to really believe this. You can see a hint of that inspired belief in his eyes when he talks of it. But also a bitter sense that he had failed or was wrong to begin with.

"Regardless of what he thinks right now, at that time, and right up to his crucifixion, he believed that he was the Son of Man, God's own chosen one. That affected his thinking and actions from that point on. He felt that it was upon his shoulders alone to help bring about the apocalypse. He had prophecies of the old prophets to guide him. He set out to fulfill them.

"Eventually, this led him to Jerusalem on that fateful Passover, and you know what happened then.

"I have tried to understand when this change in understanding of his nature happened and what, if anything, triggered it. So far, I have been unsuccessful. Perhaps it was always there, lurking in his subconscious. Are not there enough examples throughout history of men who proclaimed themselves to be the Messiah? Even in Jesus' time and before, there were Messiahs. Even today, there are men who claim to be Jesus returned or a part of God in some way."

He sighed, and suddenly looked a lot older.

"I'm sure a psychiatrist would have a lot to say about this. Perhaps someday one will examine Jesus. Oh, that will be interesting!"

He shook his head.

"Sorry to be so long-winded. The simple answer to your question is that the Jesus we have here, as far as I can tell, is simply a man. There is nothing divine about him. He cannot work miracles. He cannot walk on water. He is a man. Just a man with a vision, and depressed that his vision never came true."

It was Tamara's turn to shake her head. "But what about the claims of the gospels? That he did perform these miracles? Raise the dead? That he is the Son of God?"

Myers leaned back in his chair. "First," he said, "you have to understand and accept that God does exist. Of that there can be no doubt. But Jesus, even if he thought he was fulfilling God's will, was a man. Those who wrote of him did so many years after the events. And, for the most part, they were people who did not know Jesus, nor even know one of those who did. The gospels describe what these unknown writers wanted Jesus to be. And wanted to believe he did.

"There is a huge gap between what Jesus actually taught and believed, and what the religion named after him claims. I cannot say whether Jesus was guided by God in what he did and what he preached. All I can tell you is that he was a remarkable man who had something about him sufficiently unusual to influence people around him. He was special; but you already know that: you've met him.

"But we will talk of that another time. I am tired. And you've undoubtedly heard enough of my voice. Would you like to go to lunch with me? And Jesus?"

16. LATE NIGHT CONVERSATION

It was after midnight in the palace-like building in the tiniest country in the world. Gilded furniture and ancient painting adorned the room, along with tapestries of the finest quality depicting religious scenes. Behind an ornate French provincial desk sat a man in red robes. He was an older man, back bent by both time and responsibility, his hair only a fringe round the small cap matching the red of his robe. On his left hand was a gold ring; a massive gold ring that looked far too large for his slender, wrinkled fingers. Set in it was a ruby. On the sides were crosses carved into the solid gold.

"Your Eminence, I am sorry to call upon you so late, but it is of the utmost importance."

The visitor also wore a cardinal's robe but remained standing before his superior.

"We have a communication from America. About that... That matter we discussed yesterday.

"Yes? And?" asked the seated man. His voice was barely above a whisper but easily heard in the otherwise silent room.

"Things are happening. An outsider to the company has become aware of this Project J, as has the Projector Director of Chronodyne. Our informant feels that this may lead to a public disclosure of what they have done."

"But they have done nothing in that direction yet? It is still a secret?"

"Yes, your Eminence. It is that our informant fears the secret cannot be kept much longer. When too many people know a secret..."

"Yes, yes. But what can we do?"

"Perhaps much. At the very least we must prepare the Church's official stand when this becomes public. His Holiness will have to make a statement on it. Silence can only hurt us."

The older man looked up with watery eyes to the standing man but said nothing.

"Your Eminence, there are other possibilities, other actions we could take to make sure that this blasphemy does not become public."

"What are you suggesting, Carabelli?"

"We can eliminate this false Christ," he said flatly.

"Eliminate...? What are you saying? That we somehow kill the... Him?"

"It is not Jesus, your Eminence. Only something they made up to seem to be Christ. It may be a man, but it is not our Lord Jesus. I have tried to explain this to you. This is only a poor copy of something they plucked out of the past."

"Still, I cannot condone what you suggest. You would kill a man?"

"Others have died to preserve the Church. The potential for disaster here is more important than one man's life. And it was a created man. Like a robot. This man was not born of woman."

The seated Cardinal only shook his head.

"You will at least tell his Holiness of this?"

"Yes. I will. Perhaps that is best. The Pontiff will be guided by God to do what is right."

"Of course, your Eminence, of course."

The seated man totally missed the sarcasm and the hint of suppressed anger.

"I will tell him tomorrow. But I do not think this affair is as dangerous as you believe it to be. Nevertheless, I will talk with his Holiness. You may leave."

The other Cardinal made a slight bow and turned. As he walked across the carpet, his face was set into hard lines. "The fool," he muttered under his breath. "He knows nothing. He does not understand the danger at all!"

17. TURN THE OTHER CHEEK

The summer sun was bright, but not overly hot at that altitude. The table in the patio was set for lunch when Dr. Myers and Tamara entered the courtyard. A large umbrella shaded most of the table and the four chairs around it.

"Please sit down, Tamara. He will be here soon." Myers waited until she had taken a seat then sat down himself, easing into the chair while leaning on his cane.

"Please remember," he said in a low voice, "this man is of a different time and a vastly different culture. And there are things that we do not think it wise to let him know as of yet. So please don't talk about religion at all. At least, not current religion. You'll find he's only too willing to discuss his views."

He paused to laugh gently, mostly to himself. "I will enjoy seeing his face when he finds out about the vast Catholic Church founded in his name. Now that will be more of a shock than airplanes or TV!"

"Have you told him about the Jewish religion? A lot has changed from his day."

Myers sighed. "Yes and no. At first I told him that our people have finally regained the land God granted us in the covenant. *'And he said unto him, I am the LORD that brought thee out of Ur of the Chaldees, to give thee this land to inherit it.'*"

"Genesis 15-1," Tamara said. "*And I will establish my covenant between me and thee and thy seed after thee in their generations for an everlasting covenant, to be a God unto thee, and to thy seed after thee.*"

89

"You know your Bible well," Myers chuckled. "Well, so I wanted him to know that our people have at last obtained the land given us by God. But his first question was if he could visit the Temple in Jerusalem. Well, you can imagine my problem. If I explained to him that the Temple was destroyed only a few years after his death, that would open too many questions, and probably upset him. So I told him the Temple still is in Jerusalem. Which is the truth. Part of it still is. One wall, at least.

"And I told him that someday he might be able to go there.

"His next question was if Israel now ruled the world. If you will recall, I mentioned that he was an apocalyptic Jew. The belief of many at that time was that God would come and straighten out things. He would see that our people got back the land he gave us. He would throw off the oppressor that ruled that land. And many also believed that God would set up Israel to rule the world in an era of peace and harmony among all people. After all, this was God, the All Powerful, coming to set things right.

"I had to tell him that had not yet come to pass. I didn't mention that it was unlikely to, either."

Taking in a deep breath, Myers added, "It would be best not to let him know the true state of the world today. So please be cautious."

They were interrupted by a door opening and the subject of their conversation appearing. Jesus walked slowly along the path to where they sat. He did limp, but Tamara was surprised that he could walk as well as he did. Again he was wearing slacks and sandals, this time with a pale green sweatshirt, again proclaiming UCLA across the front.

Tamara stood when he reached the table.

"Shalom," she said.

"Shelama," said Myers. "That's how you say it in Aramaic. Means the same."

"Shelama," replied Jesus. "It is good to see you again. God's blessings upon you."

Dr. Myers had to translate, explaining to Tamara that Jesus had learned only a few words of English and they were not really trying to teach it to him.

"Thank you." She halted, however, before returning the blessing. It did not seem right, somehow, to offer God's blessing to his Son.

Myers, who had not risen, said, "Please sit down. Lunch will be here soon."

Jesus sat down carefully, as if his knees were stiff. He also eased slowly back into the chair. Back still sore, Tamara told herself. Poor man.

At that point, the door opened again and a man pushed a cart through. He was wearing a pale blue jumpsuit with the Chronodyne logo on the chest pocket. She had seen more than a few such informal uniforms around the compound. The man, himself, had darker features than Jesus, and long black hair tied into a ponytail. From his features, Tamara was sure that he was an Indian, probably Navaho or some local tribe. He began setting plates and bowls of food on the table.

As the food was being set out, Tamara noticed that Jesus was staring at the man.

Myers explained. "He had never seen an American Indian, you know. John's features fascinate him."

Jesus turned to her and smiled. Again there was that change from a tired, concerned frown to a pleasant, friendly face.

With the food set out, and each was poured a glass of

SEAN BRANDYWINE

white wine, Jesus picked up a tortilla and broke it into three pieces. Handing a piece to each of them, he said some words in Aramaic, which Myers did not bother to translate. They began to eat.

"How far are we from Jerusalem?" Jesus asked, looking at Tamara but the question was directed to Myers.

"Oh, a long way."

"Ten days of walking? Twenty?" he asked.

"If you could walk it, it would take you many times that amount. And you would have to cross an ocean."

"An ocean," Jesus said flatly.

"A big ocean. Much bigger than you know."

Jesus reached for a slice of melon, apparently letting the question of how long it would take him to walk to Jerusalem slide.

Most of the food, Tamara noted, was fruits. One plate held slices of baked fish, probably halibut. Jesus picked up a piece of the fish and put it on his plate. Joining it were grapes, slices of melon, and dates.

"Jesus enjoys lamb," Myers told her between bites of his own fish. "But, you know, he had never eaten beef! Took a while to convince him that beef was kosher. We do, of course, avoid non-kosher food. At least, anything that might upset his sense of purity. That is very important to the people of his time, just as it is to many Jews today. They must be pure in all things to please God."

Jesus looked to Myers because he had not translated his words to Tamara into Aramaic. Myers explain quickly what he had said, and then added, "I'm trying to get Yeshua to enjoy a thick, barbequed steak. Maybe if he sees you eating one, he'll consider it."

As the lunch progressed, Tamara noticed that Jesus was

awkward using his knife and fork. "He was used to eating with his fingers," Myers explained. "And a knife to cut as needed. I've told him that he doesn't have to use the silverware but he wants to fit in with the rest of us. So he tries."

"Tell me, friend Seymour, you said that the land granted us by God is again ruled by Israel. What of the Romans? Were they cast out?"

Translating his words for Tamara gave Myers the chance to compose a reply.

"The Romans left, that is true. But it was many years before the Holy Land came to the people of Israel."

Jesus paused while taking a fork of fish towards his mouth. The piece of fish fell back onto the plate. "Where they overthrown by the sword?" he asked.

"They were conquered by the sword, but it was not Jewish swords."

Jesus seemed to consider this. "There were those in our land who wanted to drive the Romans out by the sword," he said finally. "There were times when I felt that the coming of God's Kingdom could only be by way of our people taking up arms. I had hoped that God would perform a miracle, as he did when he parted the sea for Moses. But the land had been taken by the strength of our swords, and the help of God, and would most probably be done the same again when the Kingdom arrived."

"You actually considered an armed rebellion?" asked Tamara. Myers shot her a swift glance before translating.

"Yes. There were times when we had to take the land by force," he replied. "As when the land was taken from an evil king by Judas."

"What does he mean?" asked Tamara.

"After Alexander the Great's death, the Holy Land came

under the rule of Seleucus, one of Alexander's officers. One of his successors, Antiochus, began a policy of turning the land and the people into pseudo Greeks. He made possession of the Torah a capital offense, banned many Jewish practices such as sacrifices, feasts, even circumcision. Altars to Greek gods were set up in the Temple in Jerusalem and he ordered swine to be sacrificed to Zeus because roast pork was a favorite of that god. Things came to a head when the High Priest, Mattathias, refused to worship an idol of Zeus that had been placed on the altar in the Temple. He and his sons were forced to flee into the wilderness where they began a guerrilla war against the Seleucid army, led by one of his sons, Judas Maccabee, and against all odds, they won.

"They ritually cleansed the Temple and created a kingdom that lasted for a hundred years, ending about sixty years before Jesus was born."

"Oh, yes, I remember that," Tamara said. "When he said Judas, I was a little confused."

"Judas in this case is Judas Maccabee. And that was where Hanukkah came from; when a single day's supply of oil kept the Menorah burning for eight days," Myers continued. All that had been in English. Turning to Jesus, he gave a quick summary of what he had told Tamara. Jesus nodded – it was an old story to him.

Tamara was frowning. When she had the chance, she asked, "Jesus, I have trouble believing that you would suggest an armed revolt. You said so much about peace and loving your neighbor. Did you not say: 'That ye resist not evil: but whosoever shall smite thee on thy right cheek, turn to him the other also'?"

For a long time Jesus just looked at her, his food forgotten, his eyes intent upon her face. Finally he relaxed and said, "I once said something like that. I was giving advice to my followers concerning the Roman troops. I was sending them out to teach of the coming Kingdom. I knew that they would encounter Roman soldiers, so I instructed them not to resist armed soldiers. If struck, do not strike back. If a Roman soldier tells you to do some work, then do it and more. Give them no reason to kill you."

Jesus pushed away the plate before him. "Our people had tried. In the year I was born, arms were taken up against Archelaus. Roman troops from Syria came and many were killed. Two thousand were crucified!

"Again, when I was a child of ten, more were killed trying to free our land.

"I knew the Kingdom of God was soon to come. When that happened, God would sharpen our swords and we would drive the Romans before us. But until then, we lacked the numbers. We lacked the swords. Until God helped us, we could not defeat the foreigners by force of arms. I knew it was not the right time to attempt such. But soon, very soon the Son of Man would come and God would restore the land to my people. We would answer the Jewish bloodshed by the Romans with an equal amount of Roman blood.

"Until then, it would be best to turn away lest they do more than strike you upon the cheek."

Tamara did not know what to say. She could sense the hatred in his voice when he spoke of the Romans. Suddenly it was believable that this man, called by some the Prince of Peace, would led an armed revolt with all the bloodshed that would entail.

"There were no Roman troops actually stationed in Galilee at that time," Myers told her. "But he was sending the disciples out to spread the word, to tell of the coming

Kingdom and bid the people repent so they would become part of the Kingdom. He didn't want them to fail in that mission because they pissed off some Roman soldier they encountered."

Jesus was sipping at his wine. Tamara drank from her glass. It was a light Chablis.

"Jesus is fascinated by the quality and variety of wines available now," Myers told her. "Back then, he was limited to that which could be made locally. Some of the Romans had wine imported from Rome and Greece, but Jesus lived most of his life in a small rural town, and was never rich enough to afford such luxuries."

Jesus had finished his wine and was pouring another glass from the carafe. The idea of a drunken Jesus flashed through her mind and she had to keep from reacting to it. She told herself that there was no reason why Jesus would not feel the effect of a bit too much wine. Sitting before her was a man. And a man who liked wine. Nothing wrong with that. Did not the Bible say: *"...but use a little wine for thy stomach's sake and thine often infirmities?"*

The lunch was obviously over. "Jesus and I were going to talk a little bit about the layout of the Temple in those days. Would you like to sit in?"

Tamara could sense that Myers would rather she did not. The conversation would undoubted proceed much faster if he did not have to take the time to translate the Aramaic for her.

"Thank you, but I have work to attend to." She started to rise, but paused to ask, "I am curious? I'm sure Jesus was not a student at UCLA. Why does he wear that shirt?"

Myers laughed politely. "When he had recovered enough to leave his bed, we had to find some clothes for him. I had a UCLA sweatshirt left over from the days when I was a professor there. Taught Biblical History. Well, it fitted him, and he seemed to like the letters across the chest. I'm not sure why. Perhaps I should ask him. Anyway, I ordered a couple more for him. The green one is his favorite."

Tamara said her goodbye to Jesus and Dr. Myers. Walking back to the office allocated to her, she did a lot of thinking, still trying to comprehend the magnitude of what they had done here, and how incredibly different this man was from what she had expected.

18. DECISION

It was nighttime in Cairo, just after midnight, and the sounds of the latest protests had died down. Abdul Murad looked out from the office window at the nearly deserted streets below. A single vehicle, an old American brand, slowly cruised along, looking for what Murad had no idea. Perhaps it was just someone looking for trouble. It seemed to him that there was always someone looking for trouble. Uneasy times, these days.

As second in command, he had powers but had mostly been content to allow Munif to lead. The problem now was that Munif did not know what to do. He was a good leader if you wanted a protest organized, a building blown up, or someone assassinated. But when something different came up, he could not make the decisions when they had to be made. Perhaps his time as their leader was over.

Resting his head against the window frame, the young man who had gunned down men and woman, built bombs for others to destroy their enemies with their sacrifice, and helped lay plans for spreading terror among the enemies of Islam, thought upon what he had heard from the infidel Americans. They claimed to have created *Isa* the *Masih*, the Messiah, whom Allah sent to guide the Children of Israel with the new *injil*, the new Gospel! After much reflection, he found he did not believe their claim. It must be a trick of some kind. They could not have brought one of Allah's messengers from the past to today. The infidels wished to confuse and delude the faithful.

But Abdul does not see this clearly! He does not see the need for immediate action; instead he talks with the *imam*, asking for guidance. While he waits, these Americans will bring this false prophet to the world, spread their lies, and there are many who will believe.

Murad stood away from the window. The slow moving car had passed from sight. In his heart, he knew that Allah has chosen him to act as his sword. Why else would this news have come to him? Why else would he feel so deeply in his heart that he was right?

He began preparations to go to America.

19. DEBATE

Tamara sat at the desk and rested her fingers lightly on the keyboard of the computer terminal they had given her. A lot was going through her mind: amazement, confusion, surprise and more than a little awe. As a teenager she had always been interested in religions, but especially that mystical and powerful time two thousand years ago when Jesus walked the dirt paths of what is now Israel. Although not a religious person herself, she was fascinated by the whole story. Perhaps it was just a part of her nature to dig into stories and root out the facts. She had turned that interest and ability into a good career working for the government. Perhaps it was simply that the whole story of Jesus was one great murder mystery she felt compelled to solve.

Or maybe, were she honest enough to admit it, she simply wanted to know the truth behind what happened all those years ago. Was Jesus just a man, or something divine? Was he The Son of God? Which was, of course, just a part of a bigger question: does God exist? She was never sure of the answer, but, like most people, she wanted to know, to have something to base her understanding of the world and existence.

"Hello."

The voice startled her, and she looked up to see a man standing in the doorway. He was of medium height but quite slender. The lab coat hung loosely on his gaunt frame. More bald than not, what was left of his hair was a fuzzy fringe around his head and streaked with gray. His features were thin, his eyes dark behind thick glasses. Had he not been wearing the uniform of a lab scientist, she thought he would have looked appropriate in the black suit of an undertaker.

"I'm Hans Buerer. I'm a research assistant on Project J. Dr. Fielding tells me that you are now cleared to our little secret. He asked that I help you to access any records you want."

"Hello, Dr. Buerer. I'm Tamara Graves. Nice to meet you."

Stepping in, he offered his hand. It was a very weak handshake, she noted, almost feminine.

"Please, have a seat," she told him.

"Thank you. If there is anything I can do for you, you'll find my extension in the directory. It's off the main menu," he added, gesturing to the computer screen. "Oh... I guess you have already looked there. How else would you know to call me Dr. Buerer?"

"It is true that I looked over a list of personnel," she told him with a smile. "It is the first thing I do in any audit. But there are so many PhDs around here, it would be a safe guess to call anyone doctor."

He laughed at that, an undertaker's mild chuckle that just reinforced that image. "Well, I'll get going. Just wanted to introduce myself and see if there is anything I can help you with."

"There is one thing," she told him. "What is your impression of your... ah, guest?"

He frowned. "My impression? Had I not been with this project from almost the inception, I would say that the man there is simply an approximation of a man who lived long ago. However, I know full well just how accurate the Machine can reproduce something from the past, down to the sub-atomic level. All the neurons of the human brain have been created in the Machine exactly as they were at the point in time when the original existed. Exactly! That man has the exact memories and behavior patterns of the original Jesus.

"You do understand, don't you, that he is a copy? Not the original brought here through a Time Machine."

She replied, "I've had enough science background to understand the principle, as hard to believe as it may be. The Jesus I have met has the body and memories of the original, I'm sure. But what I wonder is if there was something in the original that could not be copied."

"Ah, you have hit upon something that has sparked much debate! Does the Machine recreate the soul? Or is that something beyond even our advanced science? Was there something else in Jesus that did not come to us?"

"How do you believe, Doctor?"

For a brief second his eyes turned hard, but the look was gone as quickly as it had come. He laughed mildly. "That, my dear, is where I differ from most of my colleagues. I believe that this man is only a shell of what Jesus was... and is. I believe that there is no way technology can create the spirit within. That man is an automaton, like an organic computer programmed to respond in totally human ways but lacking the inner soul."

"But he seems so very real!" Tamara protested mildly. "I have talked with him. I have seen him show emotions. I have seen him reason. Is there any way to distinguish this Jesus from a totally naturally created human?"

"I can think of none," he admitted. "Yet, I believe this man is no more than a copy. He may seem to be Jesus but he is not." His frown turned into a mocking smile. "How can a machine create what is beyond the physical? No, Miss Graves, this is not Jesus Christ."

Tamara could sense the sincerity behind his words. After he had said his polite goodbye and gone, she sat there for a long time, thinking. And finally coming to the conclusion that, as so often happens in religious matters, it boils down to a matter of faith.

Which left her no closer to the truth than she had been before. With a sigh, she turned to the computer to do some of the work she had been sent there to do.

20. QUESTIONS

The last of the setting sun's crimson beams were illuminating the mountains to the east, turning into reddish brown and giving testimony to why they were called the Sangre de Cristo, Blood of Christ, Mountains. Tamara stood by her Corvette outside the housing assigned her and watched as the disappearing sun lit up the distant peaks. It reminded her of her childhood home in Colorado where incredibly beautiful mountains, sunsets and sunrises were the norm. She had finished dinner in the Chronodyne cafeteria, an excellent lobster bisque followed by basil salmon *terrine*, all good enough to convince her that the chef *had* to be a Frenchman.

The evening progressed, the mountains turned darker and darker red, and she finally went into the small apartment that was her temporary home. On a small desk in the front room was a computer. It was not connected to the Chronodyne network but did have the Internet, so she brought up Pandora radio and tuned in to her favorite classical station. Beethoven's *Pathetique* piano sonata filled the room. Slipping her shoes off, she flopped on the bed and allowed the music to comfort her.

In the morning, she knew she would have to have another talk with the Chronodyne Project Director, Dr. Stryker. She had spent a good part of the afternoon tracking down some of the unaccounted Machine usage. Knowing about Project J's hidden usage in bringing Jesus to life, she was puzzled by some remaining occasional additional discrepancies. They were hidden pretty well for most people, but she was a very good auditor and considered the attempts rather crude. She had a list of unauthorized usages and knew who was responsible for them. All that remained was to inform the Project Director and let him take it from there.

She sighed, and tried to push her work out of her mind. The discrepancies were really minor and would be taken care of, but the fact that she had had lunch with Jesus Christ was still hard to accept. Likewise, his insistence that force should be used, but only when you have a good chance of winning. Or maybe, to put it more accurately, when you have God on your side, assuring you of victory. It did not match up with the pacifist image of him years of Sunday school had instilled in her mind. His "turn the other cheek" had been only telling his disciples not to mess with the Roman soldiers.

The Internet radio shifted to Johann Sebastian Bach, a cello solo she did not recognize.

There were still so many unanswered questions filling her thoughts. Was Jesus really a descendent of King David? And, as such, did he have a legitimate claim to the kingship of the Jewish people? What part did that play in his actions? Did he really know that he would be killed, and in such a gruesome manner? Or, more precisely, when did he come to that conclusion?

She felt like reaching for a pencil and paper to write down all the questions. At the very least, she should talk with Dr. Myers some more. She considered it likely that he had already asked most of those same questions of Jesus. She remembered that she had been offered the video recordings of the interviews. Perhaps it would be a good place to start. But then, she had to remind herself, she could not stay there forever. She had been sent in to do a job that should not have taken more than a week. Sooner or later her bosses, one nasty woman in particular, would be wanting to know what was taking so long. And she was not in a position to tell them the truth.

For that matter, there was the question of when the project would be announced publicly. It seemed inconceivable to her that such an incredible accomplishment would be kept secret from the world. In a sense, the world had a right to know. At least, that was how she felt. Not only the scientific advance they had made, but also the important person they had brought back. How many millions of people would love to have a chance to talk to Jesus? To hear from his own lips of the events during and at the end of his life.

While lying there, thinking about that, she became aware of a growing sense of unease. What if the world was told? What would the reaction be? Cheers? Or rioting in the streets? One thing was certain; there would be strong feelings about this.

With a big sigh, she began undressing for bed. As was her wont, she would read in bed for an hour or so before turning out the light. As she did, she wondered if the people here, from the Project Director on down, really understood the powder keg they were sitting on.

21. MORE QUESTIONS

"I want to know."

Tamara had just asked a question of Dr. Myers and was awaiting his reply.

"My dear, that is a complicated question. I'm not sure I know the answer."

"It can't be that hard," she told him as she paced in front of his desk. "Just tell me: did Jesus arise from the dead?"

"You do know that we retrieved him just before the point where he died."

"Yes."

"So there is no way that we can ask him what happened after that point."

"True. But your Machine has the ability to see the past. How else could you have identified the time and place to grab him? Or any of the artifacts. Hasn't someone wondered what happen after that? It wouldn't be too hard, would it, to simply watch what happened after his death?"

Myers sighed. "At first, it was decided that we would not use the Machine to determine what happened postmortem. The whole issue of his resurrection has serious religious ramifications, as you can understand. This is a very emotional issue with many people. If we determined that he did appear to his disciples, it would confirm the basic principle of the Christian religion. Likewise, if we do not find any proof of a resurrection, that could well undermine the faith of millions."

She frowned and said, "You say 'at first'...?"

Myers sighed and shifted in his chair. "So I did. Well, as you can imagine, there are those in the project who were curious. A lot of debate ensured over that issue. Finally, the side that wanted the truth – no matter what it was – won out."

"So you did use the Machine to look..."

"We did."

"And?"

"After his apparent death on the cross, we observed several people taking his body down. They wrapped it in a cloth and carried it away. Jesus died surprisingly quickly. He was on the cross only a few hours. Normally, the victim was simply left to die. However, if the soldiers wanted to speed up the death for some reason, they would break the victim's legs."

"Break the legs?"

"You have to understand, death by crucifixion usually does not come from dehydration or starvation. Even if left up for a day or more, the victim, already weak from a whipping, loss of blood and shock, usually dies of suffocation. When he can no longer support his weight by his arms and legs, his thorax closes and he gradually suffocates. Breaking the legs prevents the victim from supporting himself and death comes faster.

"Pilate expressed surprise that Jesus had died in less than six hours. Mark 15:44: *'And Pilate marveled if he were already dead; and calling unto him the centurion, he asked him whether he had been any while dead'.*"

"And then...?"

"Let me quote you a little more scripture.

"John 19:29: *Now there was set a vessel full of vinegar: and they filled a sponge with vinegar, and put it upon hyssop, and put it to his mouth.*

"*When Jesus therefore had received the vinegar, he said, It is finished: and he bowed his head, and gave up the ghost.*

"*The Jews therefore, because it was the preparation, that the bodies should not remain upon the cross on the Sabbath day, (for that Sabbath day was an high day,) besought Pilate that their legs might be broken, and that they might be taken away.*

"*Then came the soldiers, and brake the legs of the first, and of the other which was crucified with him.*

"*But when they came to Jesus, and saw that he was dead already, they brake not his legs:...*"

"But one of the soldiers with a spear pierced his side, and forthwith came there out blood and water," she finished the quote.

"Yes," he nodded. "We saw them break the legs of the other two, then stand there to watch them die. They would be taken down after they died and cast into a pit, not buried. That was the fate of most who were crucified. Only if the family or someone wanted the body and petitioned for it, would the body not be tossed into the pit.

"But Jesus, apparently already dead, was taken down by the soldiers. Now here is where things get interesting. Keep in mind that when he was crucified, it was the afternoon before the Sabbath. And to Jews, a day begins at sundown. It is also a Jewish requirement that the body of a dead man not be left exposed, even for one night. The Torah clearly states that it must be interred to avoid defiling the land. So, instead of remaining on the cross after sundown, alive or dead, his supposedly dead body was taken away.

"Since you know your Bible so well, I'm sure you know the part about Joseph of Arimathea asking Pilate for the body. Joseph was a *Sanhedrin* rabbi, a respected member of the Temple Council. Since it was the high priest and others of the priesthood who feared Jesus and wanted him out of the way, why would a member of that council want to treat his body with respect even to the point of placing it in a cave reserved for his own body eventually? And another rabbi, Nicodemus, also a *Sanhedrin* member, helps in this act? Why not his disciples? They were nowhere to be seen.

"So, Jesus is taken to this nearby cave. There, two women, Mariam of Magdala and another Mariam, the mother of one of the disciples, have the task of washing away the blood and filth. Joseph of Arimathea had given them money to buy burial ointment, olive oil mixed with myrrh and aloes. That's what the Bible says.

"Now, if you are a conspiracy theorist, there is much here you can pounce upon. The whole series of events seems to have been planned. Why did he die so quickly? Did it have something to do with the vinegar given him on a sponge? John said, *'When Jesus therefore had received the vinegar, he said, It is finished: and he bowed his head, and gave up the ghost.'*

"Is it possible that there was something more than vinegar on that sponge? Perhaps a drug to render him unconscious and apparently dead? If he were alive as sundown approached, he would have been left there or his legs would have been broken so that he would die before sundown."

He paused to push back his chair and turn to a side table on which sat a coffee maker. "Would you like some?" he asked.

"No thank you, I prefer tea. But what I would like to know is if what you saw agrees with the Bible."

"For the most part, yes. I have seen the recording made through the Machine. It is surprisingly good quality. You can see a lot of details.

"I saw Jesus nailed to the cross. By the way, you would probably be surprised but the cross was not as depicted in all those paintings. He was not hung on a tall pole well above the heads of the soldiers. His feet were actually only about eighteen inches off the ground. His head was barely above those of the men around him. Same with the other two. If you think about it, that makes it a hell of a lot easier for them to hang him up and eventually take him down.

"Anyway, that made it easy for someone to give him a drink of vinegar in a sponge. I saw that. I replayed that part several times. The man who gave the sponge to Jesus was a Roman soldier, but he looked to a man on the side before he did it. I got the impression that the soldier was given a clue when to perform that supposed act of insult.

"Now comes another interesting part. As soon as Jesus apparently passes out, the same Roman comes up and jabs him with a javelin or spear. Some blood comes out. But Jesus does not react. To the centurion in command of the soldiers, that was proof that Jesus was dead.

"Almost immediately, the man secretly directing this little scene comes forth and talks with the centurion. Equally quickly, Jesus is being taken down.

"His body is wrapped in a piece of cloth and carried away by two men. Those men were not disciples. From their dress and appearance, I believe they were Jewish and of the priestly class, or at least wealthy.

"Now, consider this. Sundown is coming soon. This man, whom I believe to be Joseph of Arimathea, gives a silent order and Jesus is drugged, probably by a bribed soldier. A spear pokes his side and gets no reaction. Immediately he is taken down and hauled away. Apparently Joseph had already gotten permission from Pilate to take the body – I think the Gospel got the sequence of events a little out of order there. It is also apparent that they wanted him down quickly before he suffocated to death.

"The prophecies..." Tamara said.

"Yes, the prophecies. *'A bone of him shall not be broken.'* And *'They shall look on him whom they pierced'.*

"Well, the recording follows Jesus' body away from Golgotha, rather hurriedly, I might add. He is taken to a cave. The inside had been prepared as a family tomb, one of many in that area.

"Here an interesting part occurs. He is put on a ledge. Then, instead of calling upon the women to do the job of cleaning the body, one of the two men pours a liquid into his mouth from a small jar. They try to get him to swallow it. They wait a minute, and then they try again. And a third time.

"Finally, they realize that apparently he is truly dead. Only then does one of them leave. Not long after that, two women come in to clean the body and wrap it loosely in a linen cloth. The day after the Sabbath, they will come back and anoint the body with oil and wrap it tighter. Then it will sit in the tomb for one year. At the end of that time, the bones will be placed in a stone box called an ossuary.

"After they leave, that is where that part of the recording ends. He is wrapped and lying there."

"You're saying that the men tried to revive him?" Tamara said, sounding shocked. "That it was the plan that he not die on the cross?"

"I told you what I saw. I can only add that I was able to see the faces of the two men, Joseph and Nicodemus, both rabbis who agreed with Jesus' teaching."

"But..." She seemed at a loss for words. What finally came out was, "Did you follow up? The next day. And the third day? To be sure?"

"Yes. The Machine recording skipped forward in time.

His body was still there on the Sabbath, Saturday. Later that night, the two men returned and took the body away, to another tomb, I imagine. The next day, after the Sabbath had ended, two women came to finish the preparation of the body."

"So he never arose..."

"I'm afraid not. But the women thought that he did. My guess is that they were meant to think that by those who took away the body. And then the story grows from there, because it was written by people who were believers. Suddenly there are angels sitting in the tomb and such."

The two of them were silent, each lost in their own thoughts. One was a Jew, the other not really a believer, so the facts were believable to them. Had either been a true Christian, that might have been impossible.

Finally, Tamara said with a weak smile, "You could prove your conspiracy theory."

"Oh? How so?"

"Use the Machine to make a copy of the sponge. Then test it for drugs."

Myers frowned, and then shook his head in wonderment, not disbelief. "That thought, my dear, never occurred to us."

22. CAUGHT!

When they knocked on the door to his apartment, Timothy Williams yelled, "Go away!" So they kicked the door open.

Three men entered the front room of the small apartment, two armed Federal Marshals with automatics drawn, and a tall man in a black business suit. On the couch, looking surprised as hell, was Williams. Also there was his live-in girlfriend, Daisy. Both were naked and engaged in sexual intercourse. Or they were, until interrupted so abruptly.

"What the shit!" exclaimed Williams. Daisy said, "Eck!"

The federal agents were frozen in their tracks, guns pointing at the couple. If they felt any surprise, it did not show on their faces. The third man, one Carl Manhusen, Chief of Security for the Chronodyne Dry Wells Project, smiled faintly, fighting to keep in a laugh.

"Get your clothes on," he told them.

The clothes in question were scattered around the couch. As the two hurried to get clothing on, Manhusen noted that Daisy appeared to be the kind of woman who would appeal to Williams: big breasted, long blonde hair which a quick glance proved to be from a bottle, and a not-too-smart look on her face. When the man had been hired to be an operator on the Machine, he had cleared background checks without problem, but it was noted in his file that he was of limited intelligence. His hiring had been marginal, and the initial doubts had now proven to be correct.

"Timothy Williams, I place you under arrest for theft of Chronodyne's property." One of the agents read him his Miranda rights. As soon as the two had enough clothing to be decent, Williams was handcuffed. Daisy's eyes lit up. "Oh, kinky!" she said. Manhusen sighed.

"Miss Miller, we are not arresting you at this time. However, if it appears that you were a willing accomplice to the crimes, you may be so charged at a later time."

"Huh?" she said.

"Search the place," Manhusen told the men. As they spread out to the different rooms, he began a survey of the front room. His attention was immediately drawn to the coffee table that had been pushed aside to make more room for their lovemaking. Resting atop some magazines was a crown. It appeared to be made of gold, with *fleurs-de-lis* and *crosses pattee* and two arches surmounted by a cross. The inside was of purple velvet and it had a white ermine border at the bottom. Many precious stones were set into the gold. Manhusen whistled when he saw it.

"Timmy, you've been a bad boy," he said with a smirk. "This is, unless my memory fails me, St. Edward's Crown. The original is, of course, in the Tower of London with the rest of the Crown Jewels." He lifted the crown. "Heavy. But then it is solid gold, almost five pounds of it."

Williams was looking at the floor and said nothing.

"You weren't giving this to your girl here, were you?"

The guilty man's silence spoke loud enough.

Manhusen laughed. "Not many girls get a gift like that!"

The others began bringing objects into the room. First was a large leather bound, very old looking book. "A Guttenberg Bible, oh my," said Manhusen. There followed a couple gold bars, each of which weighed twenty-five pounds, then a bag of loose, cut diamonds, a suitcase filled with stacks of banded one hundred dollar bills, all fresh and crisp straight from the mint, and finally a large single diamond.

"The Hope Diamond?" Manhusen asked. "Well, never mind. You do know that you would have been caught sooner or later? Most of this stuff is too hard to fence. The money would have been easiest, but since these are duplicates you copied, they would have duplicate serial numbers. If you sold them one at a time, you might have made some money off the diamonds. If you were careful."

Williams looked up. There was a small tear trickling down his cheek. "I didn't do anything wrong. These things are just copies. You know that. I didn't really steal anything."

"Copies, yes, but copies made with a Chronodyne machine and therefore the property of Chronodyne. Take him away."

As the agents led Williams out the door, Manhusen turned back to the confused Daisy sitting on the couch. "Don't expect to see your boyfriend for a long time, sweetie."

23. EXCREMENT STRIKES!

"The shit is hitting the fan!" exclaimed Dr. Stryker, his face red with anger. He jabbed at a remote on the tabletop. A large screen monitor on the wall of the conference room came to life. After a moment, a scene appeared showing a female newscaster seated behind a desk. Projected behind her was a picture of the Chronodyne headquarters building with the company's logo clearly visible.

"In a surprising announcement, Representative Norman Stockman, Chairman of the Committee on Science, Space, and Technology, today said that he wanted his committee to look into allegations that Chronodyne has developed a time machine. He said that he was informed of the development by sources he declined to name but that he does believe accurate.

"The time machine is supposed to be able to travel back in time to view events in the past, and possibly enable humans to travel back into the past and return. Since Chronodyne is the recipient of several large government contracts, Stockman wants to know why his committee hasn't been informed of this breakthrough. He also states that he wants an investigation alleged use of this time machine by the CIA and other agencies for spying purposes.

"When contacted by this reporter, Physicist Dr. Malchom Chilton of the Caltech stated that time travel is impossible, and he scoffed at reports of the existence of such a machine. 'Stockman should not believe such rumors,' he said.

"In other news..."

Stryker turned off the screen. Those around the table were silent.

"Well, how the hell did this Congressman get this?" he demanded. "Someone within this project must have blabbed."

Those present, which included all the sub-project heads, looked at each other but no one spoke. A couple looked in Tamara's direction.

"Miss Graves, you are the only person here who is not a part of the Chronodyne team. You show up and a few days later this happens. Have you told anyone about this project? Perhaps someone back in the DOD?"

"I have not," she said firmly, irritated that anyone would believe she could not keep a secret. "I have the highest clearance and am well aware of security requirements. I assure you that I have told no one – repeat, no one – any information about your project."

For a few seconds Stryker glared at her.

"Colonel Manhusen will be conducting an investigation," he finally said. "If there is a leak, we must plug it. This is not a good time for a general announcement to be made public. Especially not for certain projects within Dry Wells." He looked to Tamara as he said that.

She started to open her mouth to speak, but closed it when she realized that he was referring to Project J. Not everyone in the facility was aware of the true nature of Project J, which meant that some of those present did not know that Jesus was walking around only a couple of buildings away.

"What about that operator just arrested for misuse of the Machine?" asked Dr. Fielding. "Maybe he sold information as well as stolen objects."

Manhusen stood up. "I have been investigating him thoroughly, and I am convinced that Williams is a thief but did not ever think of selling information. Why should he? He was making profit with items obtained from the Machine, why endanger the whole project?"

"Then who did?" asked Juliette O'Neill. "Someone did."

"And I will find out," Manhusen told them sternly. From his six foot four inch height, looking down at the seated people, he was the image of undeniable authority.

Manhusen put in a request that anyone who has any information contact him. There did not seem much to say after that. But as the meeting was about to break up, Tamara spoke up.

"Dr. Stryker, may I make a suggestion?"

The Projector Director turned back to her. "Yes?"

"There was something that Dr. Brown suggested," she said, gesturing to the man. "He said that maybe the animals he was bringing to our time could be shown to the public as clones. You know, the Jurassic Park thing. If you did, you could just say that your project here was to clone extinct animals from DNA. Show them the dodo. And Smiley should really get attention. A Saber-Tooth Cat! Imagine how that would look on the evening news!

"But, you also release a statement that someone found out about this project and mistook it for a time machine. You could even say that one of your own scientists referred to it as a 'time machine of sorts,' and that maybe was the source of the confusion. Get a couple other scientists, not yours, to state that time travel is impossible. Might shoot down this problem before it gets out of hand. You don't want Congress actually investigating you, do you?"

Stryker shook his head, and actually smiled at her.

"Sounds like a good idea," said Fielding. "Might just work," added Dr. Crane. Stryker looked around the table.

Noting no objections, he said, "Brown, come with me. Let's see how we can set this up."

The room emptied quickly, leaving Tamara to wonder where the security breach might have come from. There were, at the current time, exactly one hundred and seven Chronodyne employees on site, plus one DOD visitor. That was a lot of possibilities, even if you figured that some of those were support staff, such as cafeteria crew and guards, who might not know the true nature of Dry Wells. Still left a lot of possibilities.

It was early afternoon and she decided to visit Dr. Myers. There were a few questions still bothering her. She wondered if she might have an interview with Jesus again.

24. BAD NEWS

The American Southwest reminded Khurram Murad of his homeland: it was hot, dry and had vast areas of emptiness. He watched from the window of the airliner as it descended in the landing pattern at Phoenix Sky Harbor International Airport. His cell phone beeped. The text message it had for him was simple: "Comet." It was from the only person who knew of his mission to the United States.

Since all the publicity about the American NSA spying on its own people via the PRISM program, they had reduced their cell phone communications to simple code words. 'Comet' told him there was a news item of importance he should look at. Bring up the smart phone's browser, he touched the key for CNN. The eighth item down the list caught his attention. Touching on that title, he brought up pretty much the same as the newscast displayed by Dr. Stryker only a few minutes prior as Murad's plane began its descent.

Keeping his face emotionless, he turned off the phone and put it back in his pocket. This piece of news did not please him. The news about what he thought of as the "False Isa" project was beginning to break. In a country where the press was not as muzzled as in his country, that meant that soon the headlines would be screaming of Jesus' Second Coming, or some such lurid crap.

The land below began to show many houses, and he knew that soon they would be landing. He would have to get his team together as quickly as possible. There was no time to lose and much to do. There was transportation to arrange, weapons to acquire and a team to assemble and brief.

Taking a deep breath, he prepared to go through the airport security once again. His Middle Eastern appearance always attracted attention when he flew.

He had to prevent the Americans announcing this fake Jesus. He had to. It was Allah's will.

25. ORDERS

In the same office where he had twice before met with a high ranking church official, a nervous man sat staring out the window at the city lights spread out. Not far off, a freeway showed a broken string of white headlights approaching and red taillights retreating. Even though he had met with the Bishop before, he still twisted his class ring nervously around and around on his finger.

A noise made him jerk, and he turned around to see the expected two men enter the room. Immediately he rose and accepted the offered hand, kissing the large gold ring.

"Have you any news?" the heavy-set man said as he sat behind the desk.

"They have decided to announce a part of the project as the cloning of extinct animals. Not time travel."

"I know. We have other sources for information. We would like to know who it was leaked information to that Congressman. That wasn't you, was it?"

The man standing before the desk shivered under the sternness in the Bishop's voice. "No, your Excellency! I have told no one but you!"

"It is too bad that news of the time machine has been leaked. It may lead to a public announcement; something we do not wish to happen."

The fat man settled back in the chair and folded his hands over his ample waist. He did not see the man behind him showing a faint smile. "I have been in touch with the highest

127

sources in Rome," he began, as if confiding a great confidence. "We cannot allow this false Christ to be presented to the public as if he were the real one. I hope you do understand that?"

"Yes, your Excellency. I understand. But what do you want...?"

He was silenced with the wave of a hand. "I will tell you what we want you to do." He gestured, and the second man handed forth a computer tablet. "This tablet has been programmed with information of a specific type. All you have to do is turn it on and touch the icon that will appear. Then you hand it to the false Jesus..."

26. DISRUPTION OF THE QUIET

Tamara did not get that interview with Jesus. That afternoon, Dr. Myers was "in conference" with his star guest and not to be disturbed. She left a note for him requesting to see him the next day, and returned to finishing up the report she was going to have to turn in sooner or later to her bosses.

It was not an easy report to write. In the end, she simply stated that she had found inappropriate use of computers and other equipment. And that the person responsible had been arrested and charged with several counts. A few other minor discrepancies in accounting practices were noted, along with their correction by the Dry Wells staff.

The report was done. But Tamara did not attach it to a cover letter, encrypt it, and email it off to her superiors. As soon as she did that, they would expect her to return for another assignment, and she did not want that. There was too much she wanted to know; too many questions. She might get in trouble for it, but so long as the Project J staff allowed her to remain, she fully intended to do so.

Closing and saving the file, she checked her email. There was one from Dr. Myers, informing her that he would be happy to see her any time the next morning. With a look of satisfaction, she turned off her terminal and left her little temporary office for an early dinner at the cafeteria and then some relaxing in her apartment.

The next morning, she set off for the Project J building after a good breakfast. She was getting spoiled by the food here. Not like most company cafeterias she had eaten in.

When she first awoke, the morning sky had been showing a few scattered clouds, but as the morning progressed it had become overcast with dark thunderheads over the mountains and a thickening patchwork ceiling above. She knew from her experience that there would be rain soon, the hard summer storm rains that pelted the earth with heavy drops and passed as quickly as they came. She began to walk a little faster when she heard a familiar sound behind her. Spinning around, she looked to the front gate just beyond the parking lot. The sound was gunfire, and it came from the two guards at that gate, both of whom were standing beside the small shack and firing at an on-charging truck. The truck, a two and a half ton, green painted version of the military M35 medium duty truck, was heading directly towards them at high speed.

One guard sprang to the side, narrowly being missed by the truck as it plowed through, the impact snapping off the wooden gate and sending it flying to one side. The other guard stood his ground, letting off rapid fire at the vehicle. Tamara could see bullet holes appearing in the windshield, but the truck did not waver or slow down. He was knocked viciously aside as the large truck shredded the side of the guard shack, and then it was through and speeding across the parking lot, almost straight towards her.

For a brief second she was frozen by this totally unexpected event, but she backpedaled rapidly as the truck neared her. As it passed only a dozen feet in front of her, she saw the driver looking out at her. In that brief split-second she noted his youth and the Middle Eastern appearance. A teenager, was her thought. A god-damned teenage terrorist!

The truck screeched to a halt beside the very building she had been walking towards. Four men jumped out, all armed with assault rifles. As they rushed to the entrance to the building, Tamara snapped out of her shock and began running towards them. She had no real plan. The only thought that raced through her brain was that they intended to kidnap or harm Jesus!

Before she reached the open front double door, she heard gunfire from within – three quick shots. The smart thing to do would have been to turn and run. Let the guards take care of this. But she did not flee. Instead, she ran through the glass doors and into the small lobby.

The terrorists were nowhere in sight. On the floor by the desk lay Murphy, a guard she had met a couple times when she went to visit Jesus. A pool of blood was spreading out under his body and three near holes in his uniform explained why.

Without thinking, Tamara knelt and took his gun from the holster. He had not even had the chance to draw it when he was gunned down. With an anger filling her, she stood and raced off in the direction she knew the courtyard and Jesus' apartment was.

The passageway to the courtyard was long enough for her brain to begin to function a little bit. First, it told her she was stupid for thinking she could do anything. Second, it told her to check the weapon. She cocked back the slide and chambered the first round on the .45 automatic. Then she hurried on.

Ahead there was the sound of more gunfire. Christ! she thought. They're killing him! And she tried for more speed.

When she burst into the courtyard, she found the terrorists. Two of them were lying on the ground, one still, the other writhing in pain. The other two were standing with their backs to her, facing the door at the other end of the courtyard. Apparently there were more guards in the building than just

Murphy, for there were two more uniforms standing at the end of the courtyard, facing the terrorists.

One of them was holding his leg and trying to bring his weapon up for a shot. The other was standing there, braced on wide-spread feet and taking a two-handed grip on his .45. Possibly he was the one who had downed two of the terrorists.

An unfortunate fact of life is that a .45 automatic is no match for an assault rifle in a firefight. The standing guard got off one more shot before a line of holes cut across the front of his uniform. His body was thrown back to hit the wall with a thud. Then assault rifles turned on the other guard and he was cut down also.

Tamara really had no time to think. In a couple seconds those men would be through the door and hunting down Jesus. She had to stop them.

Not one for dramatics, she did not yell for them to halt. She simply took a stance much like the guard had done, pushed the .45 out in front of her with both hands holding it, and took aim at the back of the closest terrorist.

Two shots rang out, and the man she was aiming at lurched, his body arching forward as the rounds struck the middle of his back. The gun bucked in her hands but she brought it back down to aim again. Calmly, as if she did this every day, Tamara turned the weapon to the other man. He was turning, swinging his weapon in an arc that would bring it to bear upon her.

Again she double tapped, squeezing the trigger firmly but without jerking it. The .45 bucked again, then lowered and fired the second shot. Almost as if in slow motion, she saw the deadly end of that AK-47 coming around, and knew that in only a fraction of a second it would be spitting lead at her. She willed herself to fire again, another double tap.

The second double tap was not needed. Of the first two bullets, one passed through the man's vest, missing his ribs by half an inch. But the second bullet, as is often the case in double tapping, was more accurate. It entered his chest on the right side, tore its way through one lung and ripped into his heart. The man was dead but did not know it yet as his turn made the assault rifle swing wildly upward. Two shots fired as his finger jerked, but that was all. They went wide over Tamara's head. The man twirled around and spun to the ground.

The sound of gunfire had been loud in the small courtyard, and her ears were ringing as she watched the man twitch once and then lay still. Off to one side, the only terrorist left alive was screaming and holding his belly. Slowly she turned towards him. For a woman who had just been so fast on the uptake, her mind suddenly slowed down. She watched as the man's hand reached towards his fallen assault rifle, a contorted mask of hate and pain on his face. She watched, unmoving, as he drew the weapon towards himself and fumbled to get his hand onto the handle and his finger into the trigger guard. The barrel was lifting in her direction when another two shots rang out and the man jerked violently. The rifle fell from his lifeless hand.

Looking around, Tamara saw another couple guards who had just come through the same door she had. Both had guns drawn.

Feeling her legs going weak, she stumbled over to one of the chairs and flopped into it. She put the .45 on the table. When one guard came up to her, she looked at him with a puzzled expression on her face.

"I just killed two men," she said simply. "I've never done that before."

27. DEBRIEFING

It was quiet in the conference room as all present watched the surveillance video on the large screen. Taken from a camera in one corner, it showed most of the courtyard. Not high definition quality, but good enough to recognize the people.

The video showed an empty courtyard for a few seconds, then four men burst through the far door. They held assault rifles at the ready and headed directly across the courtyard at a trot. Suddenly two guards came into view along the right edge of the screen, drawing their guns.

From that point, things happened very fast. Four assault rifles came down just as the guards were squaring off to fire. The shots came almost together; one from the rightmost terrorist, and two from the guards. One terrorist dropped his rifle and began collapsing to the ground, holding his stomach. One guard jerked around, hit in the leg, his gun no longer aimed across the courtyard. But his first shot had been true. The rightmost terrorist was falling backwards, a small hole in his front and a larger one in his back, along with a spray of blood.

At that point, another figure came through the far door, Tamara, holding a .45 in her hands. The two remaining terrorists, while still advancing, had their weapons up and began firing at the guards. In less than a second both guards were dead. A second after that, both terrorists were dead, shot by a good looking civilian girl.

The video screen went dark.

"Well, that pretty much tells the tale," said Security Chief Manhusen. "Tell me, Miss Graves, where did you learn to shoot?"

Tamara, still shaken from the experience, admitted weakly, "From my dad. He was a county sheriff and insisted I learn how to shoot. I liked it. He taught me a lot about shooting. But I never expected to have to actually shoot at a person. It was more like a game. How good could I get on the range – you know."

"Well, you got pretty good," admitted Stryker.

"Yes," added Fielding. "If those terrorists had gotten through that door, they would have been in Jesus' quarters."

"Was this just a terrorist act? Something random?" asked Stryker.

"No," replied Manhusen sternly. "This was no random act of terrorism. Those men had a target." He pulled a folded piece of paper from his pocket and opened it for all to see. "The lead man has been identified as Khurram Murad, a member of an Islamic extremist group. They had a hand-drawn map of the facility. They knew where they were going. They intended to kill or at least kidnap Jesus. From their techniques, I'd say they intended to kill him."

No one said anything for a minute as that fact was absorbed into stunned minds.

"What I don't understand is why Islamic terrorists want to kill him?" said Juliette. "He is a prophet in their religion."

"They may be afraid of what he might say," answered Fielding slowly. "Or of how the faithful might react to him. Hell, I'm surprised it wasn't the Catholic Church!"

"They wouldn't do that," said a frowning Juliette. "Would they?"

No one answered her question.

"Unless we want investigators from Homeland Security, the CIA, NAS, the Boy Scouts, and who knows who else to be knocking on our doors soon, we will have to keep a lid on this," said Manhusen.

"How can we?" asked Fielding strongly. "That group, whoever it was, may attack again. If they know where Jesus is located, maybe they'll crash an airliner into the building next time."

"We will increase security at this facility," Manhusen told them. "A whole lot. This has already been declared secure airspace by the FAA. I'll see that the nearest Air Force Base is notified to scramble jets if we get an intrusion."

Fielding snorted in disbelief. Frowns on some of the others apparently indicated they agreed that it would be too late by the time any jets got there.

"Meantime, I would rather that we do not try to relocate Jesus. We can protect him better here than someplace else. If you want, I'll see if I can get an anti-aircraft gun put on the roof."

Fielding looked as if he were about to speak again, but he said nothing. Juliette O'Neill also looked aggrieved.

"We'll put a better gate in front, one that will include concrete blocks a truck can't drive through," Manhusen continued. "And more guards. And security measures on that building so no one can just walk in."

Dr. Stryker, who had been looking deep in thought, added, "I think there will be more security upgrades than that. As soon as our government spooks hear about this, they'll move in a division of soldiers to protect our precious Machine. They think too highly of it." He paused to look around the table. "They may not know about Jesus, but they will know of the attack and assume the target was the Machine itself. So get ready for more security. A mouse won't be able to get in here."

The meeting broke up after some plans were made to clean up the mess. Dr. Fielding came over to Tamara as the others were leaving to say, "I want to thank you for your brave action."

"It wasn't really bravery," she laughed weakly. "If I had a second to think about it, I probably wouldn't have done a thing. In fact, when it was all over, I was trembling like a little child. I even cried some. That's bravery for you."

He smiled at her. "Bravery, I believe, was once defined as being afraid but doing the job anyway. You did it." He laughed. "That makes you unique among people. You actually saved Jesus Christ's life!"

28. PLANTING A BOMB

The man walking down the corridor tried not to appear nervous but it was hard to do with his knees feeling weak and his stomach knotted up. Although he was perfectly within his rights to be where he was, the fear that someone would stop him and ask what he was doing there was strong. The tablet in his hand seemed to burn his flesh. He had viewed what was recorded on it and had a fair idea what it was, even though he did not understand the words. What the recording showed was innocent enough, but it was still as dangerous as a bottle of nitroglycerine. To get caught with it would be at least the end of his professional career, if not worse. But duty required he obey orders, a duty far beyond that owed to Chronodyne or any person.

He avoided crossing the courtyard because he knew of the security camera there, and even though it was the middle of the night, he did not want any record made of his visit. It was important that no one knew it was he who delivered this dangerous tablet. The side corridor bypassed the courtyard and allowed him to enter the apartment-like area where Jesus was living. Pausing before the door, he felt his mouth going dry. But then it usual did when he was in Jesus' presence. With a shaking hand, he reached for the doorknob.

Jesus was lying on the bed, eyes closed, apparently asleep – just as this man had hoped. Moving very, very carefully, he slid across the room to the small table about six feet from the bed. Ever so slowly he lowered the tablet to the table, taking care not to make a noise, although his heart was pounding so hard that the sound must surely wake the sleeper. The tablet finally in place, he touched the button on the side that activated it. A single word appeared on the screen, green letters on a black background, only one word, "Start," inside a circle.

Backing away, his heart almost stopped when he bumped into the door. But the sleeping figure did not move, and then the intruder was gone, closing the door behind him.

29. DISASTER

Tamara knew that something was wrong when she walked into the building. It was mid-morning and she was entering the Project J building to see Dr. Myers, to ask him about another interview with Jesus. The guards – there were two of them now – double checked her ID and seemed extremely nervous. As she walked down a side corridor to Myers' office, an assistant hurried by her, not even bothering to say hi. When she reached the office, it was empty. She was about to leave a note when the doctor entered. He looked flushed and on edge, stopping suddenly when he saw her standing there.

"Miss Graves..." he began, and then halted as if he did not know what to say.

"Please, call me Tamara," she said with a smile, but inside wondering what was upsetting the mild-mannered Jewish historian.

"Now is not a good time," he began, and then stopped again.

"Dr. Myers! What is wrong?"

With a sigh, he walked around behind his desk and settled into the chair wearily. "Please, have a seat." When she was seated, he rubbed his forehead before speaking again. "Something terrible has happened."

"What?"

"You are aware how careful we have been to keep some knowledge from Jesus? Well, someone gave Jesus a computer tablet. On it was a video recording outlining the history of the

Catholic Church, Christianity in general, and other historical events. I have seen it! If you wanted to create something that would upset Jesus, you could have done no better than what was on that tablet."

"Why? Why would some history upset him?" she wanted to know.

"Why? Can't you imagine? He is a sensitive man, a truly religious man. Can you imagine what he must have thought when he saw what had become of his teachings? What has been done over the centuries in his name!"

Tamara felt herself grow cold. Fielding and the others had been right to keep many things from Jesus; she had never disagreed with that.

"Can you imagine what he feels when he sees what the Catholic Church is today? All the idolatry? All the ornate churches. Saint Peter's Basilica? The Vatican? The Sistine Chapel? He was a man who believed God did not want you to worship idols.

"Can you imagine what is going through his mind when he finds that his disciples – and many others – are prayed to as saints? Or that his mother is revered as a holy virgin? Look at the millions who worship the Pope! And the wealth of the Catholic Church? At the wars that have been fought over which is the true Christianity? Or even over what was the true meaning of some of his words?"

He shook his head sadly. "Let alone the fact that Rome is the capital of the massive church created to worship him."

He rested his head on his hands, elbows on his desk. "Whoever created that video was a sadistic bastard! Oh, but he knew what he was doing. Not only was it filled with visual images, it was narrated in Aramaic! They found someone who speaks Aramaic to make sure that Jesus would understand every word."

He looked up at her again, sadness in his eyes. "Please...
Remember that Jesus is a first century Jew. He was never
anything else. He believes in the Covenant, the Torah, all the
rules thereof, and absolutely in God's promise to his people.
He passed out on the cross believing that God would save him
and that he would become the anointed one to lead his people
into the Kingdom of God. Now, he wakes up to find that two
thousand years have passed and a massive church has grown
up in his name but not teaching what he actually taught. The
Temple in Jerusalem is no more and the Jews have to fight for
their existence almost every day.

"He went through so much when we fetched him to our
time. The unimaginable ordeal of the crucifixion, if nothing
else. We tried so hard to make this easy on him, not to shock
him too much."

For a few long seconds he said nothing. Then, "This is
nothing short of an attempt to destroy his fragile mind."

"How is he taking it?" she had to ask.

"How? He won't even talk to me! He just pointed to the
tablet. He looks like a man who is in shock. His whole world
is turned upside down, to say the least. I think he blames me
somehow. Or all of us."

"Let me talk to him," she said softly.

"You?" There was disbelief in his voice, but it was
replaced by sadness. "Might as well. Can't make anything
worse. He likes you. He told me so himself." He laughed
sadly. "Maybe partly because there were damned few blondes
in that part of the world."

As he rose slowly and reached for his cane, he advised
her, "I think this is going to be an important conversation, not
just chatting over lunch. It is important that shades of

meaning and context come across correctly. I will try to translate the colloquialisms of his time and place into English but keep the original meaning as best I can."

"I'm sure you'll do fine," she told him. "Let's see what we can do in the way of damage control," she said firmly, rising from her chair. "Come on."

30. DAMAGE CONTROL

He was in his room, a plate of food untouched on the table. He lay on the bed, almost curled up into a prenatal position.

"Jesus, I want to talk to you," Tamara said, and Myers translated. Jesus barely glanced up at her, and then he turned his head away. "I won't go until we have talked," she told him, and received no reply. Gently, she placed her hand on his arm. It took a few seconds, but his head did turn around to face her. His lips barely moved when he said, "I failed. I was not good enough for God."

"You did not fail. You tried your best for your people," she said firmly but kindly, unaware she was echoing Myers' words. "And the church that grew up in your name has done a lot of good."

He sat up slowly. She saw that his eyes were red and there were tear streaks on his cheeks. "Do you know of this church called Catholic?"

"Yes. Everyone does."

"And that man they call the Pope? Is he just the high priest or is he the Anointed One? The chosen by God?"

She hesitated. The look on Myers' face told her to tread carefully, and then he said, "He is not the Anointed One in the way that you mean it, Rabbi. He is not the Messiah."

Tamara took it up from there. "Some of the people of that church believe he hears the words of God. But it is my belief that the Pope is simply a man. Someone has to lead a church."

He seemed to think on that for a few seconds. "If he is not the Messiah, and I am not the Messiah, then where is he? Where is the Son of Man?"

Myers shook his head sadly. "No one knows," was all he could say.

Jesus digested that, and then said, "That thing showed pictures of Jerusalem and the Temple. Is it true that the Temple was destroyed? That a single wall is all that remains of it?"

"This is true," Tamara said. She turned to Myers and whispered, "I think it's time for the whole truth." Myers nodded. Turning back to Jesus, "A few years after your... your time, the Jewish people rebelled and Rome was harsh in its treatment of the land and people. The Temple was torn down. Many were killed. A great many."

"But Jerusalem is now ours again?"

"Israel is an independent nation. A strong nation of good people." She felt bad about not truthfully answering his question, pushing aside the question of whether Jerusalem, the city itself, was ruled by the Jewish people.

"But it is not God's Kingdom. Not what was promised our people by the prophets and by God." He seemed to almost be pleading with her. "It was to be a Kingdom of good and peace. Of all men being pure and obedient to God."

"That Kingdom has not yet come," she told him. It was a simple half-truth, in that it implied it might yet come to pass. "The Jewish people are many, and a good people. They live in all the lands of the Earth."

She was tempted to go on in that vein but instead returned to Jesus himself. "Your teachings have reached more people than you can ever believe. And many sincerely try to lead their lives by those teachings. Later, I will show you a book that tells of your life and your teachings. It is called the Bible. You have done much good for people of all races."

Her words seemed to both calm him and, oddly enough, stir up an anger within. "But I failed! God had chosen me to bring about his Kingdom. I am the Son of Man! I am the Anointed One!" Then doubt came into his eyes. "But the Kingdom did not come, even though I gave up my life for it." He closed his eyes and took in a deep breath. "I tried so hard. Some people listened to me and believed. Some understood how they might become pure and be accepted into the Kingdom. But others cursed me. Even when I cured the sick and cast out demons, so many did not believe. So many did not believe." His hands were clenched into fists and he looked on the verge of crying again.

Anxious to keep him talking, Tamara asked, "When did you know you were the Anointed One, the Son of Man?"

He looked at her sharply. Was he thinking that she might be mocking her? Quickly she tried to reassure him, "Was it when John baptized you? Please, I want to know."

The anger fled, and his face took on a sadness but was calm.

"I grew up with the words of the Torah; the words of the prophets. They foretold of a good time to come. Of a return of our people to God's graces. They told of a man who would be chosen by God to bring this about. I always knew these words were true; that this would happen. We lived in the land that God had given us, but it was not ours. We had to pay taxes to Rome. We had to put up with their soldiers taking what they wanted and making us work. Of them defying the Temple. It was only right that God would give back to us what he promised if we were pure and free of sin." He looked firmly into her eyes as he said, "And that time was to be soon! It had to be. We had suffered enough."

After pausing for a moment, he went on, "I heard of John teaching by the Jordan, telling of the coming Kingdom, telling people cast aside their sins and become pure. In the living water of the Jordan, he washed away the sins and made ready the path into the Kingdom. I went to him.

"It was not easy. I had to leave my family and all that I knew in Galilee. When I saw John, he was as the prophets of old. He lived in the wilderness and ate of the land. But there was a holy glow in his eyes when he spoke of the coming Kingdom! He understood! It was good that I followed a man who knew and loved the old words as I did. And I learned so much more from him. I spent a long time with him.

"Then, one day, soldiers came and took him away. Herod Antipas took him away because he feared that John might incite the people to rebellion. But he was wrong. John did not say to take up arms. He taught only repentance and obedience to God's will, so that one would be ready for the Kingdom."

Jesus paused for a few moments, reflecting inwardly of a time so very long ago. "You know," he said calmly, "I believed then that we were so right to teach of the coming Kingdom and the man who would come forth to announce that Kingdom, the Son of Man. When John was taken away, I went back to Galilee, back to my home. I felt compelled to continue the teaching of John, to make people understand what they need do for themselves and for our people. Oh, it would be so good and proper when God came! I knew in my heart that day would be soon. It had to be!"

"You told the people," she prompted, "but they did not believe?"

"Some did. Some did. But not all. I tried. There were

some who believed me and wanted to follow me. I stayed out of the cities. There was too much that was impure there. And too many of the priests. To tell the truth, I was afraid. I did not want what happened to John to happen to me. My message was so important. People had to understand what they must do to make ready for the coming Kingdom.

"A few times I went down to Jerusalem for a holy festival. The Torah tells us to visit the Temple for Passover, Shavuot and Sukkoth. Oh, the Temple was so beautiful! You could sense the presence of God within. I longed to be as the High Priest and go into the Holy of Holies, the place of God.

"But I found much that was not right. The priests dressed in costly garments and displayed riches like the noble Romans did. The moneychangers and sellers of animals were right there, inside the Temple! It was as in the cities; mammon was more important than holiness. I was angry. I wanted to tear out those unholy things!"

He took a deep breath. "That was what really got the priests angry with me, you know. The last time I went to the Temple, I could not hold in my anger. I overturned some tables and cursed the people there. Got a lot of people upset. I got out just before the Temple police came. But the Pharisees were against me even more after that."

"That was near the end," Tamara said. "Was it in those last few days that you came to know that you were the Son of Man?"

"No. I knew before I cast out the moneychangers. When I heard of John's death, in the days that followed I was thinking about what John had said, about the coming of the Kingdom and wondering when that day would be. Soon, I knew, but when? Then, suddenly, as if God were speaking inside my mind, I knew. He had chosen to open my eyes! I was the one who had to make the prophecies come true. I was the one God had chosen! It washed over me like the cold waters of the Jordan years before. Suddenly it was all so clear! I was not just continuing the words John taught, I was the one he talked of. The Son of Man. The Anointed One.

"It all made sense. I was of the line of King David. I understood better than any other man what was to come and what had to be done. The prophets and the words of God guided me."

As he talked, he became more animated. Tamara could see the depression fading away as he spoke of what he considered the most important in all of times. It would be an event that would set the whole world right.

"I tried to make those who followed me understand, but I think most of them did not really know the meaning of my words. My good friend Judas understood better than the others. And John. And my wife, Mariam, she understood. My mother knew what I was talking about, but I could sense she had her doubts about my being the Son of Man even though she believed with all her heart of the coming Kingdom. It was my beloved wife who believed most. She knew what I was saying. She understood what I would have to go through to bring about the Kingdom. It saddened her, I believe, but it was also a source of great comfort to both of us to know we were part of God's plan."

Myers paused for a breath. "I hope I'm getting his meaning correctly. These are things we never talked about. I've never seen him open up like this before."

"I'm sure you're doing just fine," she told him. Then, to Jesus: "So you went to Jerusalem one more time."

"It would be the right time and place. I had to be near the Temple, the most holy place of all. It had to be a time when there were many people to see. I had to fulfill the prophecies exactly."

"But you knew that you would be killed?" Tamara could not stop herself from asking.

31. ANSWERS

"Yes, I knew." He paused for a moment. "You know, I thought that it would be the hated Romans who would kill me. But I was not surprised when it was the Pharisees who forced Pilate to issue the order. They would have killed me themselves but for the law. I don't think Pilate understood at all the importance of what was happening. He thought of me as a minor rebel, a nuisance, little more. But this was as it should be. As the prophecies foretold."

"The prophecies! Like the donkey you rode into Jerusalem on," Tamara asked, "you arranged for that, didn't you?"

Jesus actually smiled. "I had friends who lived in Jerusalem. They would help me because they understood and believed. Yes, when I said go and find an ass at a certain place, I knew it would be waiting for my followers. That was one of the prophecies."

"Did the people really greet you as the coming Messiah?"

"Some did. Some of the people coming for the festival from Galilee had heard of me. And there were those who came with me. They placed palm branches down and made a cheerful noise. But, to tell the truth, we had to pass through a lot of people who ignored our procession."

"And the Last Supper? Did that really happen?"

"The last supper? Oh, I know what you mean. Yes, we had a celebration meal. I told my followers again that they should remember God's gift to them when they ate of bread and drank wine. I told them to imagine that the bread was my body, and the wine my blood. And I again told them that I was the Anointed One, but I doubt they all really believed that."

At that point Myers interjected a question of his own, "In whose house was that meal?"

"Joseph. My good friend, Joseph from Arimathea. His house was within the walls of Jerusalem, not far from the Temple, in fact."

"And what happened then?" Tamara asked.

"It was a time for thought. I went to a nearby garden. It was always easier to think when I was alone. I had made Judas understand that he must inform the Pharisees of my location. It was necessary for them to play their part in fulfilling the prophecies. He did not want to go. I had to yell at him. He left with tears in his eyes."

"And then..."

"The night grew late as we waited. The other followers did not know what was to happen. I could not trust them that far. Some of them would have tried to prevent what had to happen.

"I went off to think. I am ashamed to admit that I had my doubts. Was I really doing what God wanted?" Jesus turned to Myers and said, "I never wavered in believing that it was time for God to act. I want you to know that."

Then he lowered his head. "The night became cold. I prayed. I remember how brightly the stars shone down. How beautiful they were. It came to pass that I felt myself calming. A sense of peace came to me. I was doing as God wished. I was to be a part of his grand plan. I was in his hands."

He sighed deeply. "So when Judas came with a group of men, including Temple police, I simply stood there."

"Did he kiss you to show them who to arrest?" Tamara asked.

"He kissed me. But it was because he loved me. As I did him. There were tears in his eyes.

"They took me. As I had feared, a couple of my followers wanted to fight them, even grabbed swords. But I stopped them. If there was a fight and my followers killed or arrested, who would there be to spread the word?

"I went with the Temple Police. I was taken before Caiaphas and a few of the Sanhedrin. They all seemed angry, but most of all Caiaphas. He seemed to take my teachings as a personal affront. He ranted and raved and I said nothing. I saw Joseph was there."

"Joseph of Arimathea?"

"Yes. But he could not defend me. He knew what was to pass just as I did. We had talked of this. But that night it was the other Joseph who did all the talking. It was to his house that I was taken. I tried not to speak for I knew I had to force them to do what they must do. The prophecies, you know."

"What other Joseph?" Tamara asked.

"Joseph Caiaphas, the High Priest, of course. He asked me if I had claimed to be the proper king of the Israel. I said nothing. It is true that I am a descendant of David, but I had not claimed to be the King of the Jewish people.

"Caiaphas grew angrier. He slapped me and yelled at me to say something. I held my words for I knew the right time was yet to come.

"When Caiaphas asked me if I was the Son of God, I could no longer hold my tongue. 'You say I am,' I told him. Truth is, I had never claimed to be the Son of God. I am the Son of Man, one who is chosen by God to do his purpose. But Caiaphas did not ask me that, he asked if I were the Son of

God.

"That was all he needed. He ordered that I be taken to that Roman Prefect, Pilate, by the Temple Police. It was not yet morning. We walked through the empty streets of Jerusalem. At Herod's Palace I had to wait in the courtyard for a long time. It was early in the morning, the sun barely visible when Pilate himself came out."

Tamara could not help but cut in. "Wasn't Pilate staying in the Fortress of Antonio? That's where the Roman soldiers were. Right?"

"Roman Perfect stayed in Herod's Palace, as he called it. It was a large house on the Western Hill."

"Oh." So much for that theory, she thought.

"Pilate didn't like being presented with a problem so early in the morning. I think he had been drinking the night before and was not feeling well. This man, in the fine robe with bad breath was the man who would fulfill part of the prophecies. He slumped into a chair and looked at me with blurry eyes. "Why do you bring this Jew before me?" he asked. They told him that I had claimed to be the proper king of the Jewish people. He put his hand on his forehead and lowered his face away from me. "And are you King of the Jews?" he asked without even looking at me. I spoke Greek well enough to understand what he was asking. I said, 'that is what you say'. He groaned and, without looking up at me, said, "Crucify him," then waved his hand in dismissal."

Jesus sighed, and went on, "Pilate, who understood nothing of the coming Kingdom beyond that it was a myth favored by the Jews, could, however, understand a claim that I was king. But he was not stupid. I am sure he fully understood it was the priests who wanted me killed for some reason of their own. And anything they wanted, he would normally be against. It was a battle between him and the High Priest. But that morning, he did not feel like continuing their battle, so he gave in and ordered me crucified. He had no idea he was playing out his part of the prophecies."

"Was there a crowd of people there?" Myers asked on his own.

"No. There were many in the city for Passover, but this was early.

"I was taken from that house to the Roman fortress and flogged. I had not expected that. A Roman flogging is terrible. I tried not to cry out, but when I felt the flesh of my back being torn, I fear I screamed.

"So there was no crowd who demanded your death?"

"I don't remember any onlookers," Jesus said. "I do not think that Pilate cared what the people might have said anyway. He let the priests have what they wanted. Just as the prophecies said he would."

"And then?" Tamara prompted again. She wanted to keep him talking. It was beyond fascinating listening to his words describing a scene from two thousand years ago.

"I was taken out. They made me carry the cross beam I was to be crucified upon. I had seen this done before, so I was not surprised by it. They wanted the condemned to be shown to the people, so he had to walk through the city to his place of death."

"Did anyone have to help you?" Tamara asked, thinking of the Simon of Cyrene.

"I fell. The beam was so heavy and I was weak. Then there was someone else carrying the beam. My back hurt so much."

Tamara felt a sense of excitement within. This incredible narrative was approaching its climax.

"I stumbled all the way to Golgotha. When they lay me down and spread my hands on the beam, I heard a scream. I could not see, but I knew that it was one of the other two men as his wrists were being nailed to the wood. Then it was my turn. I tried not to, but I think I cried out. The pain was bad but not as bad as my back felt when the whip tore my flesh."

"Were you scared?" asked Tamara, having to endure a look from Myers before he translated. He also told her, before asking Jesus if he felt fear, "His back has horrible wounds on it. He was going to be killed in a most terrible way."

Jesus replied, "I was, at first. But I kept telling myself that I was doing as God wished. It was something that had to be done in order for God's Kingdom to come. You understand?"

"I understand," she told him with great sympathy truly felt.

"They lifted the beam up and fixed it on the post. It hurt so much. There was a peg in the post and I was told to put my feet on it. I did. That helped because I could stand on it. They tied my feet to the post.

"After a while, someone put some thorns on my head. They were big thorns and pierced my skin."

His hand went up to his forehead where two small scars showed. As his hand lifted, the sleeve slid down and Tamara could see the wrapping that still covered the terrible wounds on his wrist.

"After that, someone put a wooden plank on the post above my head. I could not see, but I heard one of the soldiers say, 'King of the Jews.' The Romans always put a sign telling why the person was being crucified.

"It was hard to breathe," he continued. "I hurt. I could just see one of the others also condemned to one side. Another was behind me. The one I could see was begging to be taken down. As I hung there, I remembered the stories I had heard about men who had been crucified living for one or two days before dying. You asked if I was afraid. At that thought, I was. Would it take so long for me to die?

"Then I saw Joseph standing nearby and I remembered. I still believed that God would save me ultimately, but I admit I was greatly afraid. It had been too easy to think about this while in the garden or eating with my friends. But to be there, like that..."

He shook his head slowly. Tamara felt strong empathy.

"Did you say much?" she asked. Here was a chance to clear up the discrepancies of the Gospels about his last words.

"I think I said some things. It was hard to talk."

Tamara remembered reading that crucifixion causes asphyxia, making inhaling air difficult and painful, and talking difficult.

"I think I said that I forgave those who were doing this to me. They were only playing their part in the prophecies. After a long time, I remember asking aloud if God had forsaken me. I wanted his assurance that this was worth it.

"Finally, I could take it no longer. The sun was low in the sky, and the Sabbath was coming. I called out that I thirsted. That was the signal."

Suddenly Tamara became more alert. She could sense Myers also tensing. "The signal?" she asked.

For a while, Jesus did not answer her question. Finally, he said softly, "That was so long ago. It matters not today, so I will tell you of it.

"Days before, when I was with Joseph and we were talking of what had to come, he told me that he would arrange that I should not suffer too greatly. He told me when I said aloud that I was thirsty, he would have someone give me a drink. In it would be a potion that would make me unconscious.

"I agreed, although at the time I did not think that I would have need of it. And it would be as with the prophecy."

"Psalms 69:21," Myers added. *"...And in my thirst they gave me vinegar to drink."*

"Later, only a week before Passover, Nicodemus said to me that the plan was all in place. Nicodemus believed in the coming Kingdom as I did, but he did not think that I had to die to fulfill the prophecies. I asked what plan, and he explained that he and Joseph had arranged that when I had been given the potion and appeared to be dead, they would get me off the cross and into a tomb nearby where they would revive me.

"I think he assumed that Joseph had given me all the details of their plot.

"I told him that it was God who would attend to me. It was not necessary that they do anything. If God wanted me to return to life, He would do it. And that I did believe He would. Was I not the Son of Man, the chosen one? The one who would sit in judgment as the Kingdom of God came to earth? How could God not help me fulfill the prophecies for Him?

"He said he understood and left me. Then I remembered that Nicodemus ben Gurion was said to have performed miracles himself. Perhaps he knew of a potion that would make me appear to be dead. But I was firm. God would do what had to be done. I heard no more of it."

"Did you say anything else on the cross?" Tamara asked. There were still some quotes attributed to him in the Gospels.

"I remembered a saying I always liked. *'Into thine hand I commit my spirit'.*"

"Psalms 31:5," Myers added.

"I think I said that aloud," Jesus said. "Then I said I thirsted. I felt weak and tired, and in great pain, and could take no more suffering," he added.

Myers and Tamara looked to each other. The narrative was now to the crucial point. That was the point when their Machine had fetched the man from near death. Jesus would be unable to tell them more from that point. He would only remember waking up in their hospital room.

Tamara reached out, took his hand and held it in both of hers.

"We will talk of this again," she told him. "I want you to see that your death has inspired many people to do good deeds, that you have done good for the world."

If Jesus believed her, it was hard to say. He merely looked at her with tired, tired eyes.

Before the interview broke up with promises to return soon, Jesus looked to both of them with his sad eyes and said, "How can they use the cross I have so much reason to hate as a sign of me?"

162

32. WHAT MORE?

In the silent apartment, a man sat and stared at the faint morning sunlight coming between the drapes. He had the lights off. Heavy were the thoughts running through his mind. In his hands he held a well-worn Bible, his since his early days.

He had done as he had been instructed and delivered the tablet with that recording. Upon returning home, he could not sleep and sat up in the dark, his mind a turmoil of confusing thoughts. Had he done the right thing? What was the right thing? Was that all he need do? He longed to talk to the bishop again, to hear his soothing words telling him that this was right and proper and approved by his Holiness.

In his troubled thoughts, he understood what that recording was meant to do. It was meant to disrupt this image of Christ that he had helped create, to upset the delicate balance of his mind and render him unusable as a tool against the Church. If the project could not present a sane, rational man, he would not be believed as Jesus, and no one would believe that he was the Christ come again.

He remembered the incident only that prior morning. The truck ramming its way into the compound, the noises of gunshots, and then the blood. There was blood on the ground, blood on the walls; it seemed to be everywhere. He shivered at the memory of that blood. That attack had failed, but he had heard that the target had been Jesus, only they failed to get to him. Perhaps it would have been best had the terrorists succeeded. Then he would not be so confused and unsure.

Off in his bedroom, an alarm clock emitted annoying beeps. The night had passed and still he could not sleep. He rose slowly and made his way through the semidarkness to quiet the clock. Then he would shower and dress and go to the project, as he had on so many mornings. He would see what his midnight sneaking had accomplished. Then he would hope to understand what he had to do next.

33. LET IT PLAY OUT

The late evening shadows stretched across Saint Peter's Square as three people met in an ornate office in the Papal Apartments on the top floor of the Apostolic Palace. In a pure white cassock with white cape and wide silk sleeves, the current successor of St. Peter sat, while two cardinals stood before his desk. An old man, having achieved the highest position in the Catholic Church at the age of seventy-three, and now approaching his eightieth year, he was squinting at the two before him, Cardinals Carlo Lucarelli and Gaetano Milanesi.

"I cannot believe what you are telling me," he said, nodding his head as if agreeing despite his words. "Jesus? You say that Jesus has come again?"

"No, your Holiness," Lucarelli was quick to respond. "It is not Him, but a copy. The Americans reached back into time and made a copy of Jesus. It is a man who looks as Jesus and has his memories, but it is not Jesus Christ."

The Pope's gaze wandered from one to the other of the men. His hand, resting on the desk near a fancy silver cross, was shaking slightly. "Jesus..." he said slowly. Now his head was shaking from side to side. "How can this be?"

"Science," Lucarelli said, and offered no further explanation.

"Think of it like a video, looking like Jesus and talking like him," Milanesi cut in.

"We are afraid that the American scientists will announce

this copy to the world," Lucarelli took up. "That would not be good for the Church. I fear we must do something about this."

For a minute, the two thought that the Pope would not answer them; his gaze was at a spot between them, perhaps on the distant wall. But then he regained Lucarelli's eyes. "Yes, we must do something. You say this is not Jesus, but he has Jesus' memories? And he is alive?" A tiny spark of the man's old inner fire shone in his eyes. "Can he talk to us?"

"Yes, he can talk," Lucarelli admitted. "But that is what we fear. Who knows what this false Christ will say? If people believe it is really him..." He sighed and held his hands out to his sides.

The Pope stared hard at him. "Perhaps you should not fear this man. When I was young, we had a man come into our village. He claimed that he was Jesus returned to earth. He even had scars on his palms. Of course, he was not Christ, as we found out quickly, but just a poor cobbler named Marco, a maker of shoes. But he was a kindly man and meant well. If this man is not Jesus Christ, then we will find out soon enough. And if he is... Well, maybe this is God's doing."

The two cardinals were speechless. What does one say to the Pope when you think he's diving off the deep end? How could they show him the error of his logic?

"Your Holiness, I really must..." Lucarelli began.

His Holiness continued as if the cardinal had not even spoken. "We should let this play out as it will. Let them bring forth their man, their copy as you call him, and let us see what he has to say. Yes, that would be best. It would be most interesting to talk to this man, would it not? Let me know when I can speak with him. Meantime, trust in God."

He waved his hand in dismissal.

The two bowed in silence and backed away. Outside the room, Milanesi slammed his palm against a wall. "His is senile! He does not understand at all!"

"But he is the Pope," protested Lucarelli mildly.

Milanesi glared at him. "Do you have any idea what the press will do with this story? Especially the Italian press?"

Lucarelli nodded. "It would be a circus."

"And with the Church in the center ring," added Milanesi. "We cannot let this happen."

Lucarelli looked as if he were about to protest, but then snapped shut his mouth. With a deep sigh, he said, "You are correct. Even if we win out and this copy is proven false, it can do no good for the Church. It would be best if this did not become public."

"You said nothing about the tablet we had our man give Jesus."

"I thought it would serve no purpose to bring that up. His Holiness need not know."

"Especially since it apparently, from the last word I have received, has not had the desired effect." They began walking down the corridor. "It is good that we have someone within their group, someone who will obey."

Suddenly Lucarelli stopped. With no small amount of sadness in his eyes, he told his friend, "Then see to it that this false messiah does not become public." Much more than just those words passed between them in their looks. Milanesi nodded and walked briskly away. Behind him, still standing there, Lucarelli sighed and crossed himself.

34. ANOTHER DEBRIEFING

Tamara was in Dr. Myers' office, discussing what they had heard from Jesus. And trying to come to grips with what they had learned.

"So, Jesus had an escape plan," Tamara commented.

"His friends did. At that point in his ministry, I suspect those two were more important than the twelve disciples. Did you know that only one of them showed up at the Crucifixion?"

"The Beloved One," she said. "But one unnamed. Don't most scholars think that refers to John?"

"That disciple is mentioned only in the Gospel of John, and there six times. That term is used nowhere else in the Gospels. Some think it refers to the author of that gospel. But then there are those who do not think that the disciple John was the author of the Gospel of John at all. It can be confusing."

Tamara, who had always had a fascination for the subject, added, "The other Gospels do not mention a disciple being present at all. Just a group of women. But they were written well after the fact."

"Joseph of Arimathea and Nicodemus were the prime movers at that point," said Myers, returning to his first statement. "They set up the plan for him to survive, even though he rejected it. From what we saw through the Machine, they did try to revive him after taking him from the cross. It is undeniable that they were, at the very least, co-

conspirators in his plan to fulfill the prophecies. It is believed by some that both of those men were priests, and wealthy. They would certainly be in a good position to help Jesus."

"The prophecies, yes," Tamara mused. "So much depended upon making them come true. If Jesus truly believed in them, why did he feel he had to cheat? I mean, he admitted that he arranged for the ass or colt or whatever it was to be where he sent his disciples to find it. And a great deal more of the story was also deliberate planning on his part with the prophecies in mind."

Myers turned to a side table and turned on a small, automatic coffee maker.

"You have to keep in mind the times and beliefs. Many Jews believed in the coming of a Messiah and the Kingdom of God. And the only 'proof' they had to back up that belief is the words of the old prophets.

"Now, Jesus could not read, he told me so himself. Very few of his time could, especially among the poor farmers such as lived in Nazareth. The Torah was mostly handed down as an oral tradition, to be learned by listening to the rabbi. Jesus, being very religiously inclined, listened well. He knew the old prophets by heart. They formed an integral part of his religious upbringing. If the Messiah were to come, it had to be as the prophecies proclaimed it would be. It could be no other way."

"Then why didn't he simply sit back and let them happen? If God were really manipulating behind the scenes..."

"For the same reason many people today do things in the belief God wants them to. He thought of himself as an instrument of God. That it was God guiding his hand and actions."

Tamara shook her head. "It gets confusing."

"God moves in mysterious ways..." quoted Myers. "And people believe."

"And the words that Jesus said while on the cross," she said, "they were sort of the same as what the Gospels say, but different."

"Again, remember, the Gospels were written down only years after the events they speak of. Until that point they were only oral traditions."

For almost a full minute they were silent, until Tamara spoke. "That pretty much solves the problem. Answers the question."

"You mean about the resurrection? And his divinity?"

"Yes. If your Machine did not see him arise, then he simply died and all else was made up by those who followed him."

"So it would appear," was Myers' only comment.

"That's going to upset a lot of people when it gets out."

"If it gets out..." he said quietly.

"If...? You mean you would hide it from the world? I thought that what you and Fielding and Juliette wanted was the truth? That's what I have always wished for: the absolute truth."

Myers clasped his hands together. "But what is the truth? I saw the video showing him dying, the failing to revive him, and the taking away of his body from the tomb he was supposed to be buried in. But did we see everything?"

"What do you mean?"

"There are a few in the project who believe that what we created was only the shell of the man. It may be a perfect automaton and perform exactly as the real man would, but it would not contain that part which is not made of protons and neutrons and quarks. That there is something that the

Machine could not bring through. Call it the soul. Call it the spirit. If Jesus was the Son of God, as so many proclaim, then maybe we did not get that part of him. If we could, maybe our copy could walk on water and raise the dead."

"But you said you saw the recordings showing that he died and it was human hands that took him from that tomb."

"That is true. But what if he was placed in another tomb and did arise from that one on the third day?

Tamara was shocked by that idea. "But couldn't you use the Machine again to follow his body to where it was taken? Follow it for days until you're certain he did not arise?"

He sighed. "Perhaps. But would it prove anything? There are those who maintain that the arisen Jesus was not the physical body, but the spirit of Jesus who came back to talk to his disciples. Our Machine could not record that."

"Then you're saying that we can't be sure we have the truth?"

"I'm just a humble Jewish historian. What do I know of God's mysterious ways?"

35. DANGER FROM WITHIN

They returned to Jesus that afternoon. He was willing to have some lunch with them, and seemed much closer to normal than he had been. It was raining, so they sat in a small conference room near to his apartment to eat and talk.

"All those things I saw in that picture thing, they are true?" he asked when they were settled and the lunch begun.

"I have seen it and it is a record of true facts. It is a biased presentation, but an accurate one," Myers told him. "But, understand that it is only part of history. There is much, much more since your time."

"I know that you have hidden facts from me," he told them. "Will you now be truthful? Will you answer any question I ask and not lie?"

"Yes, I will, rabbi. What we say may be hard for you to understand sometimes, but I... we will try our best."

He seemed to think about that as he took a piece of melon. Finally, he said, "This church, the one called Catholic, is it as the pictures showed? It is filled with golden images and fine robes? Do crowds of people worship the high priest, the one called Pope?"

"Parts of the Catholic Church has much wealth," she told him. "But some parts are like the small synagogues of your time: humble people meeting to worship God. There are many religions in the world today."

Please, let's not get into Islam and the crusades and things like that, Tamara wished silently.

"The priests in the Temple wore fine robes," Jesus said slowly. "And they defiled the temple with their greed for mammon. They made a sacrifice to God not what it should be."

He settled back in the chair and sighed. "You know, I had come to realize that the sacrifices of animals may not be what God wanted. I know that was what God asked for, according to the prophets, but I came to doubt. It is right to pay homage to God, but was a sacrifice the only way? I thought upon that. Could we not honor God in other ways? In our hearts? Each time we ate or drank? It came to me that a prayer each time we took bread, or each time we drank wine, a quiet, private dedication to God, might well be more pleasing to Him than the noise, confusion and almost impersonal way that the priests slaughtered so many animals. I told those who followed me to make the meal a sacrifice to God. At the end, when I knew that I was the Son of Man, the Appointed One, through whom God would work his wonders, I told them to remember God each time they took up bread or wine, that the bread was my body and the wine my blood. That was because the spirit of God had entered into me, and the blood that I would spill and the body that I was to give up were as the body and blood of God."

He sighed again. "I do not believe they understood." Then he straightened up and changed the subject.

"Now tell me of what happened after I died? What became of my friends? My wife, Mariam, what happened to her? And my children, Judas and Deborah? Where did my followers go?"

Myers sighed, and began to talk of history. And he was honest. Some of the facts shocked Jesus, such as the disciple Judas killing himself. Judas was his close friend, so much so that he even named his firstborn son after him. And he was both glad and saddened at the fates of his followers. He seemed particularly interested in how the Jewish faith fared after his time, and in the beginnings of the church that came to bear his name. Some of the news depressed him, some seemed to lift his spirits. He was depressed that nothing was known of his children, or his wife. That his mother was now revered by millions seemed to amuse him. He said that it would also amuse her no end. That his disciples were now saints, installed in heaven and prayed to by many seemed to confuse him. "I told them they would sit on twelve thrones and rule over the twelve tribes when the Kingdom of God came to the earth, not to be taken up to heaven and be prayed to by people."

Also confusing was the importance to the new religion of a man named Saul, then renamed Paul. He had never heard of this Paul, but seemed to grasp that it was he who had changed much of the direction of the early church and installed some principles that Jesus never intended.

A few times, Jesus muttered words mostly to himself, words that Myers did not always translate. Later, he told Tamara that Jesus was saying that he did not understand. To her, however, it sounded more as though he was praying. Or maybe cursing in that quiet voice of his.

The afternoon wore on, and when they departed Jesus was much as he had been before the disclosures of the tablet. "He's coping with a massive amount of information rather well," Myers said later when the two were having a dinner meeting with other members of the team.

"I agree," Tamara told them. "He's pretty much gotten over the shock of what he saw and heard on that tablet."

Myers shook his head. "Maybe. I still feel that he has yet to come to grips with all that he saw."

"Either of you two have any idea who gave him that tablet?" asked Fielding. When they both replied that they did not, he went on, "I'll talk with Manhusen. He'll be investigating." He was looking at the innocent looking device as it sat on the table. "Maybe he can get some fingerprints off it. Or maybe trace the serial number and find out who bought it."

"It had to be someone within the project," Juliette said. "Who else could get into his room?"

"I'm wondering why this was done, rather than something stronger," said Fielding. "I mean, if someone could sneak into his room at night, they could have done much worse than leave a tablet that would upset him. They could have killed him."

Each of the six people in the room looked at each other. The idea that someone would want to kill the most famous man in history was at first a shock, but then it slowly sank into their minds that the very type of thing had happened so often before to so many famous men, and had happened to Jesus himself two thousand years prior. Almost as strong was the shocking idea that it had to be someone connected with Project J, or maybe one of the other projects. A lot had happened over the last few days and their little secret was not very secret any longer. Many of those who should not have even known of his existence had come forward asking if they could meet Jesus in person.

"So, what do you intend to do next?" asked Tamara.

"Just continue as before," was Fielding's reply. "We have ongoing research into improving the Machine. Dr. Myers will continue his interviews with Jesus. I thank you, by the way, Miss Graves, for your help with our guest. Seymour seems to think that Jesus is strongly attracted to you and opens up more to you.

"I will, of course," he went on, "ask that security be increased. It may be good to limit access to Jesus. Maybe it would be best were I to install rules to the effect that no single person should be alone with him. It would be better that there always be a second person present. Except, of course, Dr. Myers. I will also add more security cameras. I don't want any more such problems."

The meeting continued for a while longer, the others anxious to know what Dr. Myers and Tamara had learned when Jesus finally opened up and talked about those crucial last days.

For a few days, things settled back to normal. A part of the Project B team was relocated to another laboratory in a distant city where they could show off their "cloned" extinct animals. As predicted, Smiley, the growing Saber-Tooth Cat cub was a great hit and filled the news for a few days. The team was constantly asked if they were cloning any dinosaurs, but Dr. Brown would laugh and tell them that was impossible. In private, he was lobbying for a chance to bring back a few dinosaurs – small, harmless ones at first, he said. Seems he had gotten the notion that a real Jurassic Park would be a great idea.

The Chronodyne Project Director spent a lot of time with some high-ups from three security agencies trying to convince them that their work with the Machine would continue uninterrupted. The terrorist attack had them very upset. They seemed to think that it was aimed at shutting down the Machine. But, of course, they did not know of Project J, and Jesus. Secrets hidden from the secret masters, as it were.

So life went on within Project Dry Wells, the shock of the terrorist attack and the revealing of the future to Jesus fading, but leaving him in a much more communicative mood.

36. TAMARA STAYS

Tamara turned in a report on her audit of the Chronodyne facility. It said nothing of Project J, and attributed all the misuse of the Machine to one employee using it for personal gain.

Normally, Tamara would have returned for reassignment, but she wanted so to learn more that she drew upon some of the vacation time she had coming to stay at the site and continue working with Dr. Myers. Fielding and the others accepted her as part of their team, Myers even going so far as to ask if she might be hired on. Jesus seemed to prefer working with her, even with the language difficulties.

A strict policy of not having any single person alone with Jesus was put into effect. It was unlikely that it would be perfect, but it was a good attempt at protecting him. It was the accepted idea that there was a single person within the project who had tried to sabotage it. Until they found out who that was, caution was the watchword of the day.

All was going smoothly, and no one noticed the slight signs of change in one of the team members.

Tamara was the one who pushed the idea that Jesus should be allowed more freedom, even if it meant security problems. She argued that the man had been confined like a prisoner for weeks, constrained to the courtyard and a couple indoor rooms, and should be allowed to see more of the world.

It was almost like watching your child's first visit to Disneyland or the zoo. There were so many things that were new to Jesus. It was as if he were discovering a whole new world, as, indeed, he was.

At first, he was allowed outside the Project J building for short periods, accompanied by Dr. Myers and Tamara. The first time he saw a car being driven, he was amazed, so Tamara arranged for him to be given a ride. It was only around a couple buildings, and he was filled with wonder that something could move without animals.

Then they introduced him to CD players and music. Not that he had not known of music, but even the simplest pieces of modern music were far beyond anything he had ever heard. They were careful to not overwhelm him with too much, and kept his CD collection to carefully selected music. He seemed to love classical music so long as it was melodic.

After a few days of sunshine, another summer storm moved in, curtailing his walks outside the building. Jesus was in his room, taking an after lunch nap. Tamara was in Dr. Myers' office, writing some notes about a small talk she had had with Jesus that morning. She had asked him about who was present during the Crucifixion. Did he notice his mother watching? And who else did he recognize?

She suggested that they could use the Machine's viewing capabilities to simply look at the scene, but Myers laughed at the idea and asked her if she could recognize the people there. They had figured no way to get sounds from the past, only vision. They discussed, for a while, letting Jesus see a recording of the scene, but decided it might be too much for him. So they settled for asking him questions.

That morning meeting, as did most of the meetings, included a lot of time answering questions of his own. There were times that his inquires could simply not be answered. For example, when he wanted to know what had become of Joseph of Arimathea and Nicodemus. But on the whole he seemed to be accepting what they could tell him.

Afterwards, in a debriefing that had become a standard part of their routine, Tamara asked how hard it would be to get some time on the Machine.

Myers told her, "I believe Dr. Stryker has stated that the Machine's usage was to be very limited and under much stricter control. Any time on the Machine would have to be approved by him. What did you have in mind?"

"Well," she said slowly, "why couldn't we use the Machine to make a recording of the Crucifixion, but only of the spectators? Keep the viewer trained away from the crosses?"

"I guess that would be possible. Ah, you're thinking that then we can show them to Jesus and he can identify the people. That would clear up a lot of controversy about who was there."

"Yes. Once again, the Gospels are contradictory, or at least incomplete."

"Well, let's ask the good doctor," Myers said with a smile. "Worst he would do is say no."

"No!"

Stryker was adamant about it. "I do not want you using the Machine to play more games with Jesus. You've created enough of a headache for me already."

Myers only smiled faintly. Tamara wanted to argue with him about the historical value of the information gained, but was only forming the argument in her head when Myers spoke quietly. "That is your prerogative, of course. But you do agree that since we have Jesus here, shouldn't we learn as much from him as possible?"

"I wish you could send him back, but that's not possible. Yes, I guess learning about history is part of our main goal."

"Jesus asked about what happened after his death," Myers went on. "Particularly, he wanted to know about his wife, Mary Magdalene as we call her, and his mother. Also, some of his friends and his children. If we can use the Machine to help him in this respect, it would make learning other things from him much easier. I think he would trust us more and be more cooperative."

Stryker only glared at the older man. The longer he stared, the more his expression faded from anger to resignation.

Myers cleverly sank the hook in. "What man wouldn't want to know about his children?"

"All right, I'll authorize some time. But if the spooks come in, you immediately cease and vacate the Machine for their use."

"Don't we always?" Myers said with a smile.

"And, for Heaven's sake, don't let them know what you're looking at!"

Fifteen minutes later they were talking to the operator, and ten minutes after that, the Machine's viewer was powered up and reaching backward in time almost two thousand years.

"By the way," Myers told Tamara as the Machine began probing in the past, "did you know that we've isolated the date of his Crucifixion. It was in CE 30. And he was thirty-four years old at the time. The New Testament was a little vague about that also. And Josephus. He seemed to have his time scale mixed up also."

The screen before them cleared from the dancing but meaningless color streaks it had been displaying, and a scene formed. "I think I've got it," said the operator, a friendly young man named Jacques Bretel. "Basically, it's the same coordinates as you used to bring him back the first time."

"That's right," Myers agreed. "But this time we want the scene to be on the spectators. I'd like you to get a close up of their faces, if possible. Keep the recording going; I'll edit it later."

"You still haven't let Jesus see his own death?" Jacques asked as he adjusted dials on the massive console.

"No, and we're not going to. Jesus has been through so much shock, why add to it by showing him the grisly way he died?"

"Guess you're right. Okay, I'm coming up on the sequence where the soldiers put him up."

Tamara stared in fascination at the images on the screen. It was a barren landscape around the dozen or so posts set into the ground. A ravine ran along behind the posts, and the area was littered with small rocks and weeds. In the distance, behind the ravine, some trees could be seen. A group of soldiers were standing around one post. When one of them moved, Tamara could see the man lying on the ground. With a shock she recognized the Jesus she knew. But this was a different man. His back and sides were streaked with blood. There were bruises on his arms and legs from mistreatment at the hands of the soldiers. He looked only half aware of what was going on, and his eyes often closed.

One soldier was holding Jesus' arm out to the side. Under it was a beam of wood, crude cut and flat. Another soldier placed a large iron spike against the upturned wrist and immediately pounded on it with a large wooden mallet. Jesus cried out, jerking his head up. The soldier pounded again, driving the spike deep into the arm and the wood behind it. A third strike and he was done. Only the spike's flattened head was visible against the tanned skin of his arm.

The soldiers shifted around and one's back blocked the view of Jesus' head. But she could see his other arm being pulled out to the side and held against the wooden beam. In eerie silence she saw the spike being placed and then pounded into his flesh. The hand jerked into a claw and trembled. Watching this cruelty, she felt sick inside.

Four of the soldiers lifted the length of wood and placed it into a notch cut into the post. Jesus' feet hung down very close to the ground. Kneeling soldiers gathered his feet together, placed them on a small peg set into the post, and bound them to the post with rope. Stepping back, the two of them stood there for a moment, gazing upon the hanging man. Another was standing behind the cross, lashing rope around the crosspiece and his wrists near the spike.

"That's to make sure that the spikes won't pull out," Myers told her quietly.

It was then that Tamara saw, in the background to the left, another man positioned in the same manner on another cross. His head was bowed but his chest was rising and falling as he gasped for air. Jesus was also breathing heavily, pain written in every line of his face. Tamara's heart ached at the sight. One of the soldiers tore the last of his clothing away, leaving him naked to the world.

"Nudity was shaming to the Romans," Myers said. "So they made sure that those being crucified would suffer that shame."

The soldiers were busy with a third man. He was also bloody and battered, but he was fighting the soldiers as they forced him down onto the crosspiece. The watchers could see him screaming. His body writhed in agony as the spikes were being pounded in. He was still screaming as they lifted him up on his post. He even tried to kick out with bare feet at the soldiers. Quickly they had him secured. They had done this many times before.

For a time, the soldiers stood back, perhaps admiring their handiwork or maybe contemplating life and death.

"I've seen this three times now," Jacques said, "and it still chokes me up."

Tamara silently agreed. It was the most dramatic, powerful images she had ever seen. A tear trickled down her cheek.

"Okay, I overshot what we wanted," Jacques said as he began adjusting the controls. "Now I'll get those people standing around for you."

"That is my mother."

The words were barely audible as Jesus said them.

They were in a conference room, watching a playback on a large screen. To make sure that Jesus understood what he was seeing, Tamara had shown him how she could create a video recording with the camera built into her cell phone then play it back. He got the idea even if he considered it magic. So, when they began the edited recording, he immediately grasped that these were scenes from when he was killed.

It was strange seeing his face as he recognized his mother standing not far from the posts. He loves her, Tamara thought. Standing next to Mary was another woman, much younger, not much more than a teenager, to judge by her face. She was holding Mary, helping to support her.

"And that," Jesus continued in a voice that almost choked up, "is my wife, Mariam."

"Whom we call Mary Magdalene," added Myers to his translation. "Did you know that in the Bible, she is mentioned by name thirteen times? That's more than most of the apostles."

Jesus was weeping silently, his eyes moist with tears and a most tender look on his face.

"During the crucifixion, she stayed by him all through it," Myers said. "The disciples all fled. Except for one. We know that she was one of the two women who initially prepared him for burial. The other woman was possibly another Mary, Mary of Bethany, the sister of Martha and Lazarus. Or it may have been another Mary."

Myers was taking notes as he talked. Perhaps to give Jesus time to collect himself, he continued describing elements of the scene to Tamara.

"Matthew's Gospel says that 'many woman' were watching from a distance. Then he spells out Mary Magdalene, Mary the mother of James and Joseph, and the mother of Zebedee's sons. That was another Mary. Entirely too many Marys to keep track of.

"Luke said that there was the 'Daughters of Jerusalem' attending. Kind of nebulous.

"John says there were Marys, including Jesus' mother. But there is some uncertainty whether he refers to three or four women."

Glancing Jesus' way, he asked, "Jesus, who is this woman to the right of Mary Magdalene?"

At first it seemed he might not answer. "That is Mary, the mother of James," he finally said.

"He's not talking about his brother James," Myers added. "And who is that young man standing beside them?"

"John." Jesus seemed to choke up for a moment.

"Called the 'Beloved One'?" asked Myers.

Jesus looked to him. "He was beloved. Next to Judas, he was the one I trusted most of them all. He believed in me and in God's coming. When the others ran away and hid, John stayed." There seemed to be some bitterness in his voice, most likely directed at those who had abandoned him.

Myers frowned, and thought for a few seconds. "Was there more than one follower named John?" he asked.

"Yes. Two. There was John the son of Zebedee and Salome and brother of James. And there was John of Capernaum. I met him while I was in that town, teaching those people who would listen. He came to listen and stayed to talk with me afterwards. Then he began to follow, as the other did. That John was as a brother to me, nay, more than a brother. Yes, you could call him the beloved one."

Myers said to Tamara in a quick aside, "Two Johns! History will have to be rewritten!" Turning back to Jesus, he asked, "Did you expect your followers to stay with you?"

"I had thought them of stout heart. But they were weak. They ran away for fear of the soldiers."

"Did not some of them try to fight for you when the soldiers came to arrest you?"

"Two did. But I knew that my arrest was inevitable. And I wanted it. It was to fulfill the prophecy. The Son of Man was to be prosecuted by the priests."

Myers looked to Tamara with a serious expression. Turning back to Jesus, he said, "Did you truly believe that if the exact prophecies did not come to pass, then the kingdom would not come?"

Jesus sighed, and seemed to slump in the chair. Myers turned off the recording.

Jesus looked to them earnestly. "Yes. They were the

words, the promises of God, given to us through the words of the prophets.

"John, who baptized the people in the waters of the Jordan, taught that the coming Kingdom of God would begin with the coming of the Son of Man. I believed that was true. The Son of Man was a messenger of God. He would sit in judgment of men, preparing them for the coming Kingdom.

"For many years I believe this and taught others of the glory of the coming of God's Kingdom. Our people would be given back the land promised us. Our oppressors would be vanquished. All men would live in peace."

He smiled, and said, "The lost tribes would be found and reunited to make the kingdom of Israel whole again."

He turned to face Myers. "Do you know that I... we, expected that to come any day? The Son of Man would come to earth. He would fulfill the prophecies. He would bring forth the perfect world. So I was taught and did teach others. Some opposed me, for they wished the world to stay the same. Some did not understand. They did not believe me. But a few did.

"The days passed and the seasons came and went. Still there was no Son of Man. The prophets could not be wrong. They spoke with the words of God! Then, one day, as I told you, after we had been debating going to Jerusalem for Passover, I was walking alone by the Sea of Galilee. It came to me. The Son of Man was already here. I was him! Suddenly, everything fell into place. I saw myself doing as the prophets said, fulfilling their prophecies. It was so incredibly simple! I was the chosen one, of the line of King David. I had endured years of teaching by John. It was I who cured lepers and cast out demons. I could not have done that without the hand of God guiding me. I was the one!"

He paused, a growing excitement flushing his face. "I was the one," he repeated. "I had to do it all! I made the decision to go to the Holy City and that the prophets would guide me."

Suddenly he was tired and lowered his head. "But I failed. The Kingdom never came. Has not come yet." He looked up again. "How long did you say has passed?"

"Two thousand years," Myers told him. Both he and Tamara had the feeling that Jesus could not comprehend such a long time span. "You have done a great deal for the world, my friend. Rabbi Jesus, you have done more than you could ever imagine."

"But the Kingdom did not come. All I did. All I sacrificed. All in vain." He seemed on the verge of tears.

Myers spoke softly. "Let us follow your mother."

Jesus looked up, and then turned back to the screen. He looked as if he were going to cry again. "No," he whispered. "She is a strong woman; she will survive. I want to see of my wife and my children. What became of them?"

37. A GRIEVING MOTHER

Myers was visibly surprised. "We... I thought that you would want to see what happen to your mother, Mary," he said. "We followed her only. We didn't have enough Machine time to do more."

"I want to know of my wife and children," Jesus repeated quietly but firmly. In his voice and the look in his eye, Tamara saw some of the fire and strength that had made him a leader of men.

"And you shall. I will make sure we get more Machine time."

Myers clicked on the video display again, and all heads turned to it. "This is the point after you were given the vinegar on a sponge. Almost immediately, you apparently died."

Tamara grimaced. She knew that the death was not apparent. Right after that point, the Machine had grabbed Jesus and reconstructed him in their lab. Shortly after that, perhaps only minutes, Jesus was dead – perhaps even before he was taken down from the cross.

On the screen the spectators did nothing, only stared straight ahead. They were looking at Jesus, but it appeared they were looking in the eyes of the viewers. The women all looked incredibly sad. Mother Mary was crying as Mary Magdalene supported her on one side and John on the other. For over a minute nothing changed, then John leaned close to Mary's ear and said something. The watchers did not know what it was because the Machine could not pick up sounds, but it was not hard to guess. He was telling her it was time to depart. It seemed as if she would refuse for a bit, but she did allow him to lead her away.

Mary Magdalene stayed for a few moments more. There were tears running down her face, but an oddly resigned expression on it. As his closest confident, she undoubtedly knew of his acceptance of what he considered fate. She had undoubtedly heard him talk of the prophecies and, at a certain point, his revelation that he was the chosen one, the Messiah, the one to lead the Jewish people into a new age. So maybe she understood his mind more than his disciples or his friends. And maybe she accepted his sacrifice as necessary for the good of the people. It was even probable that she knew of the prophecies that he would rise from the dead. Of Psalm 16:10: *"For Thou wilt not abandon my soul to Sheol; neither wilt Thou allow Thy Holy One to undergo decay."* And **Hosea 6.2**: *"After two days he will revive us; on the third day he will raise us up, that we may live before him."* And Isaiah. Even in the story of Jonah, for as Mark 12:40 says, *"For as Jonah was three days and three nights in the belly of the whale, so will the Son of Man be three days and three nights in the heart of the earth"*

Jesus was certainly well aware of those and other prophecies, Tamara thought. Very likely Mary Magdalene knew them as well. Was that almost a proud look on her face? Then Tamara shook away the thought and saw only grief written across those young, dark eyes.

The view followed John and the women as they left the scene. The motion was jerky as the Machine operator adjusted the settings to keep up with them. They followed a trail leading down the hillside and away from the massive city behind them. When they came to a road, there were more people hurrying along, anxious to reach their homes before sundown and the beginning of the Sabbath. At that point there occurred a jump in the scene, which Myers explained was an edit out of their walk. Now the party came upon a house made of roughly quarried stone with limestone block used on the corners and door lintels. About ten feet tall, the house was square and had only two very small windows showing on the outside. They passed through the door into a courtyard. Once inside, the windows were larger to allow light into the rooms that surrounded the courtyard. The room they went into was only ten foot by ten, the walls covered with a rough coating of mortar made of mud and clay. The roof was a series of wooden beams covered over with bundles of reeds, and a mortar laid over those. It was dark inside, for the setting sun cast little light within. An oil lamp was lit but offered only a flicking glow over the people.

"That is the house of Mary, the mother of James and Joseph and Salome," Jesus told them.

Two young men stuck their heads in and a discussion followed. One shook his head at the news, the other just looked sad. After they left, a teenage woman came in, brushing flour off her hands and going over to hug her mother. She looked as if she was going to cry.

There was little discussion among the people, and what there was seemed subdued. Mary, the mother of Jesus, sat in a chair and stared at the floor, ignoring any who tried to comfort her.

Tamara glanced over to Jesus. He was watching the screen intently, hands clenched together on the table. Her heart went out to him. How heart-rending it must be for the man to watch his own family mourning his death.

There was another edit cut, after which the scene was mostly unchanged. After a few moments a young man came in. Rapidly he spoke to Mary Magdalene. The other Mary came to stand beside her. The two women spoke with each other, then gathered cloaks, took up baskets and left with the young man.

The scene on the screen went black.

"They are going to prepare your body for burial," Myers told them. "Joseph of Arimathea and Nicodemus failed to revive you. You were already dead when they tried."

For a while, none of them spoke. Slowly, Jesus took in a breath. "I want to see it," he said.

"See what?"

"My death."

38. ON THE CROSS

Jesus' statement stunned Myers and Tamara.

"It's not pretty," Myers told him. "Are you sure?"

Jesus only nodded.

Myers sighed, and then picked up the tablet he had been using to control the video display. A menu came up and he begin working his way to another of the stored video files. Without comment, he started the video.

This began right after Jesus had been lifted to the pole and the soldiers were busy working on the third man to die that day, the one who was fighting them in a losing battle. They could not hear his cries, but it was not hard to see the terror on his face and on his mouth open in a scream as the spikes were pounded into his wrists.

Tamara glanced over at Jesus. How would he take watching the Roman soldiers crucifying him? So far, there was no emotion on his face at all.

On the screen the view switched back to Jesus. A soldier was binding his ankles to the post. Tamara realized that was why Jesus could walk so well; there never had been nails driven into his feet! So many of the depictions of the Crucifixion showed spikes in the feet, often crossed. But then, most of those depictions also showed the spikes going through his hands, and she had known from the first that was not true.

The video continued for several minutes during which Jesus only turned his head slowly from side to side as if looking around. Several times his head drooped but picked up almost immediately. It was obvious that he was having trouble breathing. Tamara noticed two trickles of blood crawling down from his forehead. Blood was likewise leaking from the wounds in his wrists. He looked very tired.

Myers leaned towards Jesus to speak to him quietly. "This goes on for almost four hours. A few times you seem to be saying something." As he said that, a Roman soldier came into view. He had a short stool of crude wood that he placed next to the post. Mounting it, he reached over and inserted a small wooden board into a grove atop the post. There was writing on it but hard to read. It looked as if other writing, probably in charcoal, had been wiped off and fresh letters applied. It was hard to make out the characters, and the view never closed in on the plank.

Jesus said, "The soldier laughed at me when he was up near me. He called me 'King of the Jews.' I guess that's what the plank said." He glanced at Myers and Tamara, and then explained. "It was the Roman custom. I could not see the other two who were with me."

"The Gospels say that they were labeled as thieves," Tamara said.

"A more accurate translation is bandits," Myers said. "Do you know, Rabbi, who they were?"

Jesus sighed. "No. The Romans often crucified people who they thought were rebels or might be rebels. The Romans saved crucifixion for those convicted of sedition against Rome. Common thieves did not merit such."

"Did you say anything to either of them?" asked Tamara.

"I don't remember saying anything."

Myers did something on the tablet and the scene sped up. Jesus looked surprised to see the soldiers moving around at high speeds and his head jerking from side to side. Those moving around were almost a blur.

Finally, as a time index at the bottom of the screen showed a setting he was looking for, Myers caused it to revert back to normal speed.

On the cross, Jesus' face had taken on a paleness. His eyes hardly stayed open. He assumed the appearance of exactly what he was, a man dying. His lips moved silently. A few moments later a man's back came into the picture. He held up a sponge speared by a branch and dripping to Jesus' lips. It seemed that Jesus would not – could not – drink of it, and it was pushed harder until some of the liquid must have dripped into his mouth. Then the man withdrew.

"It was so hard to breathe," Jesus said.

"You told us of Joseph of Arimathea's plan to revive you," Myers said. "Tell me, Rabbi, did you think it would work?"

Jesus looked between him and the image on the screen before answering. "I expected God to come to my aid. Yet I knew that it was God's plan that I die. And would be resurrected in three days. The prophecies foretold of that." He looked again at the pitiful figure on the cross. "But at that point I was not sure what to think. I wanted to beg of God that he end my suffering; oh, how I did suffer! I may even have called out to him. I am not sure."

Turning a sorrowful face to the others, Jesus told them, "I am afraid that I was weak. I cried out that I thirsted. I knew of Nicodemus' plan. I knew that there would be something in the vinegar." He sucked in air. "I could take it no longer. I greatly feared that it would take days for me to die up there. Or that they would break my legs. I could not let that happen. It would be against the prophecies. Those were God's words given through prophets of old. I could not allow them not be fulfilled."

Without comment, Myers touched the tablet a few times and the scene shifted to the inside of a cave. There were only two oil lamps and the light was poor. Still, they could see two men carrying in the body of a third. They rushed their actions, placing the body on a rock ledge with a pit dug next to it. They stood in the pit, one lifting Jesus' head while the other took a small flask and tried to pour some liquid into his mouth. Several times they tried but got no reaction. The man was dead.

"Enough," Jesus said wearily. "I have seen enough."

"Later, your body was taken someplace else," Myers told him. "When Mary Magdalene came to finish preparing you, she found the tomb empty. She believed that you had risen. She did expect that, did she not?"

"Yes. She understood the prophecies as well as I did. On the third day, God would lift up my body and I would give proof to all that his Kingdom had arrived."

"Those who followed you believed that you had risen," Tamara told him. "And that began a whole new religion."

Jesus looked at her strangely. Then he shook his head sadly. "I believe in the Law of Moses, the Torah. In the prophets' words passed down from ancient times. There was no need for a new religion. There is God, and His promise to our people! He would give us that land forever. And he would come soon to fulfill that promise. I wanted to prepare our people. I told them I was the Light and the Way, that they might listen to my words and obey."

He stopped suddenly and looked from one to the other of them. "That was all I wanted. I never wanted people to worship me, only to follow God's will."

39. WHAT TO DO ABOUT JESUS

After the promise to follow up on the lives of the two Marys, Myers and Tamara walked back to his office.

"I could use a cup of coffee," he told her.

"Maybe something stronger," was her reply. "Can you believe him? How can a man sit there calmly and watch his own crucifixion?"

"Jesus has a strong will."

"Still..."

Immediately he switched on the coffee maker.

"He seems so shocked that people would take his teachings and make a religion around them," she said as she sat down.

"And misinterpret them. But it is not surprising that he was shocked at the outcome of his ministry. First off, he was a Jew. First, last, and always. His concern was always with the Jewish people. So much so that he was willing to give up his life for his people. He really did not think of the Kingdom of God as belonging to the Gentiles; it was to be a natural result of God's covenant with Israel. Remember, those who wrote the Gospels had an agenda. They wanted Jesus to appeal to the non-Jewish world. To Rome, even. So they slanted his statements and actions that they reported in their writing.

"But some of his feelings came through. Remember Matthew 10:5? *These twelve Jesus sent forth, and commanded them, saying, Go not into the way of the gentiles, and into any city of the Samaritans enter ye not: but go rather to the lost sheep of the house of*

Israel.'

"And Matthew 15:24 when a 'woman of Canaan', a gentile, comes and begs him to save her daughter who was possessed by a devil. He wouldn't answer her. When his disciples told him to send her away, he said, *'I am not sent but unto the lost sheep of the house of Israel.'* When she again begged him, he said, *'It is not meet to take the children's bread, and to cast it to the dogs.'* By children, he means Israel. By dogs, he means gentiles like her."

"And eventually he gives in," Tamara added, "and heals her daughter."

"Only when she tells him that even the dogs eat of the crumbs of the Master's table." He winked at her, and then continued, "So he heals a few gentiles! It was still the Jews that he was most concerned with. As to the heart and soul of Jewish faith – the Law of Moses – he was adamant that his mission was not to abolish it but to fulfill it. Matthew 5:17, *Think not that I am come to destroy the law, or the prophets: I am not come to destroy, but to fulfill.'*"

"Would you hand me that Bible there? Thank you." She turned the pages until she found what she wanted. "The hatred of the Jewish people towards gentiles is well documented. At least, the Jews of old. I quote you from the Second Book of Moses aka Exodus.

'For mine Angel shall go before thee, and bring thee in unto the Amorites, and the Hittites, and the Perizzites, and the Canaanites, the Hivites, and the Jebusites: and I will cut them off. ...thou shalt utterly overthrow them, and quite break down their images. I will send my fear before thee, and will destroy all the people to whom thou shalt come, and I will make all thine enemies turn their backs unto thee. And I will send hornets before thee, which shall drive out the Hivite, the Canaanite, and the Hittite, from before thee. By little and little I will drive them out from

before thee, until thou be increased, and inherit the land.

"And I will set thy bounds from the Red sea even unto the sea of the Philistines, and from the desert unto the river: for I will deliver the inhabitants of the land into your hand; and thou shalt drive them out before thee. Thou shalt make no covenant with them, nor with their gods. They shall not dwell in thy land."

"Yes, and Jesus also said, according to Matthew 10:34, *'Think not that I am come to send peace on earth: I came not to send peace, but a sword.'* And again, in Luke 12:49: *'I am come to send fire on the earth... Suppose ye that I am come to give peace on earth? I tell you, Nay; but rather division.'*

"Those were rough times, Tamara. And Jesus was a product of those times."

"And then there is Joshua," Tamara said. "He ran amok, destroying cities and killing all within. At Jericho, after knocking down the walls, he did a real number on the people inside." She flipped the pages over to find the Book of Joshua, then read, *"And they utterly destroyed all that was in the city, both man and woman, young and old, and ox, and sheep, and ass, with the edge of the sword, and they burnt the city with fire, and all that was therein: only the silver, and the gold, and the vessels of brass and of iron, they put into the treasury of the house of the LORD."*

"As I said, Tamara, rough times," was his only comment. He took the Bible out of her hands and put it back.

For a while neither spoke, until Myers said, "You know, what he says does clear up a few things," he began. "Like who was present at the crucifixion."

"And the whole issue of the resurrection," Tamara could not help herself from adding.

Myers nodded slowly. "Yes, there is that. So he never regained life, never arose from the tomb.

"There are many who believe that the Gospel stories of

the resurrection were added by believers, and are not factual reporting of true events."

"I have studied this subject some," Tamara said, nodding in agreement. "And I was forced to come to the conclusion that much of what the Gospels say is added material. Or changed."

"That's pretty much accepted among scholars. The Gospels were written by believers for other believers, or potential believers, to read. They were not newspaper reports. They are not the words of those who were truly present at the events. It would be incredible if those who wrote the Gospels did not add elements or change them to suit their beliefs and purpose. The writers were only human, after all."

After a pause, Tamara said, "So, we know the truth now. What do we do with it?"

Myers gave her a sharp look, then chuckled. "Do we know the truth?" He leaned over to take the coffee pot out of the machine. "Do we really know what happened two thousand years ago? One might argue that all we know is what a copy of Jesus has told us, and what we've seen via a machine the working of which only a handful of humans would understand and most would not believe. Don't forget, we're dealing with the unknown here. Any time you're dealing with the quantum world, you've left the world of cause and effect behind. There is so much that is not known about quantum entanglement yet. It is one mysterious force of nature."

"Oh, so you're a theoretical physicist now?" she asked him good-humoredly.

He smiled. "I've picked up a lot from Fielding and Juliette and others. Did you know that Einstein described entanglement as '*spukhafte Fernwirkung*,' or 'spooky action at a distance'? What if there is something more spooky about this than particles entangling? There is evidence that some events on the quantum level exist in all possible states and only 'collapse' to one state when observed? Schrödinger's famous alive and dead cat.

"What if there are other factors involved? Let's say the belief of the operator of the Machine? What if the operator firmly believes that the object he is creating will be solid diamond. Then he tried to copy a lump of coal. Will the carbon in the coal become diamond when it appears in the chamber? Or will it stay just a lump of coal?

"Maybe what was created here was a Jesus who was totally human in all respects. A Jesus who was not resurrected because the operator of the Machine expected him to be nothing else? And that we see in the viewing of the past only what we expect to see? A dead man in the tomb instead of an awakening man?

"See what I'm getting at?"

"I'm seeing a headache coming on," she said. "So, all that we've learned may not be anything more than what we expected to learn?"

"That is possible. But the counter-argument is that some of the objects copied have properties that were not expected. For example, when Dr. Brown used the Machine to observe T-Rex in the past, he was surprised to find that some of them had three fingered hands while others had two fingered hands. Current belief had been that all T-Rex had two fingered hands. How could he have come up with the three fingered version if he did not expect them?"

Tamara thought for a moment, and then smiled. "Did you know that when the original T-Rex fossils were found, it was believed that they had three fingers? Here, let me look it up." She pulled out her smart phone, brought up the browser, and then typed in an inquiry. "Here it is," she read from the screen. "When the Tyrannosaurus Rex was first discovered, the *humerus* was the only part of the forelimb known. In other words, the fingers were missing. For the initial mounted skeleton as seen by the public in 1915, Osborn substituted longer, three-fingered forelimbs like those of *Allosaurus*. In 1989, a complete forelimb confirmed that T-Rex had only two fingers.

"So, you see, Dr. Brown, being a biologist, is probably well aware of this bit of history. When he viewed T-Rex stomping around in their native jungle, it might have been in his subconscious that some had three fingers, or at least that concept existed in his mind. So his looking at ferocious dinosaurs munching on smaller dinosaurs doesn't prove anything. If you assume your premise."

"You know, you are quite educated – for an auditor," he said with a smile. He sighed, and sipped at his coffee. "I guess we could devise an experiment that would test this hypothesis that what you expect may just be what you get. But that still wouldn't prove that we have an exact copy of Jesus. There are those believers who will simply say that we got an imperfect copy, while the real Jesus was happily resurrected back in 30 C.E., and is currently sitting at the right hand of God in heaven."

"I'll bet that what we have is an exact copy," Tamara said sincerely with a shake of her head. "I've seen a happy, playful and very much alive Saber-Toothed Cat. And... I don't know. I just feel that our Jesus is real."

"As do I, Miss Graves, as do I."

"Which brings us back to my original question. What do we do now? Will we ever tell the world about him? About the facts we've uncovered? This is damned important stuff! The world has a right to know."

"Do they? If we were to tell all we know as of right now, what would the results be? Praise by the scientific community? Perhaps. But what about the average man? Or the average believer? Remember, so far we have no proof of any degree of divinity."

Tamara was silent for a long time, as Myers sipped his coffee and looked at her over the top of his cup.

"There are those," she said carefully, "who would want to stone us, to use a Biblical method of expressing disagreement."

"Quite right, Tamara."

"And a lot of atheists who would shout halleluiah that they are proven correct." She shook her head. "We could release the news with a full disclaimer that this may not be the correct interpretation of the results."

"Then both sides will be after our hides!"

"But this is simply too big to sit on!" she protested.

Myers looked around at all the reference books and other material in his office, and sighed. "Two things, Tamara," he said. "First, I am taking notes. One day I may be able to write a book about this.

"Secondly, I'm glad that the decision is not mine to make."

40. SUBPOENAED

The decision to tell the world about the Machine and their distinguished guest was not made by them after all. Dr. Stryker was late for a meeting with the Project J staff but, just as someone was about to go look for him, he arrived, face flushed and breathing hard.

"Damn!" he announced heatedly. Some eyebrows went up. "Damned Congress! Damn Stockman!"

Those who knew him were silent, allowing him to blow off steam. They knew that he would get down to business soon enough.

"I have just gotten a summons to appear before the House Committee on Science, Space and Technology to explain new stories about our project."

"What!" exclaimed Dr. Crane.

"It's Stockman! He's gotten some new information – or so he says – about our project and wants to immediately question us about it."

"I thought we covered our tracks with them by saying that we were only cloning animals," said Dr. Fielding. "We showed them a few animals and that put an end to the rumors."

"Apparently not. He was positively gloating when he told me on the video feed that he had new evidence. He was none too polite about it, either."

Fielding spoke up, "Do you think he knows about the Machine?"

"Maybe. Maybe not. But he knows something." Stryker was calming down but still quite angry. "I hope not all the facts," he said with feeling.

"It would be nice to know what his evidence is," said Crane. "Then you could prepare a story."

That set off a not-too-productive discussion of who might be leaking information. When that subject had been beaten into the ground with no resolution, the topic switched to what to do next.

"Just refuse to go. What can he do?" was Crane's immediate input.

"Well, for one thing he can hold Chronodyne, and probably myself personally, in Contempt of Congress. And we don't need that kind of publicity. What would the stockholders say?"

"Well," said Crane, "that would at least buy us some time."

"To do what?" Stryker growled. "We can't very well hide the whole project!"

"Why not simply announce the project openly and beat Congress to the punch?" asked Juliette.

There was silence following that suggestion, but from the looks on faces, it was obvious that the idea was appalling to some, just as it was hopeful to others.

"We will have to do that sooner or later," Fielding added. "We've known that from the start. We just didn't want to make any claims until we proved the theory as valid. Well, we have certainly done that."

Juliette nodded agreement. "I'm for that. Boy, would that make the scientific world pay attention!"

"Which is just what we don't want." Stryker glared at her.

"Maybe we could announce just a part of the overall

project," suggested Buerer. "Just the artifacts, maybe?"

Stryker shook his head. "And then someone will remember that we claimed to have cloned extinct animals and put two and two together. Soon, Congress, the press and everyone else will want to know what else we've recreated from the past."

Fielding immediately said, "So we tell all. You do agree that eventually that will have to come to pass."

"Aren't you forgetting that major funding for this project came from the government via contracts with DOD and other agencies. And when you deal in secrets with the government, you have to deal with the CIA, NSA, DNI and others. Probably the FBI and Cub Scouts, too. We go public, they'll be having conniption fits."

The discussion quickly evolved into a battle of the stay-secret group against the go-public group, with the arguments becoming heated at times. Tamara, who had simply followed Juliette into the meeting despite the fact that she was not even a Chronodyne employee, could see both sides. She was familiar with security agencies and their attitude that nothing – absolutely nothing – is more important than their work. On the other hand, she could sympathize with the scientists who wanted their incredibly important work announced to the world. This project was their baby, and none of them wanted it buried under a cover of secrecy forever.

When the discussion reached a point where everyone had paused to take a breath, Dr. Myers made a point. "Gentlemen, and ladies, may I suggest that, if you decide to make any public announcement, please do not include Jesus. He had enough of a shock when someone slipped that tablet to him. He does not need to suddenly be the focus of attention for the whole world. He just could not handle that."

For the first time since the debate began, all sides agreed on something: Jesus should be protected from the harsh spotlight that would be turned on him. And, of course, from their being criticized for having created him in the first place.

The security head, who had not taken part so far, finally put in his view. "I don't think the decision will be ours to make." He looked around the table. "We know for a fact that others outside this project know of his existence. Someone gave him that tablet. And there was that gang who came blasting in and tried to assassinate him. Someone leaked information to that Congressman before.

"I fear the secret is out. Enough people know it, at least enough to assure that it will not stay secret for very long."

No one could argue with that point.

"I will call a meeting of all department heads tomorrow," Stryker told them. "I want input from the others concerning how a public announcement would affect their researches. Nine o'clock tomorrow."

With that, he stood and left a stunned group of scientists unable to decide if they were happy or afraid of the imminent disclosure of their work.

41. GIRLS JUST WANT TO HAVE FUN

Tamara was normally an early riser. The next morning was no exception; she was up with the sun. It had rained during the night and the air was exceptionally clear and fresh. She recalled Dr. Myers saying that Jesus normally took his breakfast in the courtyard, weather permitting. Picking up a breakfast tray as soon as the cafeteria opened, she carried it over to Project J's building. She noted the increased security and was grateful for that. The attempt on Jesus' life had shaken her up.

Her badge was enough to get her inside. The staff of Project Dry Wells, from Stryker on down, was grateful to her for her brave action in defending Jesus from the terrorists. It gave her pretty much open access to Project J, and probably any of the others, should she wish.

Jesus had just sat down to breakfast himself. He smiled as she came up. She noticed that he did not stand up at her approach, but then the custom of a gentlemen standing for a lady was probably not a part of his culture. She sat down, and noticed that Dr. Myers was not there. She was not used to seeing Jesus without Dr. Myers also present. For one thing, he was the only other person, other than Jesus, who spoke Aramaic.

She was a bit at a loss as to what to say. Did he understand any English? She started with the only Aramaic she remembered: "Shelama." He smiled and returned the greeting, adding a couple words she did not know. Then she tried, "It is a beautiful morning," waving her hand at the clear blue sky. Jesus looked up and nodded. Maybe he did not understand the words but the meaning came across.

They ate pretty much in silence, but it was a friendly silence, the kind you share with someone you know well. Although that might not be true in this case, she did feel a strong affection for Jesus. Partly because of how much the man had gone through, but also because she sensed a power within him, a power to influence people. And maybe something more. There was no question that he had a strong belief system, and that gave him a quiet air of self-confidence.

As she was trying to think of something to say, Dr. Myers walked into the courtyard. Leaning on his cane, he made his way to the table. "Shelama, rabbi," he said. He must have been expected, for there was a plate set for him, including a carafe of coffee that he immediately poured into a cup. There was no coffee set for Jesus.

"And to what do we own this visit, Tamara?" Myers asked after taking his first sip.

"Just wanted to see Jesus again," she replied. "There's about an hour and a half before that general meeting. Seemed like a good time to check up on our guest."

Myers did not translate but Jesus looked on, apparently knowing that they were talking about him.

"Why don't you ask him if he would like to take a little walk after breakfast? It's a nice day for it."

Myers translated, and Jesus smiled at her. She liked the way he smiled. Too bad he did not do it more often. Which led her to thinking about his condition. "Walking doesn't hurt him too much, does it?" she asked.

"No. His back is almost healed and his legs have pretty much recovered from the abuse. He says that walking is good.

I think it's mostly because it gets him out of the building. He really does want to see the outside world."

"I'm sure he does. We just have to do a little bit at a time."

"Quite right. Don't want too much culture shock, do we?"

Tamara waited until Jesus was finished before she rose from the chair. "I'll just walk around the building. Won't go far."

"The only danger is from the staff of the other projects. They know about him but most have not seen him yet. You might find him becoming the center of attraction."

"I'll be careful."

They walked towards the door, Dr. Myers staying behind to finish his coffee. She told the guard where she was taking him and they left the building. It was a most beautiful morning, really. The mountains stood out with unusual clarity. Jesus looked at them as he walked, leading Tamara to wonder if he had seen any really tall mountains in his life? Mountains big enough to have snow most of the year. Did they have any that tall in Palestine?

Would he like to see the Rockies?

A car drove by on one of the internal roads, and then slowed down opposite them while the driver stared out the window at Jesus and Tamara. Was he looking at Jesus or me, she wondered? She was good looking enough to attract men's glances. But more likely it was the noted historical figure beside her that drew the driver's attention.

Jesus watched the car drive away, and stopped. Turning to Tamara, he pointed to her, then himself, then the moving car.

"You want to take another drive!" she told him. "I don't

see why not. I guess you would be fascinated with driving. I'll have to ask Dr. Myers to borrow his car again."

All the time she talked, Jesus just smiled and watched her as if he understood every word. Tamara was about to head back towards the entrance when an idea struck her. She smiled at him and said, "Want to do a little joy riding? Come on!"

She led him across the road, along another building and down a street until they came to the apartment building. There, in the parking lot besides the building, was her bright blue Corvette, all clean from the overnight rain. She unlocked the doors and waved him into the passenger seat. "Stryker will probably kill me, but you deserve to experience a real car. Let me show you how to attached the seatbelt."

Jesus did not seem to understand why he had to be strapped into the seat, but he trusted Tamara, especially when he saw that she also put on the straps.

She started the motor, and Jesus was apparently impressed with the throaty growl of the big V-8 engine. That, or it scared him.

She backed out gently, and then pointed its nose along a straight section of the street. "Did you know this car can go from zero to sixty in three point eight seconds?" she asked him. A puzzled smile was all he showed. "I will demonstrate."

With the skill most women do not have, she put the big sports cars through its paces, starting with a demonstration of how to place a patch of rubber on the pavement. Jesus grabbed the dashboard with both hands and looked rather frightened. She had to slow down because the street was not nearly long enough to let the car really stretch its legs. She had not even gotten beyond fourth gear and still had another two to go.

"Man, what a rush!" she gushed, then turned to see if she

had overdone it with her innocent passenger. But she need not have worried. He might have been scared at first, but the thrill of that kind of acceleration is universal. All humans find it exciting. He was still clutching the dash, but he was smiling.

Continuing in the same mode, she demonstrated how well the car can corner, taking some of the turns on the Dry Wells road system at speeds far beyond anyone had envisioned. She swerved around a delivery truck and deliberately headed towards the parking lot before the main office building. It was the only patch of pavement large enough to do what she wanted. Whipping the car into the mostly empty parking lot, she snapped the steering wheel around and demonstrated a nice sideward skid.

"We'll have to find some good curves," she told him, "so I can show you drift racing."

Jesus just nodded, and kept on smiling.

One more circuit of the facility, drawing attention of most of the Chronodyne employees as she squealed the wheels and made the car growl nicely, then a last quick dash down the single long straight way. Demurely, she parked the beast and patted the steering wheel.

"They'll probably kick me out of here, but I thought you should have a little fun."

Dr. Stryker was waiting for them when they got back to the Project J building. She had never seen his face such a lovely shade of red before.

"Miss Graves," he said through clenched teeth. "Are you aware that the speed limit on company roads is twenty miles per hour?"

"Oh, sorry. The speed signs went by too fast to read." She smiled at him. 'Sometimes a conservative, staid, prim and proper auditor just has to let go,' she told herself. 'Besides,

Jesus liked it!'

"You were endangering the staff, not to mention Chronodyne property," Stryker continued.

"Before you get all steamed up, no one was in danger," she informed him. "I've raced that car in Autocross and other amateur racing formats. I was in perfect control at all times.

"If you want to kick me out, fine, but look at Jesus. He loved it!"

Her statement was obvious. Stryker, and probably no one else, had ever seen or even imagined Jesus grinning from ear to ear. Apparently sensing that she was being admonished for what she did, he reached over and took Tamara's hand, and lifting it up to his lips, he kissed it.

That cannot be ancient Jewish protocol, she told herself. But it is sort of universal. Besides, she was pleased with it. At least the ancient Jew had gotten his approval across to Stryker. Still fuming, the Projector Director stomped away.

Behind them, Myers laughed, trying to keep it in so that Stryker would not hear. "Oh, girl, you really stuck it to him! Magnificent! But have you really raced that car on a track?"

"Oh, yes. As often as I can. It's fun! I'll take you for a ride sometime."

"No thank you, Miss. My heart couldn't take it." Then he surprised her by taking her other hand, lifting it and kissing it.

Having her hand kissed twice in one morning! 'Pretty good work,' she told herself.

42. MEETING IN WASHINGTON

The Sam Rayburn House Office Building on Independence Avenue was an imposing five story building spreading out on a full city block. The outside was in keeping with the classical building style of the other Capitol Hill structures, but the inside was pure 1960s, with chrome push bars, clocks, and elevators and fluorescent lighting fixtures.

As they rode up from the basement parking area, Doctors Stryker and Crane were nervous. But then, anyone under a subpoena from a Congressional committee should be. After a thorough weapons check, it took a bit of walking to get to the section wherein lay the office of Representative Norman Stockman, Chairman of the Committee on Science, Space, and Technology. A man who also, some claimed, had aspirations to occupy the large White House down the street. But then, most elected officials in Washington did.

"Did you know when they built this, congressional leaders inserted a gymnasium into the plans without telling the public about that?" Crane said. The halls were filled with people hurrying about on undoubtedly important government business. "There is a sub-basement level with a gym featuring dozens of cardio machines outfitted with TV screen, all kinds of weightlifting machines and free weights. Did you also know that there is a shooting range run by the US Capital Police down there?"

"Where the hell do you get all those useless facts?" Stryker snapped.

"I watch a lot of Discover and History Channel shows."

They came to the right office and immediately found themselves confronted by a stern looking, older secretary behind a desk bigger than Stryker's. Her glasses hung by a cord around her neck, and she looked as if she had a serious case of constipation. "Can I help you?" she said in a tone that clearly implied that she probably had no intent to do such.

"We're expected," said Stryker as he handed her his business card.

She stared at it as if he had handed her something particularly foul, but finally condescended to admit that perhaps they really did have a valid reason to see the Representative. She touched a button on her phone and announced them. "You may go in," she said in the same tone you would tell the hired help to spread the manure on the lawn.

The inner office lacked the amenities of a true executive's office but was fair sized. There was the obligatory wall of photos of the Representative with various government officials from the President on down. There were books on shelves and assorted reports and such stacked on a table. And the ever-present computer terminal.

Stockman was shorter than he appeared on TV, seemed heavier, and his suit smelled of cigar smoke. He was having a losing battle with receding hairline, but what he had was well groomed and probably dyed to keep any gray from showing; he had the politician's quick but not totally sincere smile and a firm handshake. If you had intended to cast someone for the role of a Senator in a TV series, you could hardly do better.

"Well, gentlemen, thank you for coming. Please be seated," he told them in a deep, resonate voice, one of his best attributes.

Stryker wasted no time getting to the point. "Why did you subpoena Chronodyne and myself?" His tone was decidedly not friendly, and he did not return the smile, sincere or otherwise.

"I have once again come into information concerning your Project Dry Wells," Strockman said, wasting no time in getting down to brass tacks either. "And once again," he continued, "I have met with a stone wall in trying to get information from your corporation. I was told that your project was classified! Classified! Everything is classified these days. I represent the House and the American people, and we have a right to know where and for what our tax dollars are going. If you are developing advanced technology, then my committee is directly concerned."

"Don't give me the American people political-talk crap!" Stryker retaliated. "What is this 'new information' that you're talking about?"

Stockman, smiling rather smugly, tented his fingers before him, and said, "You do have a time machine at your facility. You call it 'the Machine' – rather unimaginative – and you can use it to travel back and forth in time."

Stryker laughed. "You need a new source. Time travel is impossible."

"You've found a way to make it possible. You have brought back from the past animals and artifacts, including a dodo and that Saber-Toothed Tiger you have shown off, pretending it is the result of cloning old DNA. You have, among other things, a copy of the Magna Carta, Lincoln's top hat, and an 1804 silver dollar." He smiled at the look of consternation on their faces and knew that he had struck gold.

"And I want to know *all* about this Machine." The greed in his eyes bespoke of a strong desire for power. He not only wanted to know about this, he wanted somehow turn it into a political advantage for himself.

Stryker looked to Crane and sighed. "We have been considering a public disclosure, but decided that this was not the right time. But, I assure you, we do not have a time machine in the sense you mean it."

"Then what do you have?"

"Would you like to come out and see?"

For a few seconds no one spoke. They could almost see the wheels turning in Stockman's head, undoubtedly trying to see what political good he could turn this into. For himself, of course.

"I am a busy man," Stockman began. "My time is valuable..."

"You want to know what we have or not? I'm willing to show you the project. It is my hope that then you will agree that keeping it classified is fully justified and in the best interests of all concerned."

"I'll be the judge of that." Stockman flexed his fingers a few times, as if doing push-ups with them. "Very well. I'll fly out to New Mexico and see your little project. But I won't forget my obligation to the American people."

No one in that room believed for one second that was truly his purpose.

An appointment was made for two days hence, which satisfied Stryker. It gave him time to prepare.

43. GO ON A VACATION

"We'll probably have to go public with the Machine," Stryker told the assembled project heads in a hurriedly called meeting as soon as he returned to New Mexico. "Stockman has gotten his hands on inside information, but does not know all the details. He thinks that we have a true time machine and can travel back and forth in time. I'll have to show him the Machine and tell him the truth about it."

"So we're going to have to go public with it," said Crane.

Stryker looked at him with a frown. "I didn't say that. I hope I can persuade him to allow us to continue under the same high classification we currently have. To that end, I think I have something that will help. Two things, actually."

He paused to look around at the project heads. "But," he said with emphasis, "There is one part of this project that I do not want him to know about." Staring directly at Fielding, "And we all know which project that is."

Fielding's face flushed, but he said nothing.

"If we can't keep the Machine secret, it won't be the end of the world," Stryker went on. "I'm sure that many of you have wanted to make it public knowledge from the very first. But if word gets out that we have Jesus Christ here... Well, the shit will hit the fan. The corporate executives, from the CEO, will be down on us like a pack of locust. And I shudder to think what the public will say. So... I want Jesus out of here. I want all traces of him erased. Stockman cannot find out about him. That is absolutely essential to the continued existence of this project. I hope I make myself clear on this matter."

"But where will we take him?" asked Juliette, looking to Fielding for help as she did.

"I don't care. I just want him out of here when Stockman comes. And any other visitors. Miss Graves here excepted, of course. Get him off site or hide him in an underground bunker, I don't care. Just keep him out of sight."

Fielding frowned, but did not complain.

"All of you, make sure that your people do not mention our special guest, not even among yourselves. Loose lips sink ships, and all that stuff. Stockman cannot get even a hint of something special being hidden from him, or he'll dig at it until hell freezes over.

Dr. Brown frowned and asked, "Why are you caving in to this man? Can't we stonewall him?"

"Because he will not let go until he's dug out all the secrets he can. They'll be more subpoenas and public hearings and a lot of crap we do not need. I think it's better to let him see just enough to satisfy him."

Turning to his right, Stryker added, "Manhusen, I want you to find out who is leaking information. Hell, Stockman even knew about the silver dollar and Lincoln's hat! Someone is feeding him info. I just hope that doesn't include Jesus."

The Security Chief nodded and, from the grim look on his face, would like very much to get his hands on whoever is blabbing.

"All right. Stockman will be here on Thursday. Have everything ready. I'll try to keep him from seeing more than I allow, but we have to be careful."

As the meeting broke up, Tamara followed Fielding and Juliette back to the Project J building.

"What will we do about Jesus?" Juliette was asking

Fielding. "We can't just ask him to stay in a motel for a few days." After a couple seconds, she tried to keep it in but a giggle escaped. "Maybe we could take him on a little vacation. How about a tour of the Holy Land?"

"Not funny!" Fielding scolded.

"Maybe that's not such a bad idea," Tamara interjected. "It would be a good idea for Dr. Myers to not be here, either. This Stockman might wonder why we need an expert on Aramaic on the staff, so why not have both of them take a short trip. You've been introducing Jesus to modern times; maybe it's time to let him see some of the country." They stopped and looked at her. "I'll bet he'll love the Grand Canyon!"

"You're as crazy as Juliette!" Fielding said with a shake of his head.

"Maybe she's got a good idea," Juliette cut in. "Why don't we rent a vacation house someplace close by to stay in for a few days, and use that as a base to let Jesus see some of the country? I'll go with them. Tamara can come also. Jesus is more at ease when she's around."

Tamara looked at Juliette. Was that a hint of jealousy she detected?

"You can sent along a bodyguard, if that makes you feel better," Juliette concluded.

Fielding did not look totally convinced. Letting Jesus out of his sight did not sit well with him. But he could not come up with a better alternative. "Very well, do that. But I want you and Tamara and Dr. Myers to stay in touch. And, please, be careful about what you let him see! We almost had him go catatonic when he saw that tablet show. We don't want our special guest to suffer from too much culture shock."

After a flurry of assurances by the two women, Fielding

left them to make their plans.

"First, we'll have to get a rental house, just for a few days," Juliette said. "Can't have him staying at a motel; too public. Tell you what, I'll go into town and talk with the real estate agent. Meantime, you go and tell Dr. Myers. The two of you can then tell Jesus he's going on a little trip." She paused to take in a breath. "This," she said with a big smile, "is going to be interesting!"

Tamara could not agree more. She was, however, worried. Every time she talked with Jesus or was just near him, she felt sympathy for him, a man ripped out of his time and placed into a strange world. But it was more than just that. There was a powerful magnetism about the man, like he was larger than life. She could understand how he had attracted women to his cause. Recalling the books she had read, she remembered some speculation that the financial support for his ministry came from wealthy women. Very unlikely it came from poor fishermen he recruited along the banks of the Sea of Galilee. But, whatever the cause, she did feel concern for him. And she was touched by his concern for his wife and children.

Dr. Myers was in his office and greeted Tamara warmly. After offering coffee, he asked what he might do for her. The explanation did not take long, and left Myers shaking his head. "I'm not at all sure he's ready to see the outside world," he said. "Think of how much we have to protect him from! Our technology will frighten him. And we must avoid contact with other people."

"That shouldn't be too hard," Tamara replied with a grin, "how many Aramaic speakers do you think he will run into?"

"It's a lot more than just ideas he might pick up. I'm not sure I can agree to this plan. Can't we simply hide him here?"

"Dr. Stryker thinks otherwise," Tamara informed. "You'll find he's pretty adamant about that. Besides, if we're based in a secluded house, we can keep down his contact with others."

"I don't know..."

"It's only for a couple days. And you'll be there." When Myers still seemed undecided, she added, slyly, "Would you rather that Stockman finds out about him and the public finds out a short time later?"

"No, I don't want that. But I still think we could simply keep him here and cut out the little walks – and you taking him for joyrides!"

Accepting that as agreement, Tamara immediately launched into the project. "Juliette is going to a real estate office to see about renting a house for a few days. Someplace not far off. We'll have to pack, of course, and I guess Jesus will also. He doesn't have a suitcase, does he?"

Myers gave her a dirty look. "Of course not. But I've an extra one I can loan him."

"Good. As soon as Juliette gets back, we'll go and tell him. It will probably be his first vacation in a long time."

Myers snorted, but was smiling. "At least you didn't suggest an ocean cruise or a trip to the pyramids."

"Maybe he's already seen them," she retorted. "After all, his family is supposed to have gone to Egypt?"

He laughed. "Yes, according to Matthew. When the Magi came searching for Jesus, or so the story goes, they asked Herod the Great where they could find the newborn 'King of the Jews.' This rattled the paranoid Herod and he ordered that all the male children 'in the vicinity of Bethlehem' be killed. But an angel appeared to Joseph and warned him to get out of town and go to Egypt. He did, and returned only when he heard that Herod was dead. That would be about 4 CE.

SEAN BRANDYWINE

"It should be noted that this story occurs only in Matthew and there is no other reference to it in the New Testaments. Further, it is possible that it was added to Jesus' story so that one of the prophecies would be fulfilled. Hosea 11:1 '...and out of Egypt I called my Son'."

"It will be easy to determine that," Tamara told him. "Let's just ask him."

Myers smiled. "Yes, let's do that."

44. EGYPT

"Egypt? Why do you ask? I've never been to Egypt."

"Well, that settles that," said Tamara as soon as the translation was completed. "So much for Bible accuracy."

"So it would appear," agreed Myers. "But we have another subject of more importance." He then launched into a long discourse that he did not bother to translate since Tamara pretty much knew it all anyway. At the end, Jesus looked to Tamara and lifted one eyebrow.

"Yes," he said. "I would like to see your land. Do you have any seas?"

"Yes, a couple of big ones. But not near here," Myers told him. Then he had to explain that they would need to pack some clothes to take with them.

"Will we walk or are you rich, like the Romans, and have horses?" Jesus asked.

"We have horses," Tamara said, "but of a different kind. We'll drive in a car." He seemed happy to hear that. Ever since she had taken him for that little joyride in her Corvette, he had expressed an interest in a repeat performance. How like a little child, she thought, happy at the simple thought of taking a ride in a car.

She let Myers lead Jesus off to pack the suitcase he had brought with him. Tamara sat at the table in the courtyard and enjoyed the warm sunshine. How every lucky I am, she thought, to be here at this exciting time. There were many more questions she wanted to ask of Jesus, and she did enjoy being with him. The aura of something special had not totally worn off, and she still wondered at the fact that she was now a friend of Jesus. Like Myers, she was taking notes each evening with the vague notion of perhaps writing a book about her experiences at Project Dry Wells. If that were ever possible.

It might be nice to get out into the countryside. Juliette had told her on the phone that she found a perfect mountain home to rent. She had to pay for an entire week, but did not mind since the home had no nearby neighbors, was only a short drive away, and had enough bedrooms for everyone to have their own. It was near Fenton Lake on the other side of the Valles Caldera. Nice Douglas fir and Ponderosa pines. Sounded good to Tamara.

Fielding came by, informing that the scheduled visit by the Congressman was still on. Tamara informed him of the house they were going to use, and said that she would inform Dr. Myers and Jesus.

When she walked into the area made into an apartment for Jesus, she saw that the bag was packed and Myers was explaining to Jesus that he really should take the pair of shoes they had for him. But he insisted that the sandals were all he needed. Tamara was amazed to see an easel set by the window. Next to it was a palette, brushes and tubes of paint. The canvass on the easel had an unfinished work on it, and it took her a while to recognize it as the Jewish Temple in Jerusalem, or at least the reconstructions by archeologists. The style of primitive, almost childlike, but the general form of the building and the perspective were pretty good for a beginner.

"You're teaching him to paint?" she asked when the shoe debate died down.

"Yes. Not really teaching him, but letting him see that you can use that medium to express yourself. Besides," he added with a sly grin, "you want to bet an early Jesus will be worth a lot of money some day?"

"Undoubtedly. Don't forget to get him to sign it."

They met up outside the Project J building, next to a Chronodyne SUV that Juliette had checked out. Jesus walked around the vehicle and looking inside, shaking his head all the time. But when Tamara waved an invitation for him to join her in the back seat, he complied with a smile. With a minimum of fuss, they were off.

At first, the road took them along pine covered ridges and switchbacks of that mountainous terrain. The scenery was gorgeous and Jesus never stopped taking it in. It took them less than an hour to reach the other side of the caldera and climb a ridge. It was necessary to stop twice to check the map before they found the small side road labeled "Horseshoe Loop" that led to the rented house.

The house itself was modern, one story, but fairly large with an attached two-car garage. The sides were painted a light blue with green trim. For a while, Jesus just stood there, looking at it. "Does everyone live in houses like this?" he asked. "Where are the other houses?"

"Some people live in such houses, rabbi," Myers told him as he helped unload the suitcases. "But others live in different kinds. In your days, not everyone lived in the same kind of houses, did they?"

"In Galilee there were the small villages and the cities. All the houses were the same and all built near each other. How else could everyone share the water from the well? How else can meals be shared? And homes protected?"

Myers was explaining, or at least trying to, how things were different from Jesus' time as they walked towards the house. Tamara grabbed her suitcase and followed along.

There were four bedrooms; Tamara's being next to Jesus' with Myers' on the other side. Tamara helped Juliette with the bags of groceries she had picked up in the village, then in putting the items away in the kitchen. When that chore was done, the two women joined the others in the back patio. The concrete patio gave way to grass, with pine trees only a few feet beyond that. To one side there was a view along a grassy meadow with hints that there might be a creek running down the middle. All in all, it was a pleasing, peaceful scene. Tamara smelled the pine scent and was happy.

Myers looked to the barbeque sitting on the edge of the patio and asked, "You did bring steaks, didn't you?"

"Of course," Juliette responded. "And even marshmallows to toast."

Both Tamara and Myers smiled at that. Jesus lifted one eyebrow and waited for Myers to translate. Just what a marshmallow was proved difficult to get across, so he led Jesus into the kitchen to show him.

"I'll bet there are deer to graze on the grass. And squirrels who will take food right out of your hand. A red-tailed hawk circling overhead. And larks, wrens and mockingbirds to wake you with their songs in the morning," Tamara happily declared.

"And not a Starbucks in sight," complained Juliette. "The nearest good steakhouse is probably all the way down in Albuquerque, and you'll have to go farther to find a sushi bar."

"City gal, huh?"

"Damned right," agreed Juliette. "Was born and raised in New York City. Best food and shows in the world."

In the interests of good relations, Tamara did not mention that New York also led the world in muggings, rudeness and traffic jams, not to mention high prices.

"Still..." Juliette conceded, "It is peaceful out here."

Dinner that night was, as Dr. Myers promised, barbequed steaks served with baked potatoes and steamed broccoli. Dessert was strawberry ice cream. From the private conversations between Myers and Jesus, she guessed that he was seeking assurance that this food was kosher. Myers had rubbed the meat with a seasoning and Tamara found the steak quite good. Apparently, so did Jesus, for he did justice to the steak on his plate. Putting butter in his potato did confuse him a little, but not for long. Tamara noted that he was still having trouble holding the silverware and cutting his meat, but Myers – who was obviously aware of the problem – made no offer to do it for him, so neither did Tamara. She could only imagine the damage that had been done to his wrists, which were no longer covered by bandages but by two wide leather wristbands.

After the dinner, they sat around watching the stars come out. The night was cloudless, and the Milky Way a creamy band of light across the heavens. Filled with a good meal, in the company of friends, there was little need for talk.

"I used to lie on my back and watch the stars turning overhead," Jesus said. "They were so beautiful. Maybe the finest of my Father's creations. They still look the same."

Myers translated for the others. "They are the same. At least something is constant in the universe."

"Then what is that bright star that moves?" asked Jesus.

"That is the International Space Station," said Tamara. "There are currently three men and one woman living there."

She could sense Jesus' head turn towards her. "Is that like the things I have seen in the sky? What you call..."

"Airplanes," she supplied. "The ISS is very much like an airplane, only it flies very high up. It goes around the world and only takes ninety-three minutes to do it."

She could just make out his head shaking in disbelief. But then, he really had no idea just how big the earth was, so a satellite in orbit had little meaning to him. He went back to watching it as it approached the zenith then began a slow descent to the eastern horizon. Maybe he would begin to get an idea tomorrow, she thought.

After a while of more silence, Myers got up to go back into the house, followed shortly by Juliette. With their translator gone, there would not be too much talking going on, but that was fine with Tamara, and apparently Jesus also. They sat and watched the stars grow brighter until there were so many that it was hard to identify the constellations.

Two shooting stars dashed across the sky, one right after the other. She wanted to ask Jesus what his people called meteors, but did not even try. The English words would have no meaning for him. So it was a surprise when, after a period of time, he reached over, placed his hand gently on top of hers and said, quite clearly, "Thank you."

"For what?" she said before she realized that was the first English she had heard from him.

"For being kind to him," came Myers' voice from behind them. Neither had heard him walk up. He spoke a few words to Jesus, and then told Tamara, "Yes, he's thanking you for all you've done for him."

"I've hardly done anything. I'm not even a member of the project."

"You saved his life."

"Does he know that?"

"Yes. I told him that zealots had broken in and you stopped them from getting to Jesus. Not the absolute truth, but a version he would understand. I suspect he thinks they were agents of the High Priest. He also thanks you for showing him your auto. I fear he is more impressed with that flashy sports car of yours than he is of most of our technology. He can relate to that more than he can some machines he hasn't seen and would never understand anyway."

Jesus started to remove his hand, but Tamara put her other hand on top of his. "You are welcome," she said slowly, wondering if his limited vocabulary would cover that. She thought she saw him nod just before he pulled his hand back.

"I'm off to bed," Myers told her. "Please tuck Jesus in when you two get tired. Fielding insists that someone be with him every minute. Of course, that doesn't include when he's sleeping."

Was there a hint of amusement in his voice? Surely the older man could not be thinking that Tamara would make any sexual move towards Jesus! She almost said something aloud when she realized that he had already left. She turned back to the showcase sky before them and thought about it. She was unmarried, but Jesus was. To a woman dead two thousand years. Did that make him a widower? Probably, in a technical sense. But to Jesus, she was certain, his wife was still alive, along with his children. There was simply no way he could have any concept of the incredible amount of time that had passed since his day.

Tamara shrugged off the idea of anything between them. She did care for him as a man, true. And here was a man who would never see his wife again. But the idea of actually going to bed with him... No! It wouldn't be right. She had to laugh at the idea of bedding down with Jesus. That would really make a good tale for the National Tattler!

The night was beginning to turn chilly, as it does at the higher elevations. If they were going to stay out watching the stars, it would be a good idea to put on a coat or something. She rose from the chair and Jesus did also. In the dim light coming from one of the house's windows, she could make out his face. Wrapping her arms around herself, she made shivering motions. He nodded and turned towards the house, waiting for her. They walked into the warmth of the house together.

Tamara showed him to his bedroom. At the door, Jesus turned to her and again took her hand in his. "Thank you," he said again. Then, with a gentle squeeze, he let go of her hand. After she walked away, he closed the door.

45. A GOOD WAY TO SEE THE WORLD

It was early the next morning, after a breakfast of warmed up leftover steak and eggs, that they set out to show Jesus the world. The first part was a road down to a small village called Jemez Pueblo where they stopped for gas. It was only a forty-minute drive, but all got out and stretched their legs. Jesus was particularly interested in Tamara refueling the car, but it was beyond her power to explain about the internal combustion engine, and would have been even if she could speak Aramaic. The concept was simply too advanced. He did, however, get the idea that adding that funny smelling stuff into that hole in the side of the car was necessary to make it run. He also stared at the handful of people around, most of whom appeared to be Indians or of Mexican descent. This was the first time he had seen more than four people at a time since he awoke.

They followed the two lane road down until they came to Interstate 25, then turned south. Before long they were entering the outskirts of Albuquerque. As the city grew, Jesus could not take his eyes off the buildings. This was also the first time he had seen so many cars driving all at once. Tamara, who was driving at that point, could hear him muttering to himself as the buildings grew in size until they were opposite the downtown portion and some of the buildings reached twenty-stories.

"You have so many people in your land," Jesus said, the awe showing in his voice and on his face.

"This is one of our small cities," Myers told him. "We have much bigger."

Jesus could only shake his head.

"In Jesus' day, Jerusalem held only about fifty thousand people maximum. Of course, that increased dramatically during the holy festivals when pilgrims flooded into the city. The population of Albuquerque is about half a million, around ten times that of Jerusalem." Myers chuckled. "He should see New York."

"Got that right," chimed in Juliette, "finest city in the world. Also one of the biggest."

When the densest buildings were opposite them, Myers leaned forward and told Tamara, "I hope you're not going any farther south. We wouldn't want to run into a border checkpoint. Remember, Jesus is an undocumented alien."

Tamara did not know if that was meant as a joke, but it was literally the truth. If stopped by authorities, how could they prove Jesus was legally in the country? For that matter, was he?

Shortly after the downtown section, they turned off the freeway and headed towards a sizeable airport nearby with commercial jets taking off and landing regularly.

"This is Albuquerque International," Tamara said. "Please tell Jesus not to worry about the noise. We're going to a business called 'Sunport Jets', and it's on the flight line. I'm sure he's never heard a 747 taking off."

Driving along a main street paralleling the airport runways, she found what she was looking for: a row of restaurants. She pulled into one called "Milton's," and parked.

"But first, lunch," she announced.

Milton's, as Tamara had planned, was an upscale delicatessen. The waitress looked at Jesus' long hair, beard and sandals with disdain, but seated them anyway. The food, as she expected, proved to be quite good and they all had a sizeable lunch. Jesus liked the turkey with cranberries and stuffing. It was a bit early for lunch, so the restaurant was not crowded, which pleased them because avoiding crowds was high on their list. Talk over the meal was casual. Jesus did, at one point, ask where they were going, but Tamara and Juliette looked at each other, grinned, and told Myers to inform Jesus that he would really like where they were going. They did not, however, inform either of the Jews just exactly where that was, but Myers undoubtedly had a notion.

An incident occurred during the meal that left Tamara in a state of confusion. They were eating when Juliette began choking, apparently on a piece of food lodged in the windpipe. When she saw what was happening, Tamara leapt out of her chair and was coming around the table with the intent of administering the Heimlich Maneuver to clear Juliette's air passage. However, Jesus, who was sitting next to the distressed woman, reached over and touched her on the shoulder. Immediately the piece of food was coughed out and Juliette sucked in air gratefully.

Jesus said nothing but turned back to his plate.

Tamara stood there for a few moments, confused and surprised. Looking across the table, she saw that Myers was also surprised but perhaps less confused. She went back to her seat, shaking her head. What had she just seen? she wondered. Had the problem cleared by itself and just happened to coincide with Jesus' touching her? Or did his touch have something to do with it? Tamara was confused. The manner in which he had acted, the calm, confident look on his face, and the results, combined to make her wonder.

No one spoke of it and the meal went on, but Tamara

was left wondering what she had just seen.

After lunch, it was a short drive to Sunport Jets. As they disembarked from the car, a 787 Dreamliner took off, its engine roar loud enough so you could not talk. Jesus stood there, staring at the aircraft in astonishment – or disbelief – as it climbed into the sky, banked, and departed into the blue.

Jesus turned to Tamara, tugged on the sleeve of her blouse and said something.

"He wants to know if that is the same thing you showed him up in the sky. I told him yes." Then he said a few more words to Jesus before returning his attention to Tamara. "You aren't going to do what I think you are... Are you?"

"Don't worry, he'll like it," she told Myers with a smile. Then she and Juliette were leading the men into the office building.

"I can't believe you're doing this," Myers commented as Tamara went up to the desk and began talking to the clerk. "Whose idea was this?"

"Tamara suggested it, but I fully agreed," Juliette told him. "Don't worry."

"I should have guessed it, coming from a woman who took Jesus joyriding around the compound."

Tamara returned to them. "The pilot is checking out the plane. We can go onboard in a couple minutes."

She turned to Myers. "Now I want you to explain to him that we are going to take him for a ride on an airplane. Make it sound like it is nothing more than driving in a car. Got that?"

Myers sighed. "I'll try."

He need not have worried about Jesus' reaction. It was positive, to say the least. Maybe he had been prepared for it by Tamara's showing him a high performance sports car, or maybe he simply liked the idea of flying into the sky. He nodded, and smiled at them all.

The clerk called to Tamara that the plane was ready. Tamara gestured towards the side door, and Juliette took Jesus' arm to escort him outside. There they found a sleek jet with twin engines mounted by the tail and swept-back wings. A young man walked up to them from the aircraft.

"Welcome," he said with a smile. "I'm Sandy Nelson, your pilot. This is a Beechjet 400. Seats eight, has a fifteen hundred mile range, and will cruise at five hundred miles per hour. I've just finished pre-flight, and you can come on board."

As he stood by the boarding ladder, he gave Jesus a funny look, then shrugged.

The inside was not overly large but did have seven seats, each a window seat. All were of soft black leather. The walls were white and the windows were round portholes about two feet wide. The second and third pair of seats faced each other, and it was into one of the forward facing seats that they placed Jesus. Tamara and Juliette took the seats facing backwards, but facing Jesus and Myers. Each seat had a good view out the adjacent window with the leading edge of the wing only obstructing Jesus' and Myers' view slightly.

Once the seat belts were secured, the pilot closed the door and made his way forward. Jesus seemed especially interested in the mass of instruments and dials visible through the small door to the flight deck. The engines came on before the pilot reached his seat, and Tamara could see a second pilot in the right hand seat. He must have been the one to start the engines. The engines sounded loud, but the jet did not move for a couple minutes while the pilot continued his checklist. Finally, he put it aside, glanced back to see that his passengers were all secured, and then pushed the throttles forward. The engine noise increased and the plane began to move forward. Jesus turned his eyes to the window and watched intently as they taxied out to the runways. For a minute they sat near one end of a runway, waiting for a larger jet to land. Then the pilot moved them to the end of the runway and pointed the nose along the dotted line. The engines increased their roar, heard mutedly in the insulated cabin, and they began their roll. Faster and faster the jet moved down the runway, gathering speed and lift. Just when it seemed the jet was straining to become airborne, their nose pointed upward and they left the ground.

Jesus grasped the seat armrests tightly as the ground fell away. The buildings were becoming smaller and farther away as he watched, awestruck. When they were high enough to begin to lose the perspective of being at a height, Jesus turned to Tamara and spoke a few words, then turned back to the window.

Myers choked on a laugh he could not prevent. "He says that this is better than sex!"

46. A VASE IS NOT GOOD ENOUGH

"Welcome to Project Dry Wells," said Dr. Stryker, trying to force on a smile as he did. Stockman was about the last person he wanted to welcome to his project.

"Glad to be here," said the Congressman as he got out of the car. An aide exited from the other side and hurried around to stand behind Stockman. Looking around, Stockman gave the impression that he was not exactly overwhelmed by the facilities. "So, what have you got to show me? I've always wanted to see a time machine."

"Right this way." Looking to his second in command, he added, "Dr. Crane, let's get right to the heart of the matter." Then he took off, striding along the sidewalk in the hot sunlight, never looking back to confirm that Stockman was following.

They arrived at building Two, an otherwise plain looking two story building with windows only on the second story. Inside, Stryker turned to the guests and handed them badges. "Put these on, please. This is a security installation, after all."

They passed the guard station, down a short corridor and through a door marked "Danger High Voltage." Someone had written under that with a marker, "Danger – Time Displacement!"

There was, indeed, both high voltages and the most advanced piece of technology man had ever created. Yet it looked rather unimpressive. Mostly it was a large console with numerous dials and screens, a few keyboards, and assorted technical stuff. Beyond the console there was the heart of the Machine, the assembly chamber, a large partial cylinder made of highly polished metal with a golden tint. Through the open slot they could see the platform where objects were created out of nothing, using a blueprint from the past. Numerous thick cables snaked across the concrete floor to the chamber, attached to it both high and low. The platform, which appeared to be made of mirrors, so reflective was the metal, was empty.

The Machine operator, a middle aged man in a gray jumpsuit bearing the Chronodyne logo, looked up as they came in. He nodded to Stryker to indicate that the machine was ready.

"Congressman, are you familiar with quantum entanglement?" Stryker asked abruptly.

"Something to do with physics, isn't it?"

"Something. Very well, I'll skip the technical part of the lecture. Basically what we do here is to reach back in time to an object. Then we force the matter of that object to become entangled with matter in the present. As that entanglement goes on, we begin building up that object in the chamber you see there. What we make here is an exact copy of the object in the past. And I do mean exact. Down to the sub-atomic level. Even down to the quarks that make up all matter."

"How do you find an object you cannot see and that exists only in the past?" Stockman asked.

"It took a long time, but we have found ways to focus a beam of entangled radiation backwards in time. We use that beam to visualize objects. Our main computer, codenamed Lightning, handles all the processing and focusing of the beam. No human could possibly do the task. Far too many variables.

"What the beam is focused on is visible on this screen."

Stryker nodded to the operator, who in turn pressed a button. The screen that Stryker had pointed to flashed on and presented a blurry picture to them. A slight adjustment and the picture sharpened into high definition, showing them a vase sitting on a table. Afternoon sunlight slanted in to illuminate the vase's rich red and black colors. On the side was the image of naked runners dashing around the vase. They were black with white borders on a reddish background. A border above and below the scene was made from a single red line forming small squares.

"That small vase is sitting in the house of a wealthy Greek, one Peisistratos by name. The year is 510 BCE, the place is Athens. Hodges will now define the object in time and space." A red frame appeared on the screen and was adjusted until it just fit around the vase. Then the scene rotated ninety degrees and another frame defined it again. A further rotation, this time looking directly down at the vase, and a third frame was locked in place.

"Now we begin the copying process."

Before them, the cylinder rotated so that the open slot disappeared.

"A lot of energy is being used to force the matter here to conform to the matter in the past," Stryker explained. "Too much to look at."

Nothing was happening on the screen. The vase sat peacefully in the sunlight, unaware it was being copied, atom for atom, twenty-five hundred years in its future. On a second screen next to it, an image was being created on a black background, a three dimensional image of a vase. It took almost ten minutes before the image was complete, but when it was, the operator shut down the Machine. The cylinder rotated again, displaying on the platform a perfect copy of the vase. Stryker went over to it and picked it up. Carrying it back to Stockman, he handed it to the Congressman, saying, "Here, a present from Chronodyne."

Stockman turned it round and over in his hands, looking at all parts of it, even inside. Then he set it on the console top, saying as he did, "How do I know you really copied this from back in time? I didn't see it being made. Besides, I don't take bribes."

Stryker was turning red in the face. But he managed to control his anger. "Very well," he said. "Suppose I show you something that could not possibly be copied in our time? Something that there is no way I could make here, no matter how I tried? Or how hard you tried?"

Stockman exercised his practiced sneer. "And what would that be? I can't think of anything in the past that we could not recreate today with our superior technology."

"Come with me."

Leaving that building, they crossed a grassy area to another of the buildings, this one marked with a "12" on the side. It was larger than most of the other buildings, but still of the same gray color and with an almost military aspect to it. Inside, Stryker walked up to another man and said, "Dr. Brown, is it ready?"

Brown, smiling like a small kid with a lollipop, nodded.

"Then let's go."

The two of them took Stockman and his aide to a double door and then through it. Inside the room, as the lights came on, they found a dozen seats, all facing a wall that was oddly made of thick steel bars, about twelve inches apart and going from floor to ceiling. Behind the bars was a curtain that did not allow any view of what lay beyond.

"A movie? And why the bars? What are you up to,

Stryker?"

"Please have a seat. The show will begin in a moment."

Brown went to a panel on the wall behind them and pressed a button. The curtain began sliding to one side, revealing a bare room behind it, but one with walls made of steel plates riveted together. When the curtain had disappeared totally, another button was pressed and part of the steel plated wall slid aside. What came through that opening almost made the Congressman soil his pants.

There was no mistaking the most famous dinosaur of all: Tyrannosaurus Rex, the Tyrant Lizard King.

The huge beast, half again as tall as a man, cautiously entered the enclosed area, his big head turning from side to side, his nostrils flaring as he smelled the air. As soon as the last of his long tail entered the area, his head turned towards the humans on the other side of the bars. With surprising intelligence, it tilted its head to one side as it eyed the creatures before it, as if examining them carefully. Those dark eyes stared right into the human's, sending shivers of primeval fear racing down their spines.

The big head tilted back and the jaws opened to reveal a mouthful of huge, razor sharp teeth. It roared, a sound both loud and fearful. It was both the roar of a predator and the roar of an animal denied what it sought. Stomping up to the bars, it tried to push its snout between two of them but could not. Its head was simply too big to fit.

The bars were only five or six feet from the first row of seats. When the T-Rex came to the barrier, Stockman leaped from this seat and edged his way backwards. His aide had already dashed for the door.

"Don't worry. He cannot get through the bars," Stryker said, the gloating heavy in his voice.

Dr. Brown walked down until he could almost touch the bars and stood there, his head only a couple feet from those teeth. The T-Rex clenched and unclenched its tiny hands as if wishing it could reach through the bars and drag this insolent human inside. "Of course, that's what they said about King Kong, and, as you know, he broke free and made off with Fay Wray."

Stryker, coming down to stand beside Brown, added, "You will note that this one is only a juvenile. Fully grown, it will stand another six or eight feet tall and weight around eight tons. This was the biggest we could get in the chamber. And he almost destroyed it."

"We plan to give it to the San Diego Zoo," added Brown. "Just as soon as we go public with this project. I'm sure he will be a star attraction."

Apparently, the T-Rex knew he could not get through the bars to these tasty-looking morsels, because he ceased trying to push his snout through and had to content himself with sniffing them and breathing a foul breath over them.

"You said you would believe something that I could not create without our Machine. Well, here it is. If you think you can create a live T-Rex, please tell me how."

Stockman, who had almost reached the door in his backpedaling, wiped the sweat off his brow with a handkerchief. "All right, I'll believe you," he said. He could not take his eyes off the beast, and the T-Rex returned the favor by eyeing the Congressman as a potential dinner.

47. BIG CANYON

Cruising at 40,000 feet, Tamara was disappointed that she could not see the curve of the earth. She had hoped to, so she could give Jesus some idea of the size of the world. The Beechjet 400 was surprisingly quiet inside once it reached cruising speed and altitude. Jesus could not take his face away from the window, and neither could Tamara. The world from that high up is an incredible sight. They could see the Rocky Mountains to the north and down into Mexico to the south. They were fortunate in picking a clear day with unlimited visibility.

"Who, exactly, is paying for this little jaunt?" asked Myers.

"Well, it's coming out of the Project J budget," Juliette answered. "Research expense. You know. Determining the effect of modern flight on a first century Jewish peasant."

Myers shook his head but was smiling, "Well, like you two predicted, he does like it."

Jesus leaned over to Myers and said something.

"He wants to know if you can see Rome from here. I told him no, it was on the other side of the world. You know, I'm not sure if he really understands that the world is round. I know that Greek philosophers before his time knew the world was round, some even measured the size fairly accurately. But the common person probably never thought of it." He touched Jesus on the sleeve and asked something. "He says that he's willing to believe the world is round – if we say so."

At that point, the pilot came back to ask if everything was

going well.

"Tell me, how much higher do we have to go before you can see the curve of the earth?" Tamara asked him.

"Well, I've been told you could see it from the Concord at 60,000 feet. But truth is you can see it from this altitude. Take a straight edge and hold it up to the window. Match the horizon with the bottom of the straight edge. You'll see a slight curvature."

"Thanks," Tamara said, reaching for her purse and the rental contract she had from their office. She held it up to the window and carefully aligned it. Was that really a curve there? Maybe.

"The Grand Canyon is coming up below us," he told them, and then went back to his seat.

By leaning, Tamara was just able to make out the Grand Canyon's eastern end coming up. From that altitude, the Colorado River was a dirty brown band surrounded by light colored cliffs. The river twisted and snaked back and forth as it worked its way south. Then the plane banked and they could see the river turning west in a big bend. Here and there, they could see white were the river bounced over rocks to form rapids.

At five hundred miles per hour, they reached the western end of the canyon fairly fast, seeing the thin band of brown turn into a darker blue of Lake Mead. The Beechjet then banked and began heading back towards Albuquerque.

"Is that a sea down there?" Jesus asked. "Like the Sea of Galilee?"

"Just a big lake," Myers told him.

"Someday I'll take you to see the Pacific," Tamara told him. Then, in a moment of reflection, she added, "And maybe someday you'll show me the Sea of Galilee."

They flew back by a southern route so Jesus could see Phoenix sprawled out across the desert. By the time they landed at Albuquerque Airport, Jesus was silent. Too much to take in, thought Tamara. Poor man.

48. THE GOSPEL TRUTH

During the trip back, Tamara took some time to talk with Myers about things that were bothering her.

"When we talked with Jesus about the period from the arrest to his death, there were some things that just didn't seem right to me," she told him.

"Like?"

"Well, the Bible states that Jesus was taken before the Sanhedrin and tried by them. But Jesus told of no trial, only Caiaphas yelling at him and then ordering him taken to Pilate. Was it really a trial in the night?"

Myers smiled before saying, "That's one point I have always wondered about. There are too many inaccuracies in that story for it to be real. The Gospels say that he was taken before the high priest and the Sanhedrin. Then witnesses were produced to testify that he had made threats against the Temple. Jesus says nothing to those claims. Pretty hard to deny when you had already gone in and made a big commotion with the moneychangers and such. Then Caiaphas demands, 'Are you the messiah?' His answer varies, depending on which Gospel you are reading, but all agree he does say that he is the 'Son of Man,' which is the same thing. And that was exactly what Jesus believed. Of course, Jesus wanted them to believe his claim so that they would do as he desired – namely, fulfill the prophecies.

"He is immediately charged with Blasphemy and ordered to be turned over to the Romans to be put to death.

"Now here is where a lot of problems occur. First off, Jewish law regarding a legal proceeding is adamant about certain points. The Sanhedrin is not allowed to meet at night. Nor during Passover. And a formal trail before them must begin with a list of why the accused is innocent. Only then can witnesses be called.

"To me, this means that whoever wrote the Gospels did not know Jewish law very well.

"Then we have the fact of his crime. If Jesus was guilty of blasphemy, then the penalty under Jewish law can only be one thing: stoning. Leviticus 24:16: *'And he that blasphemeth the name of the LORD, he shall surely be put to death, and all the congregation shall certainly stone him...'*

"This is shown by the incident with Stephen a few years later. This Christian convert makes the mistake of calling Jesus 'the Son of Man'. Let me find it. May I have that Bible you carry in your purse, Juliette?"

Since she had been following the conversation, it was not an unusual request. She handed a small, leather-bound Bible over. "Research material," she told Tamara as she did.

Myers turned to Acts 7:55 and read, *"But he, being full of the Holy Ghost, looked up steadfastly into heaven, and saw the glory of God, and Jesus standing on the right hand of God. And said, Behold, I see the heavens opened, and the Son of Man standing on the right hand of God.*

"Then they cried out with a loud voice, and stopped their ears, and ran upon him with one accord, and cast him out of the city, and they stoned Stephen, he calling upon God, and saying, Lord Jesus, receive my spirit."

He closed the Bible and handed it back.

"So you see, Jesus should have been stoned, if his crime was really Blasphemy."

Tamara thought about that for a bit, then asked, "And

what about the trial before Pilate? Jesus' account of it is certainly different from the Gospels."

Myers sighed. "What you first have to realize is that the Gospels are not historical reporting. They were not written by people who lived in those times, but later. When Jesus was alive, the only thing he cared about was the coming Kingdom of God. At the end, he came to believe that he was the Messiah, the Chosen One, who would fulfill the prophecies and make the kingdom happen. And that he thought of it as an overthrowing of the Roman rule, as well as straightening out the priests and the Temple. You've heard Jesus tell us that it was likely that, with God's help, the Jews would defeat the Romans and cast them out of their land. In that respect, Jesus was very much like many of the Jewish leaders of his time, a revolutionary at heart, a zealot even. That part of Jewish history is filled with armed rebellions against Rome, both before and after Jesus' time.

"Okay, got that picture? Good. Now comes his death. Then what? No Kingdom of God in sight. Just continued Roman rule and hard times. The only difference is that there is this little core of Jews who believe in Jesus' teachings and in him as the Messiah. They were his disciples originally, plus converts among the Jews, both the homegrown ones and those who visited Jerusalem for the holy days but lived in other parts of the world. Those people believed that he had risen from the dead and was therefore the long-awaited Messiah. Originally they were waiting for the Kingdom to follow any day. But as time passed, and no Kingdom showed up, their beliefs changed. Saul, aka Paul, had a lot to do with that. He turned Jesus' sacrifice from a fulfillment of the prophecies that God's Kingdom might come, to a sacrifice for the sins of all people that they might be forgiven. Paul changed Jesus' early believers immensely.

"I'm getting to my point. Now we have the revolt against Rome and the crushing defeat of the Jewish people. That was in 66-73 CE. There were anti-taxation protests and attacks upon Roman citizens. The Romans responded by plundering the Temple and executing about 6,000 Jews. A full scale revolt followed. Shortly thereafter, Cestius Gallus, the Legate of Syria, brought down an army to restore order. The Jewish rebels defeated them at the Battle of Beth Horon and slew 6,000 Romans. That really shocked the Roman leadership and they came down hard. Well, the short of it is that the Jews were crushed, Jerusalem burned to the ground, and many killed. Tacitus, a historian of the time, said that no fewer than six hundred thousand men and women of every age were killed. Josephus puts the number at one million. But he often exaggerates.

"This left a nasty taste in the Roman's minds concerning the Jews. It was not good to be a Jew at that time. Those who had formed a church believing in Jesus were stuck in a hard position. They did not want to be included along with the Jews who had made war with Rome, so what to do? At this point, and again thanks in a great part to Paul, the early Christ was transformed from a rebel to a peaceful preacher concerned only with man's sins and redemption.

"At this point the Gospels were written. Mark was the first, written about the time of the Great Revolt, probably in Syria. The target audience was the early Christian community. Most scholars believe that the original text of the gospel ends at Mark 16:8 with the discovery of Jesus' empty tomb and that the account of his resurrection appearances is a later addition.

"Now here's the important part. The writer of Mark did not want to antagonize the Romans. So hints of Jesus' revolutionary zeal had to go, and the Romans absolved of responsibility for his death. If not the Romans, then it had to be the hated Jews who killed him. Caiaphas dupes Pilate into carrying out a tragic miscarriage of justice. Pilate tries to save Jesus. Or so says Mark.

"Now we go to Matthew, written around 90 CE. In that, Pilate is warned by his wife to have nothing to do with 'this innocent man.' Pilate washes his hands of blame. The Jews respond, according to the writer of this Gospel, with *'may his blood be on our heads, and on our children.'* Matthew 17:1.

"Next we come to Luke, written about the same time, probably in Antioch. In this one, Luke extends amnesty not only to the Romans, but to Herod Aptipas as well. Luke 23:14 *'...Ye have brought this man unto me, as one that perverteth the people: and, behold, I, having examined him before you, have found no fault in this man touching those things whereof ye accuse him:* 23:15 *No, nor yet Herod: for I sent you to him; and, lo, nothing worthy of death is done unto him.'*

"Now we come to John, the last to be written, probably around 100 CE. In this one, Pilate does all he can to save Jesus, not because he is guiltless but because he seems to believe that Jesus maybe, in fact, the 'Son of God.' Nevertheless, Pilate is forced to condemn Jesus by an unruly mob. As if Pilate would really care what the Jewish people think. His disdain for Jews was well known. John puts words in Jesus' mouth: *'the one who handed me over to you is guilty of a greater sin.'* Then he insults the whole Jewish nation when he has the crowd chanting, *'We have no king but Caesar!'*

"See a pattern here? Those who wrote the Gospels had only one purpose: to prove Jesus was put to death by the Jews, not the Romans. The farther away from the actual events you get, the stronger that purpose is stated. Factual accuracy was of little importance.

"Now we get back to your original question. You asked why our Jesus' story is not the same. He says that Caiaphas and a few others condemned him in the middle of the night. Then Pilate makes him wait until morning. When he does see him, all he cares about is the claim that Jesus has kingly pretensions and therefore guilty of sedition against Rome.

"It is the Gospel authors, and those who later added theological enhancements and outright fabrications, who draw a picture of an innocent Pilate and nasty old Jewish priests.

"I believe Jesus," he concluded.

Tamara did not know what to say. She had studied the Bible and history, but never had the Gospels explained to her that way. Yet it made sense.

"And that's the long-winded explanation you get when you ask an old college professor a simple question."

49. SPOOKY!

"There's something else I want to show you," Stryker told Stockman as they walked out of the building. Behind them the T-Rex was roaring for his lunch. "Come on to my office. There's someone I want you to meet."

Going into his office, he told the sexy blonde secretary, "Have Adrian come on in, please."

Stockman was recovering from the shock of coming face to face with a drooling T-Rex. Just as he was about to resume his normal blustering facade, Stryker told him to sit down and wait, in a voice that said he was no longer afraid of the Congressman.

A minute later another man came in, a non-descript man of medium height, mid-fifties, business suited, and looking like a successful lawyer. Stockman gave him a harsh look.

"Allow me to introduce Mr. Adrian Connors, the Deputy Director of the CIA. Adrian, I believe you have something to say to Congressman Stockman?"

There followed a very brief, very one-sided conversation. Condensed version: "It is in the best interests of our national security that Project Dry Wells remain classified. If this is not done, we at the CIA will be very unhappy. Likewise will the FBI, NSA, Naval Intelligence, and a few others who utilize the facility here for purposes of our own."

"I..." Stockman began but was cut off.

"And when we are unhappy, others tend to be more unhappy. For example, were you to say one word about this project to anyone – repeat anyone – it may be necessary for us to release to the press certain documents concerning insider trading of Stanee Oil stocks. And some very interesting photos we have of you with a certain under-aged summer intern."

Stockman turned as pale as a ghost.

"Understand me?"

"I understand," he stammered out.

"Good. The information we are gaining via this project is far more important than any single man. And if any man endangers that relationship between our agencies and Chronodyne, he will be removed."

Stockman did not want to ask if "removed" meant kicked out of his nice, plush job in Congress, or something worse. One never knows with the spooks.

Adrian nodded to Stryker, who was grinning, and left.

"I believe you have a plane to catch back to Washington, Congressman Stockman?"

With only a quick nod as a goodbye, Stockman turned and walked out, giving his aide a nasty look as he did. In the outer office, Adrian was talking with the Security Director Manhusen about something.

Back in his office, Stryker was telling Crane, "I don't think we'll get any more problems with Stockman."

"Good riddance," Crane agreed.

"And I'm certainly glad that our hastily erected cell held back the T-Rex. I wasn't certain those bars were strong enough."

"So am I. Did you know he bites?"

50. SIDE TRIP

After an exciting day, Jesus napped most of the way back to their rented house. Since it was evening when the Beechjet landed, they had an early dinner in Albuquerque at a steakhouse called "Rancher's Roadhouse". Jesus enjoyed his first T-bone steak along with a new wine. He was quite worn out on the trip back.

The next day was spent mostly sleeping late and enjoying the scenery. Jesus and Tamara took a walk across the grassy meadow and through some of the pine forest. Apparently he had seen pine trees before, but not quite such tall ones. He seemed fascinated with the variety and quantity of wild life, from chipmunks to deer. Tamara made a mental note to take him to a good zoo some day.

They did not talk much, there being the language barrier and all, but it was a peaceful, enjoyable time for both of them. Occasionally Jesus would point to something and look at her, and then she would tell him what it was in English. He would repeat the word twice, and then go on. He laughed when she told him that little furry creature with the bushy tail was a squirrel. All she could think of was that the word meant something else in Aramaic. After a while she tried reversing the game. She pointed to a flower or an animal and lifted her eyebrows at him. Usually he would say something that she would try to repeat, but a couple times he simply shrugged his shoulders, indicating that he did not know what it was. A few times she caught him looking at a high flying airliner making contrails in the blue. Flying must be something pretty special to someone who had always assumed that it was impossible for a human to leave the ground.

When they got back, Juliette informed them that Stryker had called and it was safe to return to the project. Apparently, Stockman had not taken as long as he might have. Also, they were told, he left with no intention of bothering the project again. The three of them speculated on what might have caused his sudden change of heart. Something drastic, was all they could come up with.

They decided to make a side trip on the way back. Actually, it was a bit out of the way since where they were going was on the other side of Project Dry Wells, but all agreed that it would be an interesting visit and worth the time. So, after packing their bags, they drove off to the old town of Santa Fe, which Myers translated for Jesus: Holy Faith.

Santa Fe is a city that revels in its past. Everywhere one looked there were ancient buildings in the Spanish style – and tourists. Tamara had done a little research on the Internet the night before and knew just where she wanted to take Jesus. They parked, and walked along a red stone wall to a set of stairs that led to a double towered Spanish church, also done in red stone blocks. Myers read the sign for Jesus: "The Cathedral Basilica of Saint Francis of Assisi."

To the left of the steps was a bronze statue of Saint Francis, standing there with one hand held out and the other resting on the back of a wolf. Jesus asked who that was and was told. There seemed to be a little confusion about what a saint was and why the man had a wolf for a pet. An explanation of sorts took place while they were walking up to steps to the impressive front door. The statue seemed to bother him. Myers had to remind him that this was a church, but not a Jewish one. Images were accepted here where they would not have been in his day.

Inside the church was built as most Catholic churches were, in the shape of a cross. Rows of wooden seats led up to an altar, while pillars supported a high, vaulted ceiling. Stained glass windows allowed colorful light to spill into the church. When they neared the back, the altar held a small statue of Jesus with a panel behind him picturing fifteen saints. The statue showed Jesus holding a cross in one hand and the other raised upward to the sky. He had a most suffering expression on his upturned face. Jesus looked at that and shook his head. They sat down in a pew with Myers on one side and Tamara on the other. She told him that this was one of the fancier churches, but was still built to honor God and was a place to worship him. She told him that the priests did good in the world, and that the gilt trim, elaborate colored windows and works of art were there to show the people the glory of God. Jesus slowly shook his head.

"This is as the priests in the Temple were. Rich and fat and always taking money from the people. Do people sacrifice to God here?"

"They pray to God here," Myers told him.

Jesus looked around, and his eyes came to rest on a statue hung on the wall, a depiction of Jesus hanging on the cross. There were nails through his palms and crossed feet. His long hair and the crown of thorns upon his head were done with wonderful detail, as was each muscle in his body. The artist had even caught an amazing look of suffering in his eyes. For a long time Jesus looked at the figure, saying nothing, and oblivious to the handful of tourists or worshipers around them. Finally, he looked to Myers, then Tamara and said, "That is not what it was like." He looked down at the leather bands around his wrists.

"They do not know how it was," Myers told him, "only that you suffered for your people. That is what this statue means to them, your sacrifice for them."

"This is not a synagogue," Jesus said simply. "Not a holy place."

"It is to these people. They worship differently, but they believe in you and your teachings."

Jesus took one last long look around, and then said, "Let us go from this place."

Tamara was on the verge of tears. She had hoped to impress Jesus with how people worshiped today. But it would seem that it had done the opposite.

As they were walking out, Juliette pulled out her cell phone and snapped a few photos of Jesus, even going to far as to ask him to stand next to the statue of Saint Francis for one shot.

As they walked back to the car, Juliette waved the cell phone, and told Tamara, "That's a unique photo. Jesus in a Catholic church! And nobody recognized him!"

Tamara said nothing.

51. ALONE IN THE DARK

What was going wrong?

In the dark apartment, alone, a man sat on the bed and hung his head. Only a tiny, pathetic light came around the closed curtains, along with distant sounds of traffic.

He had done as they told him. But the tablet with the video had not done what it was supposed to. This false Jesus was still alive and being treated as an important dignitary by those who created him. He had not reacted as he should have. If anything, from what he could see, Jesus was more talkative, more at ease with the staff than before. God only knew what lies he was telling, what blasphemies spewed from his mouth.

The man shuddered. It was obvious that the Church wanted this fake Jesus stopped. They had given him the tablet. He had delivered it. Now what? They did not call him. They did not tell him what to do. Was he to decide himself? And how could he? He was just a simple believer. But now, when he needed guidance from the Church most of all, there was no word.

During the last few years, it was the Church he had clung to, and that probably that saved his sanity. His beloved wife had died at far too early an age, victim of a car crash that had left him with only bruises. How could God have taken her for no reason? Mona had been so full of life, so happy. It had torn him up inside that he had lived while she died. What possible reason could God have for wanting to take her but leaving him? For a time it shook his faith to the core. He prayed to be shown some reason behind the tragedy. But no reply came. Beginning to doubt all that he had held as true, he almost turned from the Church, and would have but for one minister who spent many hours trying to help the man come through his crisis of faith.

The kindly words of that man had shown him the truth he sought. It was really simple: man was not meant to understand God's ways. One had to trust and allow God to fill his heart with love. Only then would the pain flow away. He became as he had been as a child, comforted by the love of the Church and the peace found in true belief. It took more than a year but his faith returned. He joined the Project Dry Wells, worked hard to do the best job he could, and tried to forget his beloved wife. Then came that terrible moment in which they had created this copy of Jesus – this lie that walked and talked. Filled with doubts about this, he turned again to the only comfort he knew: the Church.

But now it seemed the Church had abandoned him. They had not called. And something must be done or soon the world would know of this false Christ. Maybe he should contact them again. His hand reached for the cell phone but withdrew after a few seconds. They had told him that they would contact him. It would not be right for him to go against their orders.

He had not turned on any lights when the sunset faded into night. It was better to sit alone in the darkness, feeling the agony of indecision, and fearing that to do nothing would be the worst thing he could do.

Someone on the project was leaking information! Word had gotten around as to why that Congressman had visited that very morning. He knew of the project and was investigating. The Congressman had left, but perhaps he would be back.

There was talk that the project would be announced to the world soon. That would be terrible. The people knowing of this fake Jesus could not be allowed to happen. The Bishop himself had told him that.

He was a scientist. He had helped formulate some of the theory behind using the entanglement to create matter in the present. And he knew that this was only a copy. It was not possible that the real essence of Jesus had been copied. It could not be. The real Jesus was divine. The Son of God. He believed that with all his heart.

His cell phone chiming made him jump. With trembling hand he picked it up. "Hello?"

It was the voice of the Bishop. "You have said that there is talk of the project going public? Is that true?"

"Yes, your Excellency."

"Will that be soon?"

"Possibly, your Excellency."

There was a silence for long, agonizing seconds, then, "That must not be allowed to happen." A pause, then, "Do you understand?"

"Yes... Your Excellency."

"Do whatever you have to."

"Yes. Does that mean...?"

"Do whatever you have to."

"Yes, your Excellency."

"Have faith to do what you must," the calm voice went on. "This is the wish of his Holiness," it lied. "May God guide your hand."

"Yes, your Excellency."

The phone went silent.

The man put his phone down and resumed staring at the wall. Yet, although he trembled with fear, his heart was gladdened. Now he knew what he had to do.

52. TRANSLATOR

"You did what!"

Stryker's voice nearly rattled the windows of his office. He face was turning a wonderful shade of crimson.

"We simply showed some of the world to Jesus," Juliette told him calmly. "You did agree that we should bring him up to date, so to speak."

"But flying him around in a corporate jet! Dining out at restaurants! You were supposed to just keep him out of sight for a day or so. And letting him visit a Catholic Church. What were you thinking?"

"It was a beautiful church, old and historic," Tamara cut in. "And churches are part of the world he is learning about." She did not add that it had depressed the poor man for the rest of the day.

Stryker shook his head and flopped down in his chair. "And the bill! My, God, did you have to rent a Learjet?"

"It was a Beechjet 400. And it was the cheapest jet they had that would hold four people."

Sighing dramatically, Stryker told them, "I certainly hope Jesus had a nice vacation. I don't suppose you introduced him to the bishop?"

"No, he was out of town."

For a second Tamara, Juliette and Myers feared they had gone too far and Stryker was going to have a stroke. But he settled down and told them to get out of his office. And not to even think of ever renting jets again.

As they walked back to Project J. Myers was explaining to Tamara why Jesus was upset at the church. "He came from a time when the only church at all like what you showed him was the Temple in Jerusalem. And you know how he feels about that and the priests who ran it.

"Not too happy?"

"A gross understatement. Remember, the high priest was the one who arranged to have him crucified. But worse, to Jesus' way of thinking, was what they had done to defile the Temple.

"Besides, what you showed him was too filled with ornamentation and finery to appeal to a Jew who was forbidden to worship idols. A rural synagogue in his day was a simple building with seats all around so that everyone could see and hear and have a chance to address the group. Nothing so formal as what he saw yesterday."

"But you agreed to let us take him?" Tamara protested.

"True." Myers stopped in the corridor. "Perhaps I should not have. I knew it would not sit well with him. But if he is to learn of our world, he should learn all of it."

Tamara grinned, and told him, "At least I didn't take him around the Stations of the Cross. Or suggest that he visit Saint Peter's in London or Notre Dame in Paris."

"Thank heaven for small favors!" Myers said with a laugh.

They got back to Myers' office where he immediately started the coffee maker going.

"I'm glad that Stryker got rid of that Congressman without any problems," Tamara said as she sat down. "But I wonder what it was he said he showed him that scared him so."

"We'll find out soon enough. It's hard to keep a secret around here."

A large manila envelope sat on the corner of his desk. Opening it, he slid out what looked like a cell phone. But it lacked the screen of a smart phones. There were only two buttons on it.

"They got it made! Very good. Tamara, this is for you. And anyone else who wants to speak with Jesus. It is a translator. English to Aramaic and Aramaic to English."

"What?"

"It is something that IT made up for me. Basically, it is a cell phone, but limited to a specific purpose. See these two buttons? Press the left one and talk into the mic and you voice will be digitized and sent to a server in our computer center. There it will be analyzed and translated into Aramaic. That will be converted into digital sound and transmitted back. You'll hear the words through the speaker. Press the right hand button to translate Aramaic to English."

"That's great! And will save you a lot of work."

"Well, maybe. You have to understand there are many problems with translating one language to another. Simple sentence construction and grammar it can handle, but otherwise it is mostly just a vocabulary translator. Keep your sentences simple for the best results.

"In the server there is a database of Aramaic words." He demonstrated by pressing it and saying, *"Eli Eli lema sabachthani?"* A moment later, the speaker said, "God God why you have forsaken me," in a monotone.

"You try it," he said, handing the device to her.

"Left for English, Right for Aramaic," she said, then, as she pressed the left button, "Gethsemane." *"Gath-Šmânê,"* it told her. Delighted, she tried, "Virgin Mary," and it told her, *"Murr-yaam Btool-taa."*

"This will come in handy," she told him with delight.

"Remember, it will work only within the wireless range here in the project."

"Got it."

After obtaining his coffee, Myers said, "If you would like to test this, there is something you can do for me. Would you please check on Jesus? I want to make sure that he's recovering from yesterday's visit to that church. Maybe I should take him to my synagogue some day. Might make him feel at home."

"That's an idea," Tamara agreed. "I'll check on him. You enjoy your coffee."

Then she went off to find on Jesus. She was sure that he would find this new toy as fascinating as she did.

53. WHATEVER IS NECESSARY

Tamara found Jesus sitting on his bed, holding a book in his hands. Puzzled, she tilted her head and looked at the spine. The Holy Bible, it read. Now who would have given that to Jesus? That was not too hard to figure out. Juliette carried a small one in her purse. Apparently she was a believer. But also a scientist. If she had any qualms about bring Jesus to life, she had not shown them. In fact, she was one of the prime movers of Project J.

Besides, it made little difference. Jesus could not read English. The thought suddenly occurred to her that it might be a Bible in Aramaic. She remembered that Aramaic was still a spoken language, and that the Bible had been translated into all languages, including Esperanto and Klingon. But the spine was in English and he was not reading it, so it was unlikely to be in Aramaic.

He looked up and said something to Tamara. Smiling, she held up the translator and pressed the English button. "Hello, rabbi." The translator spoke and Jesus lifted one eyebrow high. "This is a translator," Tamara said. The device told him. A smile broke out on his face. "Press this and talk into here," she said. Obediently, the translator repeated the words in Aramaic.

Jesus took the translator in his hand, looked at it, and then pushed the button. He spoke, and a moment later Tamara heard, "You are magicians surely!" He frowned and added, "This is not the work of Satan, is it?"

"No, only science, not magic nor Satan," she said, reaching over to press the button before she spoke. The translator seemed to have trouble with that and Tamara wondered if it could find no Aramaic word for "science."

She was about to settle down to some question and answers with their guest but a noise made her turn around. Dr. Hans Buerer was standing there, looking confused. His features were pale, as if he had been sick, or at least not getting enough sleep to judge from the dark shadows under his eyes. Slowly as they watched his features changed from puzzlement to disdain. "No matter if you're here," he said in a tight voice. His hand, which was in the pocket of his jacket came out, holding a small automatic in it. The barrel shook a bit as he pointed it at Jesus.

"Stand aside, Miss Graves," he said. "I do not wish to hurt you."

Tamara stood. Her initial confusion quickly turned to fear. His purpose was obvious. She stepped between the gun and Jesus. "Don't do it!" she said loudly.

"Stand aside," he said through clenched teeth. "I will kill you too."

Jesus' hand rested on her arm and gently moved her aside. Tamara looked to him and was confused. Did he not understand? Maybe he did not know what a gun was?

"No," she said, but he continued to push her gently aside. As soon as she was moved enough for a good body shot, Buerer lifted the gun higher and aimed it directly at Jesus' chest. His hand was shaking.

Jesus' right arm was holding her aside. His other hand came up before him as if to ward off the bullet. Buerer's hand continued shaking. Tamara saw his finger tightening on the trigger and started to scream.

A loud bang echoed in the small room. A short lance of flame leapt out, the gun bucked in Buerer's hand, and Tamara's scream sounded, all at the same time. She felt Jesus' arm pull away and, from the corner of her eye, she saw him falling backward.

Buerer stood there, mouth open, a look of shock on his face replacing the anger of a moment before.

The adrenaline surge that began when Tamara saw the gun continued to build up in her, turning her fear into anger. Her scream turned into a roar. In front of her was the chair she had been sitting on. Without thinking, she reached down, grabbed the back of the chair with both hands, lifted it and swung it in a wide arc. The chair struck Buerer's arm, knocking the gun aside and snapping him out of his shocked state.

It mattered little, however, because Tamara, still fueled by anger and adrenaline, swung the chair again, bashing it against the side of his body. Another swing drove him backwards into the doorframe. Ignoring the look of surprise on his face, Tamara dropped the chair and grabbed him by the arm. She twisted around, pulling his arm with her, until he was slammed into the wall, face first. She grabbed his hair and smashed his face against the wall. Then again. And again. When the anger faded enough for self-control to resume, he was unconscious and his face a mass of fresh blood and battered flesh. She let him slide to the floor.

Turning quickly, she rushed over to the bed.

Jesus was lying there, unmoving.

54. AFTERMATH

"I should have done something," she told the collected Chronodyne big brass an hour later. "I should have done something," she repeated.

The adrenaline high had passed, leaving her in a depressed state, trembling and almost in shock. But there were questions to be answered and she could not curl up into a ball and ignore the world like she wanted to.

"It was in no way your fault, Miss Graves," Stryker told her. "He had a gun on you and threatened to kill you."

She had described in detail all that had happened. They informed her that Buerer was alive but in a serious condition. She had cracked his skull, so hard had she pounded his head into the wall. She told them she had no regrets about doing that, save possibly that she had not finished the job. No one chided her.

With her story told and confirmed by the video surveillance cameras, there was not much more to do. Tamara felt herself drained but fought the urge to break down and cry.

At that moment, the nurse from their infirmary came in.

"He'll be okay," she told all the anxious faces. "He has a cracked rib and good sized bruise, but nothing worse. The doctor said that he was lucky Buerer used a small caliber gun. If it had been a .45 or even a 9 mm, he could have died. But Buerer had a 380. That's a .38 caliber bullet but without much power behind it. This is what saved his life."

She laid a cell phone sized device on the table. The metal

case was dented. It was the translator he had been holding.

Tamara sighed and could not help but shed a few tears – of happiness. If she had not been there, Buerer could have shot him more than once. If she had not brought that translator with her, the bullet would have entered his chest.

Then it occurred to her that maybe it was not luck. Maybe this was a miracle? She picked up the dead translator and looked at it.

"I told you it would come in handy," Myers told her.

55. PLUGGING A LEAK

The house was dark without a light showing in any of the rooms, the only illumination coming from the streetlight through windows. Outside, crickets chirps mixed with the hiss of a nearby freeway to provide a background soundtrack for breaking and entering.

An unlocked rear window provided an entrance without the need to destroy any property. A small flashlight guided the intruder through the dimly lit rooms. His target was not, however, stereos, silverware, or even a bedroom jewelry box. Instead, he entered a study/office and began going through the desk there. The fact that the desk was locked presented no problem. With a thin sliver of steel he worked the simple lock open and was quickly going through all the drawers. In the third one from the top he found what he was looking for. There was nothing special looking about the cell phone he found there but it pleased him immensely. Switching it on, he touched the screen a few times and confirmed this was the phone he was looking for. Slipping it into his pocket, he closed and locked the desk again.

Five minutes later he was in his car, driving away into the night.

The next morning a meeting was called in the office of Project Director Stryker. The lists of those called to attend was short: Stryker, Manhusen and Crane.

"Have a seat Marshal," Stryker told Crane as soon as he entered.

"What's up?" the tall scientist asked, looking from one to the other of the serious faces before him. His smile faded from his face as he did.

Stryker's' words were icy, "You can probably guess what this is about. We've found our leak to Representative Stockman."

"And...?"

Manhusen cut in. "With the help of our spook friends, we were able to trace the calls to Stockman's phone back to a certain cell phone number."

"You put a tap on a Congressman's phone?" Crane asked, his face registering both surprise and more than a small trace of fear.

"Didn't have to, it was already there. But that's another story.

"You shouldn't look so surprised. No use pretending. I found this in your house." He put the cell phone on the table between them. Crane just stared at it, a most depressed look coming over his face. After a few moments of silence, he looked up.

"I only wanted what was best for the project. What we're doing here is too important to keep from the world. There are thousands of scientists who could benefit from our work. Can't you see that?"

Stryker sighed. "Marshal, I knew you were for public disclosure once we proved the Machine would work. But I didn't think that you would leak secret information."

"It was to a United States Representative! I'm sure he has security clearance."

"But not a need-to-know. Come on, Marshal, you've

worked on other secret projects before. You know the rules."

Crane was beginning to look desperate. "This project goes beyond just being secret. It is too important to keep a secret."

"And it will be released," Stryker told him. "When the time is right."

Crane could only shake his head.

"Come with me," Manhusen told him. "There are some criminal proceedings to initiate."

When the two had left his office, Stryker sat down and sighed deeply. He had thought Crane was his friend, and trustworthy.

He was turning his chair towards the window when Miss Swanson came in with some papers in her hand.

"You know, Rachael," Stryker said slowly without looking away from the view out across the pines to the mountains, "maybe Marshal was right. It's getting too hard to keep all this a secret." He swiveled and looked at the shapely blonde. "You know, I had to let Brown grab that damned dinosaur he wanted, just to scare Stockman. Now we have to figure some way to get it to San Diego."

He glanced at the papers in her hand but did not reach for them.

"My friend blabs secrets. Another of my scientists tries to kill Jesus!

"I'm getting too old for this."

56. PURE AND BEAUTIFUL AND BLESSED

Four days after the disappearance of Dr. Crane from the project, and two days after the appointment of Dr. Fielding as the new Assistant Director, one of the technicians delivered a package to Dr. Myers' office. Tamara happened to be there when it came in.

"This will please you," he told her. "Again." He opened the box and removed four devices much like the translator that had saved Jesus' life. "This is the second generation of translators. Does the same thing but you don't have to press the buttons. Just switch it on and it will listen to whatever is spoken. It will digitize the sounds and send them to the server. The server will determine what language it is, English or Aramaic, and translate it into the other."

He switched on one of the units and laid it on the desk next to his coffee cup. "Let us test this," he said. A moment later the device's monotone spoke some words Tamara did not understand but assumed was a translation. Myers smile and repeated a sentence Tamara recognized: *"Eli Eli lema sabachthani?"* A moment later the speaker obediently said, "God God why you have forsaken me."

He pushed the device across the desk to her. "This is yours. Keep it. The others are for Fielding and Juliette. And one for Jesus to keep."

"Thank you. There are still questions I would like to ask Jesus."

"Let me ask you one. What about your job? You said that you're taking vacation time to stay here. And you are most certainly welcome. If it hadn't been for you, Jesus might have been killed – twice, in fact. I, for one, am glad to have you with us. But won't the DOD want you back?"

"I have gotten an inquiry from my boss asking just how much vacation I intend to take. But I have plenty of time coming. It seemed I was always too busy to take my vacation time." She put the translator into her pocket. "Besides, if it came to it, I would quit just to stay here. This is simply too incredible to miss!"

"Maybe I can get Stryker to hire you on as an assistant," Myers told her. "Chronodyne has more money than it knows what to do with. You'd be surprised how much they're paying me."

He chuckled, and so did Tamara. Fact was, she knew exactly what his salary was. She had been wandering around in the project's financial records, after all.

"If you don't mind, would you give this to Jesus?" He handed her another of the units. "It will make it easier if he can talk with anyone when he needs to."

"Of course. In fact, I'll go over and give it to him now."

Jesus had been released from the infirmary, so Tamara found him in his apartment. When she knocked on the open door to let him know she was there, he was trying to put on a shirt over the wrapping around his chest. Obviously it was a painful process for him with the broken rib, so she offered to help. The shirt was obviously someone's idea of a joke. It was a Tee, black in color with the only decoration being a single sentence written across the front in white letters and fancy script. Tamara had to laugh when she saw what had been a popular saying a few years back. It said: "What would Jesus do?"

She helped him with the shirt, wincing when she saw the horrible scars across his back. With the shirt on, and him sitting on his bed, she handed him the translator and showed him how to turn it on. "This is for you. A translator," she told him. "You do not have to do anything. Just talk into it." Then she waited for it to finished relating that information to him.

"Thank you," he said. "Again I thank you for saving me. That man wanted to kill me. Did he not?"

"He was sick," she told him. "Very sick." When Jesus did not seem to understand that fully, she added, "In his mind."

"There was a demon within him," Jesus said simply. Tamara remembered Myers telling her that mental illness was not very well understood in Jesus' time. Possession by demons was the common explanation for those who did not act properly. She felt the urge to ask him if he would have tried to cast the demon out, as he had been said to have done so often in the Gospels. "Did you kill him?" he asked.

"No. I did not. But he is in more pain than you," she told him, hoping that would be of some small consolation. "And he will be in prison for a long time."

Jesus looked at her strangely. From what she remembered of her studies, simply putting someone away in a prison for a fixed period of time was not a common practice back then. Prisons back then were simply places to hold someone until you decided his punishment. Capital punishment was much more common back then – almost casual, especially the way the Romans applied it to those they did not like. She decided not to try to explain the whole concept of penal institutions and correctional facilities.

"He will not be put to death?"

"Probably not."

Jesus shook his head. Tamara was momentarily taken back by his reaction. Was this not the man who had advocated turning the other cheek? And loving your enemies? She expected him to forgive Buerer. Then she remembered that the turning the other cheek had been advice to his disciples not to antagonize the Romans. Jesus himself had explained that to her once. And as for loving your enemies, this was a man who expected that with the coming of the Kingdom of God, they would drive out the hated Romans at the point of a sword – with the help of God, of course.

To change the subject, she asked him if he would like to have lunch at the company cafeteria with her rather than in his apartment or courtyard. He said that would be nice and slowly got to his feet. They walked slowly along the sidewalk, enjoying the warmth of the day before it grew too hot. Fortunately, they were at enough of an altitude that it did not become blazing hot as it did farther down in the desert areas.

Tamara held her translator in her hand so they could chat while walking.

"Rabbi, is there something that you would like to see?" she asked.

"I would like to see the Temple again."

"That may be difficult. But maybe someday." She did not want to try to explain what else had happened to Jerusalem since he last saw it. The ancient city was much more than just the Temple now. There was the division of the old city into four quarters, the Dome of the Rock, the Church of the Holy Sepulcher, and a lot more that he would have trouble relating to. It would be most interesting to see his reaction to the Church currently sitting on the site claimed to be the former

Golgotha where he was crucified and buried.

"Then I would like to see more of your land. It is very big."

"Much bigger than you imagine. I would love to take you around our country and show you everything."

She began telling him of the wonders of Yosemite and the warm, clear waters of Florida.

Lunch was eaten at one of the outdoor tables. Jesus found the array of food interesting and chose a chicken salad, while Tamara picked a crab and shrimp quesadilla. They shared a glass of Chardonnay each. Jesus never seemed to tire of trying new wines.

As they were finishing the wine, Jesus reached over to put his hand over hers. "Tamara, you and Seymour have promised that you will use your magic to let me see what happened to Mariam and my children. This I wish for."

She was touched by his devotion to a woman who had been described by some as a prostitute. "I will speak to Dr. Myers. I'm sure that we can do something for you." She finished her wine and settled back in the chair. "Jesus, there is something I have wanted to ask you. The Bible says that you cast seven demons out of Mary Magdalene. Is that true?"

When the translation was finished, Jesus was frowning. "I am not sure what you speak of."

"When we get back, I'll show you."

The walk back to his apartment was leisurely with little talking. Once there, she asked for the Bible that Juliette had given him. Opening it to Luke, she read 8-1: "*After this, Jesus traveled about from one town and village to another. The Twelve were with him, and also some women who had been cured of evil spirits and diseases: Mary (called Magdalene) from whom seven demons had come out – and many others. These women were helping to support them out of their own means."*

"And there is Mark 16-9. He says: *"Now when Jesus was risen early the first day of the week, he appeared first to Mary Magdalene, out of whom he had cast seven devils."*

She closed the book and looked at him. "Did you cast demons out of her? There are many other places where it says that you did."

Jesus frowned. "It is true that I have cast out demons. But there were none in Mariam. She was pure and beautiful and blessed of God from the first moment I saw her. This Mark does not tell true that of which he speaks."

It was Tamara's turn to frown. Myers was not kidding, she told herself, when he said that the Gospel writers had added a lot to history.

"And I suppose that she did not help you during your ministry?"

"That part is truth. I, and those who followed me, depended upon the help of others. We had no fields to tend, no trees to pick fruit of, no herd of sheep. Those who listened would share their food and sometimes give money."

"Was Mary Magdalene one of those?"

"Yes. She listened to my words and understood of the coming Kingdom. When we left that village, she came with us." He paused and a far-away look came into his eyes. "She was the most beautiful woman I had ever seen." Then he shook his head and smiled. "Except for you, Tamara."

She could not be sure but she suspected that she was blushing. "Thank you," she managed.

Jesus picked up the Bible and opened the book. For a few seconds he stared at the words he could not possibly understand, then closed it slowly. "I wish to learn to read these words."

Tamara wondered where she could find a Bible written in Aramaic. Then she remembered Myers telling her that Jesus, like most of the Galilee peasants, was illiterate. Very few people in those days could read and write. Most knowledge was passed down via oral traditions.

Well, she thought, he's still young. He can learn to read and write, either Aramaic or English. Hell, he's intelligent, probably both.

He put down the Bible. "Please," he asked, "would you talk with Seymour about Mariam?"

"I will."

57. MARY MAGDALENE

"Okay, now we follow her."

In the Machine room, Jesus, Myers, Tamara and Fielding were watching as the operator, Jacques, had set in once again the coordinates for that fateful afternoon two thousands year prior, and was now displaying the spectators at the crucifixion.

The Machine operator was resting his wrists on the console while his fingers delicately adjusted two dials. Then his hand went to the screen and touched the nose of Mary Magdalene gently. A red glow spread out from that point, covering the selected figure of the dark haired woman in the group of mourners. When it reached the edges of her robe all the red condensed into an outline of her. That flashed twice and then faded to a dim outline.

"That is Mariam," confirmed Jesus. He was leaning forward in the chair, eyes fixed upon the main screen of the Machine's console. The operator keyed in a command and the figures on the screen came to life again. One older woman was weeping and had to be supported by a man standing beside her. Mary Magdalene appeared to be trying to comfort her. Another woman stood a couple feet from that group, crying to herself.

Words were exchanged, and the man led Jesus' mother away from the scene on Golgotha. Mary Magdalene stayed, moved over to the other woman and put her arm around her. The two of them looked straight ahead, almost looking directly at the viewers in the future.

"That new tracking software seems to be working. I'm going to increase the time passage speed now," Jacques said. On the screen the two women seemed to be moving in tiny, rapid jerks. Eventually they turned and left. The Machine's point of view followed them down the hill side, along a well-traveled path, past many people hurrying about, and eventually to a house that looked like all the other ones but was one they had seen before; one belonging to Mary, the mother of James.

The Virgin Mary, to use the name most knew her as in the Twenty-First Century, was already there, sitting silently on a stool in a corner. The Beloved Disciple, John, was also there, talking to three other men.

"Please slow it down," Jesus asked. The operator complied. "That is Peter and Andrew. When the third man's face became visible, he added, "And that is Simon! It is not surprising that they would come to her house. I wonder where the others are?"

For a while, little happened. Everyone looked sad. The disciples who had gathered there also looked fearful. Simon kept glancing towards the door as if he expected to see Roman soldiers charging in at any second. Perhaps he did.

When the door did open, it was not a soldier but a young man, a teen, who Jesus said he did not know. The boy said something to John then left. John talked to the two Marys and they left the house. The Machine continued to track Mary Magdalene.

Not unexpectedly, the two women made their way to the tomb where Jesus' body lay. They brought with them linens and bottles of lotion and a large jug of water, items they would need to cleanse Jesus' body and prepare it for burial.

"Let's cut to a day or so later," Myers suggested. "Jesus has already seen enough of his own body."

Several keyed commands later the scene switched totally to black then to the inside of that house again. Mary Magdalene was there, along with others. She was just carrying a cloth bag out of a side room and setting it down next to the door. The disciples were not present.

"She is leaving," Jesus said. "Going back to Galilee and the children." He turned to the others. "Judas and Deborah were left with Mariam's parents when we came to Jerusalem. They were too young to know of what I had to do."

"Who will go with her?" Myers asked. Women did not travel alone in those times.

"John probably. Maybe others. My mother will go with her. I asked John to take care of her after I was gone."

"Then you weren't absolutely sure that you would arise from the dead?" asked Tamara.

Jesus glared at her and did not answer. Finally, his features softened and he said, "Whatever is God's will."

Not much was happening on the screen. People moved about, packed for a journey and looked gloomy.

"We won't see much for now," Myers said. "Jacques, would you please run the scan forward until they are in Nazareth. Then lock in that setting. We'll pick it up from there another time." He turned to Jesus to ask, "This where her parents are, Nazareth, right?"

"Yes." He looked at the screen and the figures currently frozen in position. "I wish I could hear," he said softly.

58. MURDER!

It was impossible. It could not have happened. Yet there it was. In the large pen they had built to hold the juvenile T-Rex taken from the upper Cretaceous Period, the vicious predator lay dead. And not just dead, but viciously murdered.

Dr. Brown stared down at the carcass sprawled on the sand and shook his head. One of his assistants was already in the pit, photographing the body from all angles. From his higher elevation, Brown could easily see what had killed the mighty beast. Slashes along the exposed flank were deep. But the worst was a large chunk of the neck directly behind the head. It was missing. Something had taken a big bite out of a T-Rex.

Stryker came up to stand next to Brown. "What the hell did that?" he asked.

Brown could only shake his head. "Damned if I know. He was fine last night when we fed him. No one could have gotten in here and done that. You know the security we have in place since that attempt on Jesus' life. And even if someone did sneak in, how the hell did they kill him? He may only be a juvenile but he was still more than a match for a man. Crap, he could swallow a man whole!"

"Do you have surveillance cameras set up here?" Stryker asked.

"Yes. They were mostly to make sure no one snuck in, but there are two overlooking his pen. I'll go over the recordings."

"Do that." Stryker noted the dark pools of dried blood half under the large body. "I'd like to know what could rip up a T-Rex."

Half an hour later, in a lab nearby, Brown was sitting with an assistant while the video recordings were being reviewed. They began with the feeding, a gruesome but interesting show in which they tossed a live sheep into the pen and allowed the beast, which some of them had nicknamed "King," to go after it. It was an unfair contest; the sheep always lost. After gobbling the sheep whole, he roared his defiance at the humans who had fed him, then settled down for a nap. They had found that he tended to take a nap after a meal, not an uncommon trait among predators.

The two monitors before them continued on showing his pen from two angles. Nothing much happened. The lights were lowered and the researcher who had been taking close up photos of his eyes (with a telephoto lens) left. In the lower right of each display small numbers recorded the time.

"Let's speed it up," Brown told the tech. "But stop and back up if you catch any motion."

Obediently the tech keyed in instructions and the displays flickered a little. For minutes nothing changed beyond the jerking motion that was his breathing. Then, extremely suddenly, there was motion on both displays. The tech stopped the recordings and backed up both to a point before the motion, then continued forward in real time.

King lay there, sleeping peacefully, but suddenly jerked his head up. He roared and twisted his body sideways. Then he was on his feet, tail lashing out, jaws snapping. But there was nothing there. He danced in a circle, snapping to his left as if something were there. But his jaws closed on only empty air.

"Freeze that!" Brown suddenly cried out. The scene on

both monitors froze. Brown leaned forward to stare at the scene. "Can you magnify this?"

"Sure."

The dinosaur's side filled the screen. Red marks appeared against his brown-gray flank, lines that opened up into gashes with blood spurting out. Two then three lines formed along the side of his leg.

"Is he biting himself?" the tech asked.

"No. But something is cutting him."

They backed out again and resumed the motion. A roar of anguish and pain filled the room as King twisted his head around. Suddenly his head snapped back and he did a little dance as he twisted around to the other side. That jaw filled with teeth snapped shut on nothing. As his body turned, they could see two more slashes appear on this right side, at the base of his neck. He continued to turn in a circle, trying to get at whatever was attacking him. Then, as they watched in disbelief, his head twisted backwards and up. Holes appeared in his neck, blood spurted out, and his whole body trembled. The holes widened and suddenly a chunk of his flesh was ripped out. It fell to the ground, where it lay bleeding.

King roared again, but there was no defiance or triumph, only pain. His head twisted around in a circle then lowered. His body collapsed to the sand. For a minute muscles twitched then were still.

Blood continued to flow out of the gash but slowed and finally ceased. The King was dead.

"There wasn't anything there!" the tech said disbelievingly.

Brown said nothing for a long time. Then he rose and silently walked out of the room.

59. IN THEORY

"What the hell happened?" Stryker asked later that morning. Assembled in a conference room were all the project heads. "You've all seen the video. Something attacked and killed our pet T-Rex. But nothing was there. Any suggestions?"

His question was met with silence. It was Fielding who finally broke that silence.

"Dr. Brown," he said to the still-stunned scientist, "Is there any natural predator who might attack a T-Rex?"

"Well, normally I'd say no. But... Ours was a juvenile. There were other dinosaurs contemporary with him who might have attacked a juvenile. The Gorgosaurus was from the same time period. A full grown one would run thirty feet long and weight about three tons. But more likely would be an Albertosaurus. They were about the same size as the Gorgosaurus but much more common during that period."

"Would one attack a T-Rex the size of ours?"

"Well... Maybe. T-Rex stayed small until about ten years of age. Then they went through a growth spurt and at about eighteen years reached mature size. I don't think there is anything that would attack a full grown T-Rex. It would be forty feet long, and weigh around eight tons."

"But a juvenile?"

"Maybe." Brown paused. "But there has been some speculation that Albertosaurus hunted in packs in order to bring down larger dinosaurs. Like Velociraptors did. A pack of Albertosauruses could well attack a T-Rex. Our King was by no means fully grown.

"But what does that mean? There's no other dinosaurs here."

"No, but there were back where King came from."

"What...?"

Fielding turned to Stryker with a frightened look on his face. "You remember the speculation early in the project about the nature of entangled matter? Our Machine creates a link between matter that existed in the past and matter that we have here and now. It uses that entanglement to force the matter here to become exactly as the matter in the past. Remember how Dr. Spencer suggested that the entanglement would work both ways? His theory was that once we created the object here, it would be permanently entangled with the object in the past."

"Yes, I remember. He suggested that anything that happened to the object in the past would also happen to the object in the present. But we tested that, and came to the conclusion that the entanglement was one way in the time stream. The object in the past could not affect the object in the present."

"Yes," Fielding agreed. "But we tested it with inanimate objects only. That was before we expanded to try it with live animals."

Everyone in the room was silent as the impact sank in.

"Maybe with a live object, the entanglement continues. Why I'm not sure, but wouldn't that explain what killed King? Let's say that we created him here exactly ten days ago. And let's further say that exactly ten days afterwards, back in 65 million BC, a pack of Albertosauruses attacked the original King. And killed him. Or it might have been a pack of some other large raptors. Those slashes on his side could have been made by Velociraptors.

"At the same time, relatively speaking, our copy became slashed and killed."

"Oh, my God..." muttered Stryker.

Fielding, however, was the first to realize what that meant to Project J.

"And entanglement works both ways. What if something had happened and we had to kill King here? If someone blew his head off here, I'll bet that the original would also lose its head."

Stryker looked sick. "Then our current theory of entanglement time displacement is flawed," he said softly.

Suddenly Tamara jerked her head up. "Do you mean..."

"Yes," Fielding said. "Our Jesus is entangled with the original."

"But the original died. Right? We saw that on the Machine."

"We saw that they failed to revive his body. We saw them prepare it for burial. Then we saw it being taken out of the tomb and to someplace else. But we didn't follow that. We just assumed that he was taken to some other tomb as part of a plan to make it appear he had risen."

Fielding looked around at the intent faces. "We healed Jesus of his wounds and pulled him back from near death here. He was in a coma for almost two days while we worked to save him. When he awoke here, in our infirmary..."

Each person there was filling in the startling results in their minds.

"He would have arisen there," Tamara whispered.

60. CONFIRMATION

The control room of the Machine was crowded. Stryker and Fielding, Tamara and Jesus, were the only ones with seats, the dozen or so who had followed them were standing behind them.

"He would have awoken about two and a half days after pick up," Fielding was saying, "based on what happened in our time. That gives us a time to look, but where? Where did they take his body?"

Tamara turned to Jesus to ask, "Do you know where they planned to take your body?"

He shook his head. "It was not planned to have to take me anywhere. They hoped to revive me where I was, in Joseph's tomb."

"Maybe, when they came back to remove the body, they realized that he was still alive even after their attempts to revive him failed," suggested Juliette. "So they took him somewhere else, not to another tomb, but someplace where they could try again to revive him."

"That might be reasonable. But where? Dr. Myers, does the Bible help in this regard?"

"All four of the Gospels tell of Jesus appearing after the resurrection. Matthew says he appeared to Mary Magdalene and 'the other Mary' and informed them to tell the disciples to go ahead to Galilee and he would meet them there. Then, in Galilee, he gives them the commission to 'baptize all nations in the name of the Father, Son, and Holy Spirit'.

"Then, in Luke, he appears to two disciples on a road but they do not recognize him. He breaks bread with them, they recognize him, and he disappears. Then he says that Jesus appeared to the eleven left and they thought he was a spirit. They gave him 'broiled fish, and of a honeycomb' and he ate them to prove he was real. Later, he blessed them and was lifted up into heaven.

"According to John, Jesus appeared to Mary Magdalene, although she did not recognize him at first. He then appeared to most of the disciples, and a week later to them again, including the doubting Thomas.

"Mark has him appearing to Mary Magdalene, then the eleven where he tells them to go out to all the world and preach the gospel.

"That's about it. But I'm not sure how this helps."

"It doesn't really," Fielding agreed. "But it does tell us in general that he appeared on the third day to at least Mary Magdalene. Then, the following week to the disciples. But where? And exactly when?"

"Let's take a look in Mary's house, the one where we saw them go after the crucifixion. No, wait! Let's go back to the tomb. The Bible had him appearing there to Mary, at least."

"Very well, Jacques, do that."

"Joseph of Arimathea was a respected member of the Sanhedrin or council of the Jewish priests in the Temple. He was also a believer in the coming Kingdom of God," Myers explained to those who might not be familiar with that. "Another member of the Council, Nicodemus, worked with him. It had been their plan to drug Jesus so he appeared dead, and then later revive him. Jesus," he said, glancing to the man sitting next to him, "says that he did not want them doing that, because he believed God would raise him from the dead."

Jesus, who had been following the conversation on his translator, nodded but said nothing. He kept the translator up to his ear like a cell phone.

The outside of the tomb appeared. It was dark, but a dim gray suggested the coming of dawn soon. Nothing moved. "This is the morning of the third day, Sunday," Jacques said. "Just before dawn." He touched the keyboard and the scene lightened quickly. Suddenly there was a blur of motion and he froze the display, backed it up, and then started it forward in real time.

A woman came into the scene, followed by another, both carrying baskets. They stopped when almost to the tomb's entrance and stood there, looking at the large rock that had been covering the entrance. It was pushed to one side. The woman, one of whom was now recognizable as Mary Magdalene, looked at each other in puzzlement. When Mary cautiously approached tomb entrance, a figure came out of it. In the faint morning twilight, it was hard to make out who it was. The figure stepped forward until he was standing directly before Mary. It was a young man, dressed in a white robe.

"Jesus, who is that?" Myers asked.

"I do not know. I think maybe one of Joseph's servants. Maybe."

The young man said something to the women. The woman behind Mary dropped her basket and covered her mouth with both hands. Mary looked shocked but composed. She said something and the man replied. Then he pointed off in the direction the woman had come from. Both of them turned and walked quickly away.

"He's telling them to go and tell the disciples that Jesus has risen," Myers said with a trace of awe. "Just as the Bible stated."

The young man waited, watching the women until they were out of sight, then he took off up the hillside.

"Well, that really doesn't prove anything," Fielding said. "Except that it was not Jesus who appeared to the women. Next we have meetings with a couple of disciples on a road, and the meeting with the whole group during the next week."

"Luke states that the after the meeting on the road, those two went back to the others and told them what had happened. Then Jesus appeared among them. I would suggest that you consider looking in the same house and room where the Last Supper was held; Joseph of Arimathea's house."

Jacques began keying in instructions.

"I would make the time at about one week after the crucifixion. Maybe five days to be on the safe side. That would be the earliest that Jesus could possibly have been strong enough to meet with the eleven. During that time, our efforts to save Jesus here were also saving him there."

The screen cleared and a room came into focus. It was large, and the walls were made of stone blocks with curtains. There was a low table but it was pushed to one side and it was empty. A collection of short sofas were also pushed to one side. They were not long enough to lie down in but would allow the person to recline while eating a meal, much in the fashion of formal Roman dinners. Jacques set the display into fast forward. Occasionally a person would dash into the room and leave. When it seemed that a group was forming, he slowed back to real time and they watched. Several times that happened, once a formal meal where the table was brought forward and the sofas arranged around it. But during these meals, Jesus did not make an appearance, and they continued on, speeding through periods of inactivity.

"It would be my guess that Jesus was in another room of

that house," Myers said. "Assuming, of course, that the entanglement theory is correct and he was alive then. I..."

He broke off because another group was forming. Half a dozen men were standing around, talking while a couple of servants were arranging the table for a meal. A few more men joined them and the servants were just beginning to set out food when a trio made their appearance from the left. Two of them supported the third between them. Their walk was slow as they made their way towards the table. The men already present stood there, staring at the newcomers in varying degrees of surprise. Or shock.

Myers heard a gasp from beside him and looked to Jesus to find an equally shocked expression on his face.

The third man, the one who needed support to walk, was Jesus! But it was a pale, sick looking version of the healthy man seated with the scientists. His wrists were wrapped in cloth and there were two small open wounds on his forehead. In the Machine's control room, Jesus' hand went up to the now-faded scars on his forehead.

When they reached the table, the two eased him down to a couch where he leaned back. The two men then stood behind him. Jesus looked weak but his eyes remained open. He had almost died, indeed would have, had it not been for modern medicine's effect on his body projected backwards in time through entangled particles, but he was alert. When he spoke apparently all could hear; it was not in a whisper. In a condition that would have had most men flat on their backs in a hospital bed, his iron self-will gave him the strength to do what he felt he had to do.

"That is Joseph and Nicodemus, isn't it?" Myers asked, pointing to the two behind the couch.

"It is," said Jesus. He then proceeded to name the

disciples who stood before his image. "Peter, John, Mark..." Those in the room who understood Biblical history did not miss the fact that he named two Johns and two Judases.

"That is Judas Iscariot?" Myers asked him.

"Yes." Jesus turned from the screen to Myers. "You told me he killed himself."

"That is what the Bible says."

"Then this Bible is wrong."

Jesus turned back to the screen. Several of the men came forward, kneeling before Jesus and talking with him. Several kissed his hand. This went on for a while, with no one certain what they were talking about.

"Frustrating as hell not to be able to hear," Myers muttered.

After a while, Nicodemus gave Jesus a cup of wine and helped him hold it to drink. Jesus seemed to be having trouble with his hands. The current Jesus touched one wrist where, under the leather cuff, there were the scars of a vicious wound.

Maybe ten minutes later, Joseph stepped forward and put an end to the discussion. He and Nicodemus gently lifted Jesus and helped him out of the room, leaving his disciples behind talking and gesturing animatedly.

"That's enough, Jacques," said Fielding. The screen froze. "Well, we know now. Jesus did survive the crucifixion!"

"Yes," Myers agreed, "but was it because of our intervention?"

Fielding looked aghast. "You mean..."

"Maybe it was only our entangling his body with this Jesus that allowed him to survive the ordeal. If we had not fetched Jesus and saved his life here, maybe that Jesus would have died and never been resurrected."

61. GOD'S PLAN?

After Stryker called for a meeting the next morning and adjourned this informal one, everyone left the building lost in their own thoughts. Myers, Jesus and Tamara went back to Jesus' apartment, all deep in thought.

As soon as they got there, Tamara asked, "Does this mean that Jesus here might die if the Jesus back then does? What will happen to the original will also happen to this... to Jesus?"

"Very probably," Myers said with a sigh. "That's what happened to that T-Rex. The original was attacked and killed, and so was our copy." He shrugged, and added, "Of course, that works both ways."

Jesus was sitting on his bed, looking down at the floor. Slowly he looked up at them. "You said I died. Now you say I lived. Why?"

Tamara tried to explain about quantum entanglement, but failed utterly. It was just too weird. Finally she told him it was a special kind of magic. A good magic, not the evil kind. She remembered Myers telling her that the Jews of that day believed most magic was done for evil purposes. In fact, to be called a magician was very negative.

Myers finally put the issue to rest when he told Jesus, "You are Jesus. That man in the past is Jesus. The two of you are the same. Yes, if he dies, so will you. I am sorry."

He was remembering, as was Tamara, just what a harsh and dangerous time and place Jesus had lived in. In fact, if

Jesus lived long enough, he would see a massive revolt against Rome started in 66 CE and end a few years later with the destruction of Jerusalem and slaughter of thousands of his people.

And that was not to mention the danger he faced if Pilate found out that he had been tricked and Jesus had escaped death. Jesus and all his disciples would be hunted down and killed.

"So what do we do now?" Tamara asked.

"Do? Why do anything?" Myers responded. "We have no control over what happens back then. And haven't we messed things up enough? I can't believe our interfering has changed history."

"Maybe it hasn't. The Gospels tell of his resurrection. They did before and they do now. What has changed?"

"I don't know. This is hard to get a grasp on."

"Classic time travel paradox?" Tamara suggested.

"Right! But... I just don't know. But what I do know is that I will suggest the Machine be shut off. This is too dangerous. The power to change history is just too dangerous to mess with."

"Amen to that!" Tamara agreed.

For a while none spoke, still trying to make sense of things.

Jesus finally reached over and put his hand on Tamara's. "I am not mad. Magic is always dangerous. If I understand... I would have died and never come here if you did not use that magic."

"That is correct."

"Then I thank you for my life. There are many good things you have shown me."

"We are glad we did, also," Tamara told him, patting his

hand gently.

"We've got to shut the Machine down!"

Fielding, once an advocate for increased use of the time machine, was adamant in his feeling. "There is too much danger!"

"I agree. But what will we tell the executives back in their ivory towers and the stockholders?"

They were seated in Stryker's office. The Project Director had just poured generous glasses of whiskey for them both.

"And the spooks! What do we tell them! Oh, Christ! I just realized – there is absolutely no way we can tell them the truth!"

"And give them the ability to change the past – you got that right." Fielding took a deep swallow. "Might as well kiss our world goodbye!"

Stryker choked on too big a drink and put the glass down. "But what can we do? We've had so much success with the Machine. Think of all the history we've uncovered. Of all the science we've corrected and expanded. We can't just say, sorry, we're shutting it down, but we can't tell you why. They'd crucify us."

Fielding glared at Stryker, but apparently the Director was not aware of the pun.

Several impractical suggestions and well into their second glasses of the strong drink, Fielding came out with, "Too bad the damned Machine didn't explode the first time we used it."

Stryker put down his glass and stared at Fielding for a long time.

"Maybe it will," he finally said.

"Huh?"

"What would happen if the Machine here were destroyed?"

"They'd tell us to build another."

"But what if we made it look as if the reason for the destruction was a basic flaw in the theory?"

"What basic flaw? The damned theory works fine."

"I don't know. I don't make a good scientist when I'm drunk."

Fielding was thinking out loud. "Maybe... No. Or... No again. Damned! There's got to be something."

"Double damn!" Stryker said with real conviction. "We're out of whiskey."

Back in Jesus' apartment, two of the three were saddened at the thought of the loss of all the potential the Machine represented. The third, Jesus himself, was happy. "I am happy that Judas did not kill himself. He was a good friend."

"What do you think will happen back then?" Myers asked him. "Where will you go? Back to Galilee? Or stay in Jerusalem?"

"I do not know. It is as I told you at first: I failed. I was chosen by God to bring our people to a glorious new kingdom. God would give back the land promised to us and we would live under his righteous rule. But I failed. I was not good enough, and God turned his back on me."

"Maybe not," Tamara told him. "Maybe you succeeded in what God really wanted you to do. Maybe he wanted a new kingdom on earth, but not just for Jews. Maybe he wanted you to do exactly what you did. You inspired a new religion! One of peace and love. One that has done a lot of good."

She turned to Myers, who responded with the tiniest of

shrugs.

"If that is what he wanted, then you succeeded."

Jesus looked unconvinced. "What of the words spoken to the prophets? I was to do as the prophecies proclaimed and he would bring about his kingdom on the earth. That was what had to be. I wanted nothing else."

Tamara felt sad inside. Jesus apparently could not let go of the idea that he was the chosen one to bring forth the Kingdom of God. And had failed.

"Well, I still believe that it is possible God arranged for you to be resurrected by having us do it for him," she said.

Myers gave her a sharp look.

"God moves in mysterious ways," she added.

Jesus still looked unconvinced.

"You can't be serious?" asked Myers.

Tamara nodded uncertainly. "I don't know," she admitted. "I... Look at what we do know. We've established that when an animal is brought back, it may still be linked to what happens to the original in the past. We've established that what happened to Jesus here, linked back to his body in the past. But, your scientists say that they established beyond doubt that inanimate objects did not retain the link, and we've also established that whatever is happening to Jesus in the past *since we brought him here* isn't having any effect on him in the present, otherwise, apart from anything else, he would know all about it. His memories would *update* with the experiences he had in the past after we brought him here. That's not happening. What does that tell us?"

"Just a quirk of quantum entanglement," Myers replied promptly. "Doesn't it...?" A strange look came into his eyes."

"Yes?" asked Tamara.

"You're not serious?"

"You're the one with the degree in Biblical Studies," Tamara pointed out. "What does it tell you?"

"You mean that there's something in animals and humans that isn't present in inanimate objects, something the Machine can't transfer."

"Not quite," said Tamara. "Or, at least, not as I see it. But I'm not a scientist."

"Go on," Myers insisted. "How do you see it?"

"All right," Tamara said, with a quick glance at Jesus. "As you said, there's something in animals and humans that the Machine can't transfer. And, it's something that can't be measured in quarks or whatever other tiny particles the scientists talk about. It can't be entangled in the same way, because it's not... well, I don't know how to put it: *it's not part of the physical world.*"

She looked at Jesus again, wondering if the translator was coping with what she was saying, and wondering whether it would make any sense to him even if it did. To her surprise, he was smiling broadly.

"Of course," he said. "It is the soul."

"I can't believe...." Myers started, and then shook his head. "No," he said to Tamara. "There's a flaw in your logic. If the Machine can't transfer the part of the person, or animal, that is life itself, then neither Jesus nor any of the animals would be alive here."

There was a long silence. Jesus was the first to speak.

"She knows," he said. "Ask her to explain. I cannot."

Tamara sighed. "So much has happened, and I'm really not sure of anything any more. All right. Put it this way. *If* whatever gives life is really not something physical – call it the soul, or whatever – then maybe, just maybe, there is only one soul for each living creature. And yet, the Machine creates an identical physical body with everything the same as the original. So, regardless of time and place, the soul, the *life*, must be in it, as it is in the original. It cannot be split; it cannot be created; it must be shared… And when either physical body is damaged in a way that comes close to the soul leaving it, the link extends back to the physical body as well as the soul, so… Oh! I'm talking rubbish, aren't I?"

Jesus put his hands together and touched his forehead.

"So much knowledge for one so young and so beautiful," he said.

62. BASIC FLAW

The next morning, a meeting of all department directors was convened by Stryker. He immediately got down to business.

"All of you are aware of what has happened the last two days," he said. "Our pet T-Rex was killed and we found that, due to our use of entanglement, Jesus actually survived the crucifixion." He paused for a moment. "Because of the danger inherent in entangling the past and present, I have decide that the Machine will be shut down."

There were a few gasps, but others just nodded their heads. No one objected aloud.

"Further, the Machine will self-destruct because of a basic flaw in the time entanglement theory. A flaw that, hopefully, will prevent anyone from constructing another such machine in the future.

"Dr. Fielding and I have worked out the details of a plausible sounding explanation. We can give you those details later.

"Project Dry Wells will be closed down. I will push Chronodyne to find projects in other areas that you may work on. Please feel free to take any of your findings with you, but nothing of the principles of the Machine. It would be better were this to die right here and now."

No one objected, but none seemed overly happy either.

"Needless to say, you will all keep the secret of what we have done here with regard to our guest," he motioned to

Jesus who was sitting there, translator to his ear. "I am sure all of you can imagine the problems if news of his presence here got out. We know that there was a leak, courtesy of Dr. Buerer, but we hope that can be allowed to die as Project Dry Wells closes.

"Dr. Fielding, do you have anything to add?"

"Only that it is too bad we cannot continue the project. But there is no way that we can keep tight enough control over it to prevent misuse."

"I quite concur," Stryker said. "The destruction of the Machine will occur at 3:12 pm tomorrow, so get anything you do not wish to have destroyed out of that building. And..."

"May I make a suggestion?" called out Tamara, interrupting him.

"Well... of course."

"I have been doing a lot of thinking about this," she began in her auditor-lecturing-auditees voice, "and I suggest that you delay the closing of the project – for a few days at least."

"And why is that?" Stryker asked.

Tamara explained.

63. AFTERMATH II

The meltdown of the Machine was not very spectacular, at least not from the outside. There was no explosion, the building was still standing, and, needless to say, no one was hurt. But the machine inside was a total loss, most of it fused into useless lumps of metal and smoldering plastic and insulation. Unfortunately, along with it, the Machine took most of the blueprints and other specifications one would need to rebuild it in a small fire that started from the main power overload.

Stryker spent a lot of time on the phone explaining to several government agencies why they could no longer have time on the Machine. Then he had to explain to irate executives in Chronodyne what had happened and why it was not really his fault. None of them questioned his explanation that a fluke of quantum entanglement theory caused the meltdown, and that it would happen again if another such machine were attempted. But then, most of them had never understood what was going on anyway. Fortunately, most of them also had no real knowledge of the extreme progress that time machine had made, including the distinguished guest they had hosted.

Stryker offered his resignation, as did Dr. Fielding, but both were turned down, most likely from fear that those two would go someplace else and make another time machine. The process of finding new positions for the staff continued, with most of the academics finding positions in education or an assignment on the new project replacing Dry Wells. It was supposed to be a continuation of the "cloning" done by the original project. Work was immediately begun on using frozen mastodon tissue to clone wooly mammoths, and an attempt to continue Smiley's line by mating him with assorted big cats. That project was headed by Dr. Brown and located in the old Dry Wells facility.

Dr. Myers went back to teaching, this time at the University of Northern Arizona located in Flagstaff, which, not surprisingly, left him only a short drive to Jesus' cabin.

Tamara quit her job with the DOD and, after a long vacation, became an employee of Chronodyne.

64. PACKING

Stryker was taking items out of his desk and putting them into a cardboard box when Fielding walked in.

"I guess this will be my office now," he told his former boss. "Did the higher ups find a project for you yet?"

Stryker paused in the packing. "They offered me a small project in New York. Research into junk DNA. You know, what it is and what it does. But, to be honest, most anything after this would be anti-climatic, wouldn't it?"

"Yeah, guess so."

"Maybe I'll retire. Get a small house in Florida and spend my time fishing."

"You won't do that and you know it," Fielding stated flatly.

"No, guess you're right." He put his refreshed personal bottle of whiskey into the box. "But you know what scares me?"

"What?"

"The basic principle behind entanglement time displacement can be found in scientific literature. You know, the theory behind the Machine is public knowledge. Based, I'm told, on the work of two physicists, a Dr. Makato Kobayashi and Dr. Robert Laughli. Any scientist can read their work. In fact, Crane once told me that he was surprised no one else had come up with the principles behind the Machine. He said it was not really that hard if you're well versed in quantum entanglement."

"Let's just hope that no one tries this again," was all Fielding could say.

"Got that right. Want to go into town for lunch and a few drinks?"

"Sounds good to me."

65. IN THE PINES

In the cool of late summer, among the Pondrosa pine forest of the Mogollon Rim south of Flagstaff, there was a newly built cabin nestled among the trees. The house had a lovely view out over an alpine meadow and was reachable only via a winding dirt road. It was far from any other inhabitation.

Tamara pulled up before the cabin in her new Jeep Wrangler and switched off the engine. She regretted the fact that she could not take her Corvette along that road, but had accepted the gift of the new Jeep, which could take the ruts and turns of that dirt road easily.

She saw the older Jeep Cherokee parked there and knew that her friend, Dr. Myers, had already arrived. Cheerfully, she opened the back of her Jeep and extracted several gaily wrapped packages. At the front door of the cabin, she was met by Jesus with a smile on his face and open arms to greet her. The packages deposited in a chair, she turned to greet the others.

Dr. Myers was seated in a comfortable recliner by the fireplace. He nodded a greeting to her and continued sipping at his coffee.

Coming out of the kitchen was a young woman, hardly out of her teens, with long black hair and a wonderful smile on her face. She greeted Tamara in Aramaic and hugged her. There was no need to translate the words.

Two children ran up to her, addressing her as "Aunt Tamara," and hugging her leg. One was a smaller but exact image of her mother, about two years old. The other was an older boy, but there was no mistaking that he had the same piercing eyes as his father.

Jesus waved his arm to the front room with its large picture window overlooking the meadow. She sat down next to Myers.

"You're looking good, Seymour," she said. "Hope you're doing well."

"Okay, if you don't count arthritis and dumb freshman students who can't read or write," he replied with a smile.

Jesus came up and offered her a large cup of hot peppermint tea. "You didn't have to get that, Jesus. I could have." She simply was not used to being served by Jesus himself.

The boy stood before Tamara and proudly announced, "I speak English good now."

"Yes, you do. And happy birthday, Judas. You're four years old today! I have presents for you."

His eyes eagerly turned to the wrapped packages. A couple others were sitting on the floor, one large enough to hold a small bicycle.

"I see you bought it, just as you promised," she said to Myers. He smiled. Turning to Jesus, she added, "I have some more boxes of food for you in the Jeep. And a couple additional blankets now that summer is almost over. It gets cold up her during winter."

"Thank you," he said. "May God's blessing be upon you."

"And you," she replied, reflecting that this man, who had been through so much, was coming to blame himself less for his perception that he failed God somehow. But she doubted that he ever would get totally over it.

"Can I open the presents now?" asked Judas. Deborah, the two year old, came up to Tamara and stood there looking up at her. The child had the sweet smile of her mother, and, for just a moment, she felt a pang of regret that she had not gotten around to being a mother herself. Maybe someday.

"Yes, you can, now that your aunt and uncle are here," Jesus told him. Tamara had automatically turned on her translator when she arrived. Jesus was learning more and more English but he and his family still spoke mostly Aramaic. It was a blessing that the translators were no longer dependent on a wireless network. All the databases and software were contained within.

Judas hurried off for the presents, and soon there was the sound of ripping paper.

Tamara sipped at her tea and felt very content. She was very happy that a few months before she had, even though not a Chronodyne employee, stood up and insisted that they use the Machine to bring forward Jesus' family before it was destroyed. It had been quite a shock for Mary. But with Jesus there to ease her through the adjustment, she adapted quickly. The children were young enough to have less cultural shock, and, again, there was their father present to help them. Quickly enough they were happy with the clean beds and new clothing and amazing variety of foods they were introduced to. Not to mention toys, the likes of which they had never seen. Tamara was pleased to see that soft, cuddly Teddy bears appealed to children of all time periods. Judas had expressed joy that there were not all those "bad" men bothering his father.

Tamara knew that Mary did not understand what had happened to her, Jesus and the children, but she seemed to accept that, as her husband told her, it was good magic.

She also knew that originally Mary and Jesus had talked a great deal about that last week in Jerusalem, and about the expectations they had and the failure of them to come true. She could only hope that the two of them would get over a lifetime of beliefs and have a happy life. It also bothered her that the life they would have in the present was uncertain. If something happened to any of them in the past, it would happen to them in the present. But then, life is uncertain under the best of circumstances, she told herself. Might as well get on with living and not worry.

Jesus was over helping Judas to unwrap the bike, and Mary was holding Deborah.

"Oh, you may wish to know that I got a copy of the report Jacques made," Myers said.

Tamara immediately turned to him. "And...?"

"Jacques spent most of the night tracking Jesus and Mary in the past. His report says that they stayed with Joseph until Jesus was able to travel. Then the whole family, along with some of his followers who were trusted, traveled down to Egypt and settled in a small town not far from Alexandria. There was a large Jewish settlement there, quite a few of whom were Essenes. As far as he could follow them, they stayed there. Hopefully, they will – no, make that hopefully they did – not try to go back to Jerusalem.

Tamara sighed contently. She had been worried that Jesus might have been found out, or, even worse, tried to return to Galilee or Jerusalem. She would discuss with Myers about helping Jesus to travel and see the world as he often expressed a desire to. Maybe, after he and his family become more accustomed to this time, he could have that visit to the Temple in Jerusalem, or what was left of it. She would like very much to go with him on that trip.

Judas was happily playing with his new toys. Mary had returned to the kitchen from which pleasant smells were emanating.

Tamara reached over and put her hand on Myers'. From the look in his eyes, she knew that he felt the same. Things had worked out well after all.

When the time came for dinner, Jesus said a very nice grace that was part Jewish and part Christian. Then they sat down to enjoy a meal and friendship. And some fine wine from the extensive collection in Jesus' basement.

The End

ABOUT THE AUTHOR

Sean Brandywine was born in 1943 of a Russian father and Irish mother, is married and has two grown children and one grandchild. He is a Viet Nam era veteran, and a member of Mensa. His main career has been in computers, ranging from programmer to systems analyst. He began programming computers in 1961 and still enjoys writing code. His B.S. and M.S. are in computer science, but in addition, he has a PhD in astronomy. This love of astronomy is reflected in many of his science fiction books.

Today he lives in Solana Beach, California, enjoying his hobbies of astronomy, fishing and fast sports cars.